TIMMY

A

MILLION

BRETT BANJO

God Gets a Gift Card

God was feeling better than he had in nearly an eternity. Out of the blue, through the Deity Postal System, a card had arrived from his mother. It was three years shy of a century since he'd last heard from her, since the ugly words had passed between them. If a God could be surprised, he was, by her cordial invitation to tea.

He had to admit it sounded delightful, tea and cookies by the lake. He couldn't even remember that last time he'd visited Hell, but he still harbored fond memories of the place. Many a youthful afternoon had been spent spelunking through the depths of Hell, swimming in the Lake of Fire and playing croquet with the demons. But in his mind it had all been tainted, not just Hell, his entire childhood and he was no longer sure he felt welcome in Hades.

If you asked him, he would have said that he hated leaving her there, but she was getting old and he had a universe to run. He had a life of his own and couldn't spend all his time watching her. Oh, he convinced himself he'd done the right thing, done what was best for her, after all they did have shuffleboard and she'd been complaining for eons that he kept it far too cold in Heaven. But deep inside he felt like he had just dumped her there, like a horse to the glue factory. Which he had, though to be honest she wasn't the only one who suffered from her exile. There was also, well, there wasn't anybody else, but God did find it very hard reconciling the stray bits of guilt that now and then surfaced over her abandonment with the joy he felt from her not being around.

And today comes a card and an invitation in her own hand, asking please come and saying how good it would be to see each other. On top of that she had enclosed a fifty-dollar gift card to Macy's, a sure sign that his mother had finally forgiven him and longed for a warm reunion.

He knew just what he would do with that gift certificate. He was going to buy some pants, nothing fancy, maybe khakis. He wouldn't want people saying God was putting on airs. They'd be surprised enough by the form fit that he hoped would highlight his junk after so many years of wearing the same old robe, the same robe he'd worn since before the Earth and Moon. It had become more than a little bit decrepit. The white sheen no longer shone. There were holes in embarrassing places. And when the wind blew up instead of across, his goods felt like they were packed in a freezer.

He'd resisted pants for centuries. They embarrassed him. He couldn't imagine why he hadn't thought of them first. The apes had figured them out, while he, creator of the earth and the heavens, had missed it. He'd spent an eternity dangling, suffering through all sorts of weather, and flashing the greater part of Heaven whenever there was a change in the wind or his robe wasn't tied right.

God would have resisted pants forever, feeling it indecent to follow the trends of glorified apes, if he hadn't, sometime last century, decided that he really had invented pants after all. It came to him through what he believed to be divine intervention. He could hardly believe he hadn't seen it before. What are pants really? Pants are little more than a modern day version of the squirrel, stretched and shaved, form fitting and weather resistant. He'd invented squirrels and had been stretching and shaving them way before they'd even existed.

Anyway, after discovering once again that he was even more brilliant than he had previously assumed, he'd begun pining for a pair, though he still worried what Heaven would think. The change might offend the conservative core. But with the gift certificate, he finally had the right excuse. After all, it was a gift and it would be pretty lousy of him not to use it. Waste not want not was another one of his creations. And what kind of God would he be if he ignored a present from his mother? He'd be the first to tell you he'd be a rather lousy God and certainly no God with whom you'd want to be involved.

The idea of pants made God giddy and he began to feel bad about the way he'd let Earth go since the Garden of Eden. Cast out of paradise? What was that all about? Thrown away for eating an apple? What the hell was wrong with him? He loved apples! Was he really that kind of God? After swearing when he was young and still under his parents tyrannical control that if he were God, he'd treat people better. After years of domination and abuse, years of being told he was less than nothing and couldn't do anything right, was he really raising his children the exact same way?

He had been that kind of God. He knew it. Everyone knew it. Oh the things he's done. He used to blame it on his mother. How they would argue! He'd blame her for anything and everything, swearing it was all her fault, that he broke his toys in response to the way she demeaned him every chance she had. Her and her snide comments:

So that's the Earth huh? That's the best you could do in six days? You must really be proud of yourself. Of course if it had been me, I would used my time to do it right, but you always were one for short cuts.

Next thing you know he was banishing mankind from the best place he could imagine. A place he had made just for them. Out of the garden and into a world of work, war, death and disease. He'd sentenced mankind to a life of pain over an apple. And the worst part was that even while he was doing it, even while he used her to justify his rage, God knew it wasn't about his mother.

Secretly, he liked being cruel. He enjoyed every hurricane, each earthquake and kept a running tally of the deaths caused by all the various wars and plagues. At night, alone in his room, when no one could see, he liked to play the best disasters over and over again, pausing to enjoy each and every look of pain.

But it was never too late to change. He could still make things right. So before God went to visit his mother, he created a tiny orb. He called it the Orb of Fertility and meant it to cure the world of its suffering; ending famines, curing disease, stamping out war, poverty, hate, discrimination, bad teeth, pimples, greed, lust, limps, reality television, gluttony, sloth, balding, hair lips, pride, envy and New Jersey. He was going to finally return the Earth and its inhabitance to a utopian, garden state.

What Hell Can't Hold

The trip wasn't everything God had hoped for. For one, Hell was even nicer than God remembered. It was clean, courteous and as far as the heat, it was more like an overzealous sauna than the soul-torturing, deep-burn described in the brochure. The place felt like a vacation retreat, a giant beach with plenty to eat and endless live music. It was like someone had taken Canada to a Disney World in Puerto Rico. Where was the punishment? What had happened to damnation?

And his mother, she was just as kind and sweat as he remembered. She had no interest in reconciliation, taking every opportunity to insult him from the moment he walked in.

So this is what Gods have taken to wearing these days?

I just got them today Mom.

And what was wrong with the nice robe I made you.

Thing was ragged as hell Mom.

It was made to last.

It had stains and holes in it that predated evolution.

You know we don't believe in evolution.

4

Maybe you don't believe in evolution, but did it ever cross your mind that while you were busy nit-picking my ice age, I might have been busy creating something complex and beautiful?

Oh yes, the mighty creator in his slick new pants.

I bought them with the gift card you sent me.

And still you come empty handed?

What did you want Mom? I'll create anything you like, fast as asking.

Doesn't really mean so much when a person has to ask.

So after all this time I'm supposed to read your mind.

Read smead, all I said was it would have been nice if you had brought something.

What exactly was I supposed to bring for a God?

I got one a nice gift card and look what he goes and does with it.

They're nice pants mom, comfortable, fashionable and functional.

So you're saying you threw away your robes, the robes I made for you, because they didn't have pockets?

I didn't come all this way to fight.

All this way? I'm sorry it was such an inconvenience.

That's not what I meant.

Taking you away from your busy schedule so full of important lording.

Did you invite me here just to insult me?

Again with the you, you, you. You came all this way. You're insulted. Did I use a gift you gave me to replace a gift you made for me?

Of course not Mom.

Of course not, after all, what gift did you give me?

Next time mom, next time I'll figure out something.

You think there's going to be a next time.

This is why I put you in Hell.

And what a fine Hell it is, just listen to all those souls riving in unbearable anguish.

I forgot how nice it was down here.

You would have known had you bothered to visit your mother.

I didn't think you wanted me to.

I'm not sure I want you to now.

You haven't changed.

And you're still the same selfish child that drove his father away so many years ago.

You can't blame that on me.

He never did like you.

5

He never liked you!

He was always ashamed.

You made him crazy with your constant nag, nag, nag!

We were happy before you showed up.

I didn't ask to be born!

Oh what, so this you didn't create, everything else you say you created, but apparently you are all my fault.

You're the reason I'm so messed up.

And you're the reason I'm all alone here, nothing to do but twiddle my thumbs for the rest of eternity by some ugly old Lake of Fire.

I sent you here because there was so much to do! The activities list goes on and on.

You sent me here so I couldn't watch you screwing up.

I sent you here so I wouldn't have to listen to you degrade everything I did!

What have you done? Heavens a mess, Earth – a joke and Hell? You call this Hell! I'd be ashamed to leave my broken toys here.

They're not broken toys.

If they ain't broken, what are they doing here?

They're sentient beings. They chose to be here, by their own actions.

Just like me.

I could have sent you to New Jersey to be with Dad.

Ah, that ass-biting lobster, I would have cooked him up and spit him out.

And you wonder why he left.

I wonder why you wear silly pants when a God needs a robe.

It was old. It was decrepit!

You can't create a washing machine, some bleach and a tailor. What kind of Heaven are you running up there?

A good Heaven! Hell, it's a great Heaven!

It ain't so great.

I'll tell you what kind of Heaven I'm running. I'm running a Heaven that doesn't need you and doesn't miss you and doesn't want you back.

Good riddance!

Screw you!

Tears splashed the parched black earth, sizzling away as God ran through Hell's mighty gates, a chorus of demons laughing at his heels. His great moody shattered, his sense of self a whirlwind of doubt and loathing.

Deep in his mind he imaged horror and trepidation. Tornadoes spun out of control across the America's heartland, wreaking havoc on trailers and cows alike. Earthquakes toppled Chinese buildings like dominos.

6

Avalanches buried yaks and Sherpas in their yurts. Rogue waves capsized ships. Trees fell on beavers. Sand storms buried camels and their jockeys. Ice cream cones fell delicious side down.

God circled the Earth, enjoying lasciviously the projections of his doubts and frustrations. In one of the pockets of his pants, one of his very useful, comfortable and fashionable pockets, he found the Orb of Fertility.

It was beautiful. He was sure, as sure as he was about anything at that moment.

He hated it. It disgusted him. It was an Earth seed, deep blue with white crests foaming above its living oceans, a thousand shades of green swayed through its forests, a billion rainbows shimmered across its fields and swirling above it all, sailed the fluffy, white and gray givers of life.

Gazing deep into the orb's folds, spellbound by its vibrations of life and spectrum of colors, God felt nauseous. He thought maybe, if he had remembered, if he had given the seed to his mother, everything might have turned out differently.

He scowled. It was too late for that now. It had always been too late for that. He knew how things had to be. He was supposed to be ambushed in Hell. Any idiot could have seen that one coming. But all the should-of-knowns in the world wouldn't make the vile shame that coated his mouth taste any more like candy.

With a curse aimed at his mother, he threw the orb with God-speed at the Earth below, watching it burn radiantly as it plummeted through the atmosphere. And that was that. The Earth was not to be saved that day.

Or was it?

The orb was made much better than God had given himself credit for. After the effrontery suffered at the hands of his mother, he just assumed everything he made was crap. He never expected that the orb could survive.

But survive it did. And while it didn't plant into the Earth and bring about a new Eden, it did land in the unassuming Erin Jameson's birth control pills and that was indeed something.

Erin would never have imagined how completely her life was about to be turned on its end. Looking back, she would never have assumed she could even survive such a radical change. But she was made much better than she gave herself credit for. She strove on and though she did not prosper, she sure did propagate. She became the queen bee, dropping babies in a never-ending stream for more than fifty years.

People called her the old lady that lived in the shoe until it became clear that there was nothing funny about the number of children that literally fountained out her door. The town's population doubled, tripped, quadrupled, quintupled, sextupled, seven-upped and so on and so on until one day the children began to disappear. Coincidently this is the same time that the doubles began to appear, but we haven't gotten there yet...

In the Unusual Way

Timmy was just a tiny baby on the day he was born, but his life would never be the same. His entrance into the world was hardly noticed by anyone. He dropped to the floor and was stepped over and around as a matter of course by the bustling family. In fact, it was a full day before his mother even noticed him, so quiet and content was this little bitty child and to be perfectly honest, so accustomed was his mother to giving birth, he was lucky he was noticed at all.

When she first caught sight of the child she only muttered. What's this! She was about to accuse one of the children of leaving the door open so any breed of newborn could wander right in, when she noticed the peculiar way he had of eating his eggs and toast. It was unmistakable. He ate them just like any other member of the family, which was, not at all.

Eggs cost money, bread does not toast itself and Timmy's mom had far too many children to start toasting. To give them each so much as half a slice, dry, would take all day, morning till night, slaving over a kitchen full of toasters and if that were to happen, there's no telling where it could lead. The children might get uppity, feel spoiled and start demanding things like butter or even worse, the other half and then where would she be? A slave to the toaster and her not even owning one. That was certainly no way to live.

That was why her children ate the same meal every day, a meal consisting of exactly what other families were having. Her children had become, out of pure necessity, master impersonators and brilliant in the art of disguise.

Whenever their tummy rumbling grew too loud, it was up to them, regardless of age, to find a home where food was abundant and convince the mother that they were in fact a starving member of her own family. Thousands of meals were pillaged from the community every day in this very manner and no one ever thought of complaining. Families just noted dully that tomorrow they would once again need to stop by the grocers.

So convincing were Erin's children, that on numerous occasions, mothers would enter their dining rooms to find that they had two or three of the exact same child clamoring for vittles. Unable to tell her own from the strays, the mother would have no choice but to feed them all and plan to see

8

the doctor the next morning. They always hoped that something was wrong with their eyes, but feared and were rather convinced that the flaw had to be of the mind.

As more and more of these cases occurred, it became widely believed that there was something in the water that caused these hallucinations. A great doctor had even been called in to diagnose the problem and while he could not get to its exact root, he did agree that the most likely culprit was some secret agent seeping into the water supply of the town. He dubbed the disease Ostensible Twin Syndrome for which he prescribed taffy. He went on to recommend that the apparitions be fed as they seemed harmless as well as ravenously hungry.

Little Timmy was the last in a long line of countless brothers and sisters. Meaning that no one had ever bothered counting them. Once, a great scholar from the big city gave it a try, but had never been heard from again. It was popularly believed that he was still in the house, that he had wandered into one of the back rooms and wasn't strong enough to battle the current of bodies back to the door. He had disappeared when Timmy was only two.

As it was, the house was standing room only. There was a line at the door of children trying to get in, fighting an equally long line of children trying to get out. At its peak, the line stretched clear to the next county and a weaker child might find himself stranded indefinitely.

Timmy was lucky he hadn't been swept away from his mother in that constantly shuffling room and even luckier that his mother was able to recognize him as one of her own by the way he ate his eggs and toast. And as we all know, when luck hits twice you can bet a third is soon to follow for Timmy was picked up from the floor and placed in a satchel that his mother wore around her waist, in an attempt to lose as few of the non-walkers as possible.

Timmy was very lucky indeed, even though the satchel was over-crowded, the turn over rates were high, since so many of the young decided it would be better just to crawl to town for a bit of deception. It turned out that there was just enough room for Timmy and the satchel made a nice temporary home for a growing boy, full of warm bodies and a constantly gushing nipple.

Being the last of his mother's multitude, Timmy was able to stay in that satchel long after his mother had introduced his other siblings to the floor. He enjoyed a comparatively pampered lifestyle, availing himself to as much mother's milk as he could drink. He stayed for six years in total, maintaining his advantageous perch, despite what would have been his mother's objections. But she hadn't a clue.

Timmy was born the master of all masters of deception. So profound were his gifts that he was able to stay safe and warm just below his mother's ample tit, convincingly disguised as her coin purse. A fortuitous choice of deception, since poverty had long left the purse too empty to bother with, yet too rare a treasure to throw away.

Timmy Leaves the Satchel

At the tender age of six, Timmy noticed the crowds that pushed and pulled through and around the delivery room his mother referred to as the kitchen, beginning to thin. The line at the door was gone and he could make out unoccupied bits of floor around his mother's feet. He hadn't seen the floor since he was only a day old and was quite startled by its flatness.

From above, it looked cool and intriguing, a place he could stretch his constantly clamoring legs. He decided it was time to make his move. He stealthed cautiously downward, first blending into his mother's pants then imitating her shoes.

At ground level everything looked different. He was very surprised at how tall the world appeared. Until then he had always considered himself breast height. Now, the brothers and sisters he had once looked down upon, towered above him and moved at incredible speeds. What had once been a crowd of bobbing heads, became bodies, below which Timmy squatted, trying his best to be a shoe.

Timmy knew that being a shoe would never do. He could not spend his life pretending to be footwear. He had given up a sweet perch at his mother's milky tit for a dank wrap around an ancient worn sock.

Fearfully, he clung to the leg, imagining his smooth transition to the floor, which he had already decided he did not want to be. He saw how his brothers and sisters treated the floor. They walked all over it and that was never going to be good enough for him. Still, he feared how he would manage as the smallest tatter in what looked to him to be a spud-crushing factory.

He might end up getting his potato mashed, he thought. But he wanted much, much more than where he was and what he was pretending to be. He boldly took his first step off his mother and claimed his first piece of floor.

Timmy Towers

Timmy was small for six years of age, weighing barely thirty-five pounds and cutting off well under four feet, but you wouldn't know it by looking at him. He had seen very few grown men, nothing with that much meat lasted long in his house, still he managed the greatest full-size man impression that anyone had ever seen. He was actual size but he looked much bigger and by all appearances he was a formidable figure standing 6'4 with a stout chest, muscular arms and a slightly crooked nose.

Turning around and seeing a grown man standing next to her, Timmy's mother let out a high-pitched scream and dropped the eggs and toast she wasn't fixing for breakfast.

Professor is that you? She exclaimed, her jaw twisted in shock and joy.

Mommy? Timmy's voice squeaked, unable to hide the surprise that came from seeing a face produce the voice he had always assumed belonged to the milk machine. He rubbed the nipple mark that still blotched his forehead and smiled at the face of his worn out mother.

My God! You scared me half to death! Are you finished with your count? His mother cackled, brought to exertion by the first man she had seen since the professor disappeared four years earlier.

The constant stream of children froze and glared, circling around, waiting for an answer from the strange man. They were not used to strange men lasting long and whispers quickly filled the air, telling what became of the last one that made it so deep into their lair. Another man that went by professor, that turned out not to be a professor at all, but an excellent roast, enjoyed thoroughly by those stranded in rooms too far back in the house to leave. The circle tightened as the children wondered, was this more sandwich meat or had the law finally caught up with them? In the end, the children were certain there was no difference.

Timmy's grown-man appearance shrunk under the pressure, as both he and the man began to sweat. Even he knew to whom his mother thought she was talking. She'd mistaken him for the once great scholar that disappeared during the widely discussed head count. Every child knew that the scholar had been eaten long ago, transcending from acclaimed university professor to meatloaf, much like the plumber, the telephone-repair man, thirty-seven mailmen, two milkmen, one encyclopedia salesman and some one-hundred-sixteen dogs, one-hundred-twenty-eight cats, fourteen bats and a never ending supply of squirrels and chipmunks lured to the window by the 'never-fail-nut' (a cunning cashew imitation conjured by Timmy's brother Roy).

Professor! Professor? His mother shook the not-there man.

Taking a deep breath, Timmy regained his composure and manly height.

Yes, Yes, What is it? A deep voice bellowed several feet above Timmy's mouth.

The count! Have you finished the count?

Count? Yes of course, been done for days.

Well?

Well?

How many are there?

Oh lots.

Well I know that.

You should.

Aren't you going to tell me?

Of course, of course I am. You've undoubtedly waited long enough.

Well, don't leave a girl in suspense. His mother cocked her head and rested her knuckles against her blown out hips.

You'll have to excuse me. This is my first time on the floor and it's rather disorientating.

Excuse me?

Actually, I've never been this tall before.

Tall?

I can hardly believe it at all! Why, just this morning I was a coin purse.

Coin purse?

Yes, your coin purse.

What about my purse?

It's missing.

She checked her satchel and looked up suspiciously.

How'd you know my wallet's missing?

Don't you recognize me?

Are you feeling alright professor?

Never better.

And my purse?

Forty-two thousand and twelve.

Excuse me?

Forty-two thousand and twelve, that's how many children I've counted since I've been here.

Wow!

Are you surprised?

I must have missed a couple.

That's alright, several don't know about you.

Huh?

Happens mostly when they hit the floor and roll.

If you say so Professor. She narrowed her eyes. I…uhh guess we should call the paper. Did you know there was a nasty rumor that you'd been eaten?

Unbelievable!

And by my children no less!

I don't know how these rumors get started.

I'm going to make the paper print a retraction. Forty-two-thousand you say?

And twelve.

Wow! She shook her head and allowed herself, for the first time in her life, to feel exhausted.

Timmy wasn't lying. He had counted forty-two thousand and twelve children in the six years he'd been alive and knew each by number. What he didn't know was how many thousands had left home before that fateful day when his mother found him on the floor not eating eggs and toast.

What he did know was that the house numbers were dwindling. At home, the number of children had reached a forty-year low, falling below twelve thousand just that week. The rest had gone in search of sustainable impersonations that would provide them with regular food. Over the years, they had spread throughout the town, the state, the country and even the world.

Timmy Steps Out

Professor Found Alive!
Says all 42,012 children are of an excellent sort and not eating anyone!

The extra edition of the *New Fanglewood Times* sold out well before they decided to go to press, faster even than the news of the professor's resurfacing could spread from one side of the small town to the other. The townsfolk agreed it was a miracle and dubbed the holy intervention 'Jonah's Upchuck'. Within half an hour of Timmy's first step from his home, wearing the guise of the Professor, the local stores had all run out of tuna fish.

Parties were launched on every corner. Bands began to play where previously there had only been fire hydrants. The town was in a frenzy. They declared it to be, 'The Day of the Great Vomit.' Schools were closed; businesses emptied; bakeries looted; and the liquor stores weren't left with enough on their shelves to cover the runt of a litter of ice-cubes.

The citizens of New Fanglewood hit the street armed with potato salad, toting chips and dip, balancing twelve packs like boom boxes, while their hips bulged with flasks and their pockets brimmed with baggies (bursting with a nearly pure baby powder concoction).

They set up quickly; lawn chairs unfolding; tasers charged; tambourines jingled; rock 'em sock 'em robots lost their heads; fireworks burst high in the air and low in the hand; and the words: 'I can't believe he wasn't eaten' dangled on every passerby's lips.

A committee was formed. A three-day festival was rapidly and misshapenly planned that included a visit by the President of Puerto Rico and an appearance by some over-the-hill pop icon showing way too much wrinkled cleavage.

The day was crowded with parades and fireworks, all swirling around the hero of the day, Professor Six-Year-Old-Boy Timmy.

The crowd quickly swelled to over 100,000, not including tens of thousands of Professor Timmy's brothers and sisters that everyone assumed to be the people that were just counted. It was like a family reunion that had interbred so many times that the newest generation had mutated into genetic strangers.

Timmy's speech went out over every major network in 138 countries, interrupting the Super Bowl, a cricket match between India and Pakistan, a speech by the Ayatollah Ali Khomeini and David Hasselhoff's comeback special. It was reprinted word for word in enough papers to fill every birdcage across the globe for a year.

High up on a slap-stick podium, concealed behind an avalanche of microphones, Timmy crooned to the world:

Not since I was an empty coin purse huddles near my mammie's bosom have I felt so at home anywhere! His voice boomed through a cheering crowd full of hoots, hollers and machine gun fire.

When I made the decision to step from my mother's shoe onto the first bit of floor that had ever appeared through the crowd of heads, I knew I was bound for greater things. I do not need to hold discarded hair clips any longer and my crevices will never again know the biting cold of expired library cards. But I never expected any of this! He paused to enjoy how the screaming sea of heads reminded him of the view from his first home.

Had I known how warm my reception would be, had I even the tiniest inkling that there could be so much kindness and support, I would have crawled out of that satchel years ago. The crowd swayed with love and two days of intoxication.

Heart-wrought passion flowed from every spigot, straining against every trouser and bounding free of a remarkable number of button down shirts. At Timmy's side, the President of Puerto Rico fought back tears and embraced the wrinkled-cleavage, butt-shaking pop star with such smoldering intensity that they disappeared, never to be seen again (except possibly at an impeachment hearing a month later).

My time spent in that great house was magical to say the least. If you could see through this façade of higher learning, you would understand how much I am starting to understand, how deeply I was touched and how hard it is for me to now leave this community after so many years of sucking at its tit. I am proud to acknowledge all 42,012 of those fine people as my brothers and sisters. I raise my glass to each and every one!

The crowd erupted like a sexy volcano. All composure was tossed to the wind as mighty cheers were passed from cup to cup and bottle to bottle. Families embraced. Men kissed their women. Women kissed their men. A car was overturned. Women kissed their women. Store windows were broken and small appliances carted off. Men kissed their men. The fire department turned its hoses on the crowd. Jell-O shots were passed around and wrestled in. Near empty bottles had unneeded shirts twisted down their holes, before being set ablaze and thrown at armored vehicles.

After feeling the embrace of such a wonder family and knowing the warmth of such a town as this, I can confidently say that my job here is complete! Timmy smiled as bits of pavement and broken bottles pass through the skull of the man he was not.

The National Guard was brought in. People were cuffed and dragged away, while others resist with hockey sticks looted from a sporting-goods store and shot guns loaded with Coco Pebbles.

Timmy wedged his little body under the podium and scrunched down fetally. Not out of fear but out of love. He thought fondly of his abandoned satchel home, never thinking once that there was anything unusual about the fires that burned, the heads that bled or the bags filled with electric eels that were hurled by the riot cops to cease and disperse.

I plan to return to whatever university I came from and continued teaching whatever it was I taught to the great credit of all the people I'll meet along the way! Thank you all! The Professor's image continued, though the riot had moved uptown and the only ones left in the square were too drunk or too beaten to understand.

Content and exhausted, with the warmth of the burning town surrounding him like a blanket made of puppies, Timmy went to sleep under the podium and dreamt of a very familiar breast that lovingly excreted eggs and toast.

Big City Shakedown

It took representatives of Columbia University no time at all to find Timmy. He had just woken, crawled out from under the podium and remembered who he was supposed to be when a small group of eccentrically uptight men and one easy spinster neatly surrounded him. They presented several outstretched and one down-turned hand to the boy.

Professor Hildenburg? A man who looked very old for being so young or very young for being so old began.

Timmy looked at him cloudily, searching the circle for a reply.

Professor Hildenburg! The young-old, old-young man urged.

Oh, you must mean me. Timmy startled.

Of course Professor. Please allow me to introduce myself. I am Dr Balvenie and these are my associates Dr. Glennfiddich, Dr. McCallan, Dr. Glenlivet and of course, needing no introduction, Johnnie Walker.

Am I sick?

I certainly hope not. We've been sent by the University to accompany you home.

I just left yesterday, have kinda outgrown the old satchel as I'm sure you can imagine and was kinda hopping to try something new.

We understand why you left and are here to assure you things have changed. You shouldn't let uncertainty get in your way until you see for yourself what is being offered. The University was rather hoping you'd consider giving, how did you say, the old satchel another try.

I'm not even sure I could fit back in. I feel so much bigger now that I've had a chance to stretch.

Ah, of course, I understand and so does the University. They are fully prepared to retain your tenure, promote you to head of the socio-economics department, with all the accompanying bells and whistles, and of course, offer a salary commiserate with your new found notoriety.

I have always liked bells and whistles.

We are very glad to hear that.

Do you have any on you now?

Any what?

Bells or whistles.

We did bring a limo for your return.

A limo you say?

Just a gesture of the Universities eagerness for your return.

Back to the satchel?

If you would.

And this limo, is it a bell or a whistle?

I suppose you could say it's the first of many whistles that will lead to many bells.

If I'm in the satchel again, I probably won't have room for more than one bell and one whistle. Umm…how long exactly do I have to stay? I'm growing all the time and I'm afraid of being smothered.

We will have no hold on you. You will be your own man. Free to stay for as long or as short as you like.

That's good, cause I already told my mother who I was and I really can't go back to being a coin purse again.

We assure you that you will never have to. Now, shall we get back to the city?

The city?

Yes, the driver should have us back in New York by nightfall.

New York?

Yes, first to your home and then the University.

And those are in New York?

Are you feeling all right Professor?

If I'm not, I sure got plenty of doctors about to fix me.

Quite cutting humor I am sure, must play very well in these small towns. Shall we hasten to the limousine?

I'm not sure what hasten means, but I'll do it if you want me too.

Great! The University will be so pleased. Do we need to stop of and pick up your bags?

No, no more bags, I promised myself that if I ever had the courage to leave, I wasn't going to be stuck in another bag for as long as I live. The one I had was more than enough.

Wonderful, then we'll bring you directly home and you can meet with the dean after the long weekend.

Home sounds great as long as there's enough space on the floor.

I'm sure more than enough room will be made for you.

Do you know how to get there?

Of course Professor.

Will I be the only Professor Hildenburg there?

With the possible exception of your wife sir.

17

Well, that does complicate things doesn't it?

If you say so Professor.

Please call me by my first name.

I'd be honored sir, but I must confess, they never told me what it was.

Oh that is a shame. I guess we'll both be surprised then.

A Short Ride to Dreams

Timmy had never seen a long black whistle with wheels before and thought it must be the loudest whistle ever. Only when he blew into the tail pipe, the whistle blew back and made him wheeze out a rather uncomfortable scream. Apparently the limo wasn't a whistle at all, but a reverse whistle. A theory quickly confirmed when, instead of putting it in his pocket, the whistle was opened and he was stored inside it.

Inside, he couldn't help bouncing. There was so much room, so much comfortable room. He leaped from seat to seat, then as the doctors climbed in, from doctor to doctor. He hadn't been bouncing more than five minutes when the world outside the whistle began to move past.

If he had known any curse words, Timmy would have used them then. Not the angry, why is this happening to me sort of curses, but the yehaw I'm driving daddy's brand new tractor across the watermelons sort of swear.

Timmy was so excited he bounced clear into Johnnie Walker's Lap. Which did nothing to please Dr. Walker who tried to get Timmy to settle down with a glass of something he called scotch.

Timmy did not like the scotch, but thought it rude to not give it the full try. It was hard work. The closer he got the brown liquid to his lips, the further his lips retracted, twitching in unsuccessful retreat across much of his face. When he did get a few drops past, his throat threw a rushing gust of half chocked air against the liquor in an attempt to push it back out again.

Fortunately, Timmy did not have to dislike scotch for very long. A mere three sips into the drink a heavy and irresistible fatigue overtook him. The glass dropped from his hand and he curled up against Dr. Walker's leg. Which did much to please Dr Walker.

Back Home Not Again

Wake up Professor, a voice hummed along to a gentle shaking. You're home.

Timmy rubbed his little eyes, then checked himself, relieved that he still appeared to be a man. He was worried, that while sleeping, he might have become the marching band he'd dreamt of, the one that ignited tiny limousines and threw them at doctors in full riot gear.

He had never thought about control before, how much he had or where he went when he slept. All he knew was that every time he awoken before, he had always been a coin purse. Go to bed a purse, wake up a purse. Go to bed a man, wake up a man. He shrugged, making a mental note to try and learn the rules. If he was going to spend his time looking like other things, it might prove important.

You must have been very tired. The voice cooed.

I didn't think so. What was in that glass you gave me?

The scotch? Why, it was forty years old if it was a day. I'm assuming you didn't do much drinking during your years of research.

I drank every day, most days I drank every few minutes.

That doesn't sound too healthy.

Being so close to the nipple, it was really rather natural.

If I lived in a house with that many kids, I'd keep it stocked with alcohol too.

I could never tell about stockings. The bigger kids did a pretty good job of keeping me off the floor.

Probably would have stomped you to death if you'd passed out there huh?

I don't know, but it wasn't long after I saw the floor that I knew it was time for me to finally get out.

Sounds like a hard time.

Not really, I just climbed down the leg and jumped off the shoe.

You're a strange one Professor.

Thank you, I like you too. Umm have we stopped?

That's what I was trying to tell you, we're home.

We are?

You're home.

We're at your home.

No Professor, don't you recognize it? Has it been that long?

You mean this is my home?

Indeed Professor.

It's much larger than I remember. It must pack a lot of children.

Two.

Thousand?

Well, I can't speak for the building, but your apartment contains two.

They must be enormous.

You'll be surprised how much they've grown.

Most of the ones I've seen were actual size, though to others they seemed bigger. Are these two really big or just pretending?

Given the amount of time you've been away, I think it's safe to bet they're pretending to be bigger than they are. But I'm willing to bet that when they see you again they'll shrink down pretty fast.

It's hard to hide from me. So who are they pretending to be?

I don't follow.

The children, don't tell me they're still in the satchel.

The satchel?

Oh never mind. I'll see for myself. Timmy opened the car door and then paused. You don't suppose, I mean, with only two children, no matter how large they may pretend to be, that they might have eggs and toast?

I'm sure it can be arranged.

After all these years, to find myself this close to eggs and toast by just getting off the shoe and being a professor.

Whatever happened to you in there is going to make a great book. I'm hoping to be on the inside track for that one, if you know what I mean.

I really don't, but if it's something you want, I'll ask about getting you there. I seem to keep getting far more than I ask for these days.

I'm glad you feel so good about this. Let me walk you upstairs.

Big Moments in a Small Crowd

A heavy oak door strained against its hinges as soon as the bell was rung. The face that met them was full of awe and surprise, excitement and trepidation. Her body twitched and her limbs shook.

My God, they called and told me, but I didn't believe them. I mean, I hardly recognize you, but it's you! It has to be! My God Charles, I thought you were dead.

I'm beginning to think I nearly was.

I mean, I want to hug you and kiss you and punch you right in the nose.

It sound nice and then it doesn't.

My God, I'm so happy and mad. You didn't call. Years and years you didn't call and here you are on my doorstep and I hardly recognize you!

I didn't have any pictures to go by.

Where have you been! You owe me at least that.

At first I was secure, but then I felt trapped. I didn't think there was room or any place to go. It took a lot of courage to get off that shoe.

All you had to do was talk to me. If you had let me know how you felt… I never wanted to trap you. I didn't even know you were unhappy.

I didn't think I was unhappy. I thought I was safe. It wasn't until I got out the door that I realized how much I was missing.

So what are you doing here now?

Dr. Balvenie was kind enough to drive me.

Oh I see. A wry smile skimmed her face before she managed shake it away. God, I'm acting like a fool. Where are my manners? Come in! Come in! It's your home too, though you'll hardly recognize the place! I just redid the living room last week.

It will be a long time before I start recognizing things.

I'm sorry. She fidgeted. I just have to touch you a little. I can hardly believe you're alive and standing here. She ran trembling hands over his face. You feel so much smaller than I remember, have you lost weight?

Do we have any eggs and toast?

She cried, pain pulling her pleasant features back toward her ears as if the back of her head were caught in a threshing machine.

It doesn't have to be right now. Timmy tried to comfort her. It was his first time comforting and he wasn't sure how to go about it.

I really thought you were dead.

The person you knew probably is.

Have you really changed that much?

You'll have to tell me.

Have I changed so much?

It's like we're strangers.

Is it really that bad?

It's got to be better than it was. Do you know what it's like when you're constantly growing but always pretending to be the exact same size?

Yes, yes I do. She bit down on what wanted to be a howl.

Then maybe we're not as strange to each other as we might think.

I really hope so. The tears dried and a dull light entered the pitch black of her eyes.

I, ummm, should probably go. Dr. Balvenie spoke low, awkwardly pacing through a short side-to-side fidget.

Go! Why would you want to go? I've never seen so much room. Timmy smiled, patting his wife and new friend on their arms then pulled them near.

All we need now is couple good eggs and some toast.

Timmy's Smallest Family

Timmy settled into his brownstone, looking forward to doing whatever it was a professor did. Timmy had achieved more at age six than most accomplished in a lifetime and he didn't know anything about any of it.

He was learning quickly, very quickly. One thing he learned was that the children in the house were neither brothers nor sisters, they were sons and apparently they were his. The eldest, nearly twice his age, topped the scale at eleven years old and the younger had reached the impressive age of eight. He learned that they were very excited to see him and a little more than curious where he had been all those years.

When he met them, the youngest threw his arms around him, while the elder hung back, a look of shy dismay twisting his face between need and anger. The younger's embrace was tight and emphatic, the elder's hesitation determined and wavering.

Where have you been? The elder braved and the younger turned to focus an evil glare.

Nowhere as good as here.

Then why did you stay for so long?

I was scared.

Scared of us?

No, I've never been scared of you.

Then what were you scared off?

The easiest answer I suppose is that I was scared off all the things I didn't know, but the real fear probably came from how crowded things were.

So, we're crowding you?

God no, I've never been anywhere so spacious and free.

So why haven't you been here?

It took some time for me to find out how much room there was.

You expect me to believe you have room for us now?

I can't imagine you stepping on me if you tried.

I thought I would hate you when I saw you. I thought I'd want to kill you. Tears streamed down the boys twitch riddled face.

But now?

I don't think I can. You're not what I thought you'd be. His eyes widened as the parts that wanted him to stay away collapsed under the weight of needed love.

I can't tell you how happy that makes me. And believe me when I tell you that I'm not what I thought I'd be either.

The boy's feet dragged him forward, his arms unclenched from his side to wrap around Timmy, who was already suffering under the weight of his younger brother. The boys hung upon him and he felt his legs begin to tremble and give, when the arms of his wife caught him by surprise, embracing him from behind, adding the strength and support that would keep them all up.

Timmy couldn't believe how good it felt, wrapped in a warm cocoon of emotion, tears of joy fell upon him from heads buried in places he didn't have. His heart thumped loud and heavy. His arms maintained just enough strength. His nose ran. He tried not to explode. And topping it all off, Timmy could smell that the good doctor had the eggs and toast ready. Once again, more than he dared to dream had come true.

Gargantuan

Victor Ramulouse was born obese. He came into the world eight weeks late and a stout 46 pounds. He had broken his mother's spirit before he made his first whimper.

The former actress thought she had done well marrying rich. After all, it's not the weight of the man, but the weight of his wallet that really matters. Her husband used to joke that he had a million dollars for every pound he weighed and he was worth a cool half billion no matter how you tallied the numbers.

After Victor Gargantuan Ramulouse's birth, the one-time actress no longer thought this was such a funny joke. In fact, she would never laugh again, nor would she ever make her long anticipated comeback, play tennis, wear a swimsuit, walk the beach, walk to the bathroom, cross her legs, close her legs, sit, stand, breathe without a machine or answer to her name.

Victor was born into excess. If there was too much of it, his family had it. If there was too little of it, his family owned it all. His home was known, by friend and foe alike, as The World. There was a wing for every continent and an ethnicity for every room. There was everything and anything. The South America wing had the best coca. The Thai wing had a booming sex trade. Opium rained from palatial towers, weapons moved through the basement and there was no end to the servants whose sole job was to kiss an obese child's ever grown ass.

Gargantuan ate chickens whole by the time he was two. By the time he was four he considered roast pig an appetizer. By the age of six he had built one of the largest harems in the free world. By ten, every other ounce of heroin passed through his greedy little fingers and at the tender age of fourteen, when he was a mere 800 pounds, he owned three countries out right (Belize, Libya and Tanzania). On his sixteenth birthday, Gargantuan hired a continuous groomer to take care of all the pieces he could no longer reach or see. That was also the year he seized control of his first branch of the U.S. government (it was the Senate, as if there was any doubt).

As much as he enjoyed the casual game of world domination, his true passion was stealing. He was often heard boasting that anything he wanted, even before he knew he wanted it, was already on its way to him.

He pirated the Louvre into his south wing, the entire complex, including the palace and all its fixing. He kept it all, with room to spare, in one of his shoe closets.

He stealthily replaced the Giza complex with what he jokingly referred to as an inexact replica, boastfully pointing out how the Spinks had too much face and that the face looked a lot like his own. He set up the pyramids in one of his inner gardens (south west wing).

More than half of the Great Wall of China, all the good parts that desert and time hadn't beaten into rubble, surrounded his compound. The Parthenon was his favorite bathroom. The Eiffel tower was his preferred place of solitude. He had leaned it gently against the Tower of Pisa, a mere fifteen-minute ride by forklift from his inner sanctum.

He would have taken the moon had he the room for it, which he would, as soon as he finalized plans for stealing Mount Everest. He intended to balance the lunar orb upon the mountain's peak.

Gargantuan set his sights on gaining a lion's share of all transaction in each and every country in time for his twenty-first birthdays. There seemed little that could stop him. He expected no real opposition, which was probably why he didn't realize that his Giza was only a poor imitation, his Great Wall was mostly aluminum siding and all the masterpieces taken from the Louvre hung in the home of his second-in-charge, a man by the name of Leviticus, who claimed his ancestors were pimpin' ho's on the Mayflower.

Leviticus was as vicious and intimidating as he was hairy and greasy. While some would argue that only made him Greek, none would disagree that he was a difficult man to catch and kicked like a mule when cornered. If you were to ask any of his enemies, they would not be able tell you which was worse; that moment when you thought you were on top only to find your fingers sliding through his oily back hair or the next moment when your hands had completely slipped free and you saw that hoof coming up to meet your chin.

Leviticus was as daring as he was stupid and as devious as he was stupid. He'd been ripping Gargantuan off since his first day on the job as the spoiled boy's wet nurse. He started simply, a pacifier here and a drumstick there. But his greed did not remain simple and his resentment was deep. He had hated Gargantuan for the entire 12 years he nursed that over-privileged, mean-hearted, bites like an alligator sucking machine. He justified his stealing as payment for the nipple damage he'd suffered over the years. And damaged they were, chewed straight down to the bone.

As Gargantuan grew, Leviticus helped himself to more and more. He stepped on every shipment, pinched every payment, deflowered the greater part of the harem and picked the best of the best from the spoils that arrived by the ton.

Beneath his modest McMansion, he'd dug a secret world a hundred miles deep and twice as wide, where he hid the good wine, the best paintings, monuments, women, drugs, donuts, sausages, polo ponies, nipple creams, statues, Noble Prize recipients, fascists, monasteries, scotches, Scotsmen, Scotch tape and embattled rappers.

Unfortunately for Leviticus, fat men sometimes know far more than they let on and while he did manage to escape with his life, he didn't manage to escape very far and his life was worth very little.

Gargantuan started with soap, hours and hours of brillo-pad scrubbing to remove the protective and corrosive oils from Leviticus's fur. Then came the strait razors, slashing night and day, sheering him down to only skin. Then came the fun part. Gargantuan stretched Leviticus slowly, a hair width every hour for days that turned into months as Leviticus turned into miles.

Gargantuan was vindictively disappointed at how far from total rule he was upon his twenty-first birthday. He blamed himself. He should never have trusted anyone. It was like a slap in the face. He had fed from that man's nipples. What more could he do for anyone? It was the greatest honor he could bestow. And for it to come to this, to such a blatant lack of respect by someone so close. Worse than that, he was fooled by someone who, while obviously cunning and devious, was at heart really, really stupid. He'd only made Leviticus his number two because he considered him the mother he'd never had. Though it didn't hurt that he was more slippery than a greased pig with a rabid horse's kick.

Gargantuan would have been completely heartbroken, if he'd had a heart to break. Instead, he gave himself the best present in the world. He decided not to worry about the stolen plunder or Leviticus' underground palace. He decided instead to make what he already had better. He encased his replica of the Great Wall and his fake Giza in real, live, one of a kind Leviticusian Leather, stretched thin and crowned by a dry, shaven head, that screamed ever so weakly and without rest.

Gargantuan smiled whenever the wind carried the gentle sounds of suffering to his ear. It was a cool and crisp reminder to always never trust anyone as well as a pick-me-up on those long days of insurmountable obesity. He was always proud of what he could accomplish when he allowed himself the simple pleasure of artistic creativity.

No Great Wall had ever looked better. Everyone agreed.

While Gargantuan was disappointed that he owned less than half the world outright, it was only a matter of time. The lessons he'd learned were beyond value, as were the lessons taught by Leviticus to all those that entered the large man's compound. The world would come, but in the mean time, Gargantuan was still able to be proud of all he had become.

Family Man

The first signs of forgiveness from Timmy's family came much faster than any reasonable person would believe. Their feelings for Timmy changed at Jerry Springer speed. Anger melted and hate had no place before the bright-eyed and eager Timmy. The difference between love and hate is never as deep as this statement.

What bridged the gap between Timmy and his new family was the extent of his interest in them and their lives. The smallest things seemed to excite him to no end. When they spoke, he looked at them with the quizzical gaze of a child. They could not help but feel that somehow his disappearance had all been worthwhile. For even in their foggiest and most skewed memories, father and husband had never cared the way Timmy did.

Timmy wanted to know about every part of their lives, from first blink threw the drooping of their eyelids at the end of the day and then into their dreams. The more time they spent together, the more excited his family became. Timmy's enthusiasm was contagious.

I started baseball last week…

Baseball? What's that like?

Mr. Freedman thought I threw a spitball…

Don't you have to spit a spitball?

No matter how much they told him about their little lives, Timmy wanted to know more. He'd seen so little that he couldn't fathom much of what they were saying. It seemed to him that the happening of the world were nearly unbelievable.

Apparently there is a brush that is used only on the teeth. There is nothing unusual about people having their own rooms. Bathrooms have more than just a bath and rest rooms are not for resting. Footballs are thrown, while soccer balls are kicked. Eggs and toast are easy to find and not hard to make. When you sneeze you should ask for forgiveness. Forks should be handled with the utmost care. Most families have two parents. Squirrels are not a snack food. His kids go to school but not where he teaches. Dodge ball is played like it sounds. Straws are not nipples but can deliver milk. When the phone makes noise it wants you to pick it up. A woman's tears leave black streaks while a boy's tears make his nose run. Children do not like being referred to as number one and number two. Wives do not like being called the old one. A bus stop is where the bus stops. Chickens do not poop eggs. If you sit on toast it won't hatch, while if you sit on a toaster it burns. Andy Silber picks his nose. Soonie Suh will kiss you for half a ham sandwich. Women at work talk behind your back and call you unfortunate, but if your husband comes home it makes them all nuts. Dr. Balvenie thinks family moments should be reserved for family. And pigeons never migrate.

Timmy learned all about his oldest son Jack, who liked to play street hockey. He was too smart for his own good, but didn't really know where he was at any given time. Timmy discovered that Jack tried really hard and never gave up and seemed to demand the best from himself at every moment, even if he was just destroying things. He also had hidden gifts, like taking things apart and not putting them back together or leaving the toilet seat up and he could out eat a racehorse. Timmy's wife claimed that he got most of these traits from him, including the toilet bowl thing. The very idea amazed Timmy.

Timmy was told all about his youngest son, mostly by his youngest son. The boy called himself Ona despite his name being Conan. He was missing a few letters but claimed to know where he left them. He was a boy that could not help but be happy. He wore his smile from habit and saw the world with so much detail that even the world couldn't tell you if it ran so deep. Ono was a sledgehammer, toppling anything in his way, with the heart of a tornado that only wished to kiss the ground lightly but couldn't help

27

being overzealous. Timmy was told by Ono that most of these traits came from himself and no one had to pass him down anything, this included his propensity to smash without knowing.

Then there was the woman, Corrinna. Corrinna the beautiful! Corrinna, with the warm eyes that sparkled. Corrinna, who complained so sweetly that you almost wanted her to have more problems just so you could hear about them. Corrinna, to whom the passing years had been very hard, raising two boys on her own, her income slashed, her social life non-existent. It had made her strong, self-reliant, had given her a sense of purpose and a mission. She kept food on the table and the heat turned on. She made sure homework was done and the kids were well-rounded. She did it all, even if that meant she was little more than a taxi driver and private tutor, chef and seamstress, plumber and disciplinarian, doctor, story teller, costume designer, barber, electrician, role model, model builder, bread winner, baker, protector, maid and father. She had held up and the only cost had been every-thing else in her life. But she didn't say these things directly and wouldn't complain. If anything she was a proud sort of overworked, marginally depressed, extremely capable woman.

Strength was what Timmy heard within her stories, it was all he could hear when she talked about her life. Her existence was plastered with family and sprinkled with the faintest dusting of personal welfare. Her life outside the family existed within coffee breaks and around the water cooler and still she was not complaining.

Timmy knew what it was to be stuck and afraid of losing the little that you had. A little seems like so much when compared to nothing at all. He had never had such a view of a mother, his own so overwhelmed by continuous birth that nurturing and affection were utterly impossible. Yet here was a woman striving to give more than anyone could expect, trying her damndest to give them at least a little taste of everything, all while Timmy wasn't there to help.

Not that she said these things explicitly. She was very generous, accommodating, restrained in what must at time have risen to a furry. She didn't seem to blame, only acknowledge, in passing, between the lines of what she described as her ordinary little life.

Touched again and again, Timmy would walk around the table to give her his knew favorite thing. A strong embrace, a hug that brought a tear and then a fountain as the boys latched on from either side and she could not decide if it was all so happy or all so sad. It didn't really matter. It was something and it had been a long while since she thought there would ever again be something.

Finally, Timmy learned that when the moon begins to rise, a red drink called wine makes one's eyes get very heavy and that a spare room means that no one is using it. It had never occurred to him that a room could be spare or that he could use it, but at night he would lay himself down on the softest thing he'd ever know and go to sleep. For the first time in his life he slept in both warmth and comfort with his legs unbent.

Rats to Eggs and Toast

Timmy didn't know what to expect. He wasn't sure what outside was normally like. The first time he'd ventured out on his own, a parade broke out and the day ended in a riot. It was the most fun he'd ever had.

Timmy knew the celebration wasn't really for him. He knew it was for the long lost and presumed eaten professor, but there wasn't any real difference between them anymore.

Either way, he quickly learned the parades don't happen every time you go outside. Near as he could tell, they only happen the first time you go outside. A fact he could not validate, for though there were plenty of people stepping outside, all around the city, he had no idea if it was their first time or not. He wasn't about to ask anyone either, not after the first guy looked at him like he was crazy.

Parade or no parade, it was nice being in New York City. He heard people complaining about the crowds, but he'd never seen so much room in his life. Except of course for his new home which was larger and emptier than he could ever hope to be. Everywhere he went in that apartment there was almost nobody.

At home there was too much room, while nearly every place in the city seems to have just enough and more often than not, more than enough, room he easily filled with a just big enough version of himself.

To fill the apartment he had to become hundreds, which he was extremely reluctant to do. He didn't think his family would be too pleased if they found their apartment cram full of him. He was glad they'd accept him at all, or believed in him, or believed he's him, which for all intents and purposes he was. Or had been for nearly two weeks, which was as long as he'd ever been anyone.

Today, he was alone, wandering the vastness of the city and feeling free enough to shrink down to his normal size and sometimes, just for fun, a little smaller. He loved walking the streets in a tight crowd composed entirely of himself, looking and thinking, his mind racing and his eyes bouncing through the urban jungle like a ping pong ball on crack.

He had never really considered what he wanted, who he was or how he might react to all that was out there. He'd never really thought of anything and was surprised when his mind started telling him things.

It told him how small he was in the big picture and how lucky. It told him that for the first time he was loved. It told him that a city block goes on forever when you've passed a thousand of them and your legs only go up to what people believe are you knees. It told him that it didn't matter how many of him there were or how big he pretended to be, he'd always feel a little bit like an empty coin purse.

Foremost, it told him he loved eggs and toast. Which was another thing he loved about the city. Eggs and toast were everywhere. He didn't have to walk more than a block in any direction to find a sign wooing him toward some sunny sides and butter melting between a ring of crust.

Since his morning breakfast at home, he'd already had three more breakfasts at three different places. That's a lot of eggs and toast! If you were to see Timmy when he's tall, you'd hardly imagine he could fit it all. As a small boy you'd be amazed to see how many eggs and how much toast he could cram into that little body. And cram he did, hardly ever leaving before he was filled clear to his tonsils.

Four breakfasts and he was far from stopping. In fact, he was on his way right then to try a thing they called an egg sandwich. If you'd believe it, they put the dang egg right on the toast, so you could hold it in one hand, or he imagined he could. His hands were not as big as they sometimes looked and he couldn't stand the thought of dropping his egg. He was also very wary of dripping yokes. Being six is hardly an excuse for being messy when you have tenure.

He reached a place where the crowds thinned and he let his own crowd dissipate. More of himself was not the kind of company he was looking for and to be honest, maintaining so many people was a little tiring to a little boy covering vast ground in a large city.

Timmy took the opportunity to enjoy being alone. It's hard to think sometimes with so many of him looking to him for guidance. They all expected him to lead. Since he was the only one that was real, he felt the brunt of responsibility. He didn't want to take care of anyone else and besides, he'd didn't want them to know he was lost.

He'd been walking for hours and while he'd seen plenty of signs for eggs and toast, he hadn't seen a single one for eggs on toast. Meanwhile, the skyscrapers were turning the world dark, depositing shadows long before the sun would have wished it. He tried to stay clear headed, but once the shadows appeared, consuming the sunny-side of the street ravenously, a coldness rose from the earth, the wind picked up and garbage roamed the street without direction. He knew he was far from home, but his brain kept telling him that it didn't matter where he was when he had yet to discover who he was.

He'd be the last to admit to himself that he was getting a little bit frightened and his brain wasn't helping with its new found logic, emotions and answerless questions. He started to yell at his mind, choosing the out loud method in an attempt at sneaking behind enemy lines and thus gain the advantage.

Leave me alone! I'm only six!

But you are alone. All alone! He heard the shadows whisper just behind his ear, sneaking behind his lines and thus gaining the advantage.

Timmy turned quickly upon a man too big and too hairy to own a neck, with tattoos larger than the boy he had let himself become.

He decided to grow, slowly, hoping that he could become a man, a big man, a bad man, before the big, bad man that had just stepped in his way had a chance to pick on a little boy.

Timmy faked nonchalance, hoping to dodge and run when the man pounced. But the man was too fast and lifted him clear off his feet, despite how he had grown.

What brings a little thing like you so deep into the shadows?

Eggs and toast. He couldn't help saying.

Many a boy has done many a thing for eggs and toast, but to go alone into the shadows is more than any chicken or any baker would have done for you.

The shadows started it.

They often end it.

What do you want?

Everything.

I have only enough money for eggs on toast.

Nothing for hash browns?

I haven't gotten around to them yet.

You should have tried the hash browns. It's like they turned bread into butter, fried it and spread butter on 'em they're so good.

On your recommendation I shall surely try them next time I am out.

Next time you are out, you'll be out cold.

But I have little money and I'm not nearly as big a meal as I've made myself look.

Oh you're worth much more than that to me, more than dollars and donuts. What I can't steal, I'll sell and what I can't sell, I'll feed to me dogs.

You should let me go now.

You should have stayed out of the darkness little boy, all by your lonesome, you won't be making this mistake ever again.

Neither will you. I'm not alone.

I suppose you're with an army.

I am!

And this army must look like sidewalk and shadows.

No, they don't either.

I'll bite, what do they look like?

Rats!

Timmy didn't know what possessed him to say rats, other than that was what he imagined his assailant to be, one big, dirty, ugly rat. Held high in the bad man's strong arms, Timmy opened into a wiggling, clawing hive of teeth and hair.

Rats surged, racing across his body, down his arms and through his sleeves. They sprouted from a spark in Timmy's darkest places. His eyes glowed yellow as theirs beat red. They festered and lunged, multiplying. A botulistic horde, spitting disease, claws pointed at the attacker's face. Leaping and swarming, they covered the big, bad man in a ten foot pile of pure abomination. Timmy became a million. His body bubbled with biting, rampaging, coarse-haired pestilence.

The big, bad man loosened his grip and Timmy dropped to the ground, landing spryly on little boy feet. His attacker was already gone, though Timmy could still hear him screaming. He grinned with vengeful satisfaction at the cowardly, yellow trail that marked the killer's escape route.

Shaking with fear, furry and power, Timmy breathed heavily as he forced his rats to settle back into boy before he crossed to the sunny side of the street. It was time to find his way back to the place he'd been calling home. Eggs or no eggs, he had a class to teach in the morning.

God's BBQ

The greatest nuisance to God, stemming from his original desire to create, was dealing with what he has created, namely us. We are always murmuring things we expect him to hear, damning him if things don't go our way and worst of all, each and every one of us wants to meet him first thing after we die. Even bugs swarm toward God when they die. In fact, everything not trying to scratch its way out of Hell expects some kind of meet and greet as soon as they enter the light, like Heaven's been waiting for them, like talking to God is a God-given right.

And the questions! We have so few questions, but each person has to ask them. What's the meaning of life? Who's my daddy? Do squirrels have souls? Why'd you make my dick so small? Are there Mormons here? If I sin in Heaven do I have to leave? Did it help when I asked for forgiveness while sinning? Why'd you put the ass so near the yummy spots. If animals don't have souls, why is it wrong to fuck them? Why'd you create herpes? If incest is a sin why are other guy's sisters so ugly and mine so hot? What do I have to do to get you to close your robe? You didn't let my stepdad in did you? If a plane crashed on the boarder of the United States and Canada, where do you burry the survivors? What did one strawberry say to the other strawberry? What's black and blue and hates sex?

The endless questions made God want to wipe out the human race and forget about the whole Earth experiment, but then he'd have billions of people all showing up at once, feeling like they have some God given right to ask stupid questions.

That was why God started the 'God Welcomes You to Heaven Noontime BBQ.' Not that he always showed up. Mostly he used God impersonators, people he only let into Heaven to keep the locals confused and off his back. They're a dime a dozen up there and work wonders in clearing up God's schedule.

Even though the God you first meet may not be the God you had hoped for, he still goes to enough of these functions to be really annoyed by people in general. He only attends at all to keep his finger on the just-stopped pulse of humanity. By talking to the newly dead he gets a unique insight into modern life or at least into what's killing people now.

You can tell a lot about a place by checking out whom they're killing off most efficiently. It's how he learned about Germany and Native Americans. One day there were just too many Jews trying to negotiate an entrance and the Indians came like a water main broke, surrounding him with a constant white man this and white man that yabber that finally forced God to put them on a reservation just outside of Hell.

It was on one of these fact-finding missions that God first found out about a small town in eastern Illinois that was struck with a most unique form of multiplicity. It seemed, as one man explained, that local families were experiencing multiple children whenever food was served. That you cannot in fact sit down to eat with less than four of the same child sitting down with you. He said it made every meal feel like a special occasion, so no one complained much, except about the grocery bill. He said his last meal was a simple family dinner where his simple family of four had been stretched into thirty. He said he never had a more pleasant time.

This caught God as being a little odd. He had never heard such a story before. Huge banquets served for ordinary families, calves roasted over open fires, pounds of pasta, hundreds of potatoes, enough Kool-aid to fill a swimming pool and the man claimed that this was the way it was for all the local families as well as for most of the county. Dozens of people routinely showed up to fill every identity.

None of it made much sense to God until the man told him about a local woman that had been spitting out children near his whole life. According to him, this lady literally dropped child after child in a never ceasing succession. She squeezed out near a dozen a day over the course of decades, but as to what happened to the children afterwards the man had no clue. He had never seen them out or about the town, but claimed that their little house bulged with kids. Every time he passed he'd see hundreds of little faces pressed against cracking windows.

What was even creepier, was that for a good half mile surrounding the place, there wasn't another living creature to be seen, not so much as a dog or cat, squirrel or bird, crickets, mailmen, African-Americans or even so much as a mosquito.

It didn't take a musician to figure out that the orb, tossed in a careless rage, did not burn up, but hatched, creating what could be thousand of future question askers. They'd be another source of pain when they died, but while alive, God saw how they had already carved themselves out quite a unique niche.

The children had developed a very specific gift. The orb was so packed with fertility that it created thousands of creatures and packed them into single bodies and it had done this thousands and thousands of times, creating a nearly infinite amount of people who turned into the greatest chameleons the world had ever known. Among them, somewhere in that horde of unidentifiable people, must be a king, someone so well disguised that he could be anything and maybe everything. God's mind reeled at the possibilities.

It was a shocking idea. If it were true, this person would have at least two of the seven qualities necessary for being a God. Only two people in all of history had even one God like quality; Jon BonJovi had God hair and Madam Currie, a radioactive vagina.

God knew if he could find a person that actually possessed two true God qualities, he could really show his mother. Just imagine if this powerful creature was also to have great hair (or a radioactive vagina). Two was a powerful number and it was well within God's power to use them to teach his mother a lesson, but if the king of chameleons had just one more God quality, then he could be assured that his mother would never have the audacity to mess with his pants again!

So that was when God created hair gel, if that answers your question.

Timmy After the Rats

War upon the meek, brought forth by the brazen, had ravaged Manhattan, leaving much of the island in perpetual darkness. The city was consumed by back-ally battles waged by every hood and delinquent from the Bronx to New Jersey. Banks were robbed, the robbers abducted and the abductors hijacked, guns blazing all the while.

The shooting never stopped, it only ducked and covered. There was enough lead in the air that buildings were being chipped away. Bystanders were falling and then devoured like pigeon feed. The honest workingman spent his nights stuffed under his bed, his hands wrapped tightly around his head, as if that might stop the bullets. Fat people lost weight just to reduce the size of their target. Skinny people gained weight hoping to cushion the impact. Tall people slumped. Short people ran on tippy-toes. Clowns took separate cars. The ice-cream man went into a deep freeze. Starving was more popular than shopping. Central Park squirrels moved to Connecticut and pigeon bones piled up under eves and ledges.

The island wasn't burning, not yet. Control was not completely lost. The rich remained unaffected. The rich always remained unaffected, at least until the guillotine gets sharpened, then it's one for all and all for one.

Much of the city lay upon the poverty line. For these people life was constant turmoil. If it could be taken, it was; and then it was again; and then three more times before it was pawned and the pawn shop was robbed. Most of the money that exchanged hands went toward buying back things that had been stolen only to have them stolen again on the way home. It was enough to turn a good man bad. As times grew worse, too many good men found themselves upon that very precipice, take by force or be taken.

What had once been reserved for moonless-nights in dark alleys, now wandered in the light. People hoped to be mugged by as few criminals as possible and prayed that the beating would lack luster, more protocol than rage.

It was a war to control the spoils in a world where everything was spoiled. But yet, not everything and not everyone had gone bad; that is too bleak. While it was true that the rich were safe in their well-tailored lives and many a good man teetered on the edge of wrong, many had not given themselves to the demands of the street. Many good, but scared men struggled meaningfully for their daily bread.

Then there was Timmy, who felt he could wander through danger unaffected. The day he became a bubbling cauldron of rats had scared and empowered him, scared him enough that he stayed on the sunny side, sufficiently empowering him to chance the dark, though he kept himself small.

As time went on he became more daring, brazen even. Since he could be anything, he often would. He would join a gang and walk cock-sure down Broadway, knowing if the tide turned, he could turn into a tank and chase them all away.

He was his own game of chicken. He'd dare himself deeper and deeper into the unknown, into the forbidden places, where he'd blend in and observe how the underbelly crawled. It became an insatiable desire, a wide-eyed sickness that didn't blink for fear of missing the next act of repulsiveness.

Timmy couldn't sleep. Images of rats danced in his head. He spent his nights amazed and amused at how deep he could go, amazed that people believe a six-year-old boy when he pretended. It made him wonder twitchily what his limits really were.

He imagined, late at night, how he could rule an army made of his imagination. He could mouse his way into the oval office or march in as the President himself. He could impersonate his way into space or present himself as some sort of divinity, but one thing he never imagined himself being was the harbinger of disease, the proprietors of plague and pestilence. He had never imagined rats.

He had never even seen a live rat before he moved to the city. Oh sure his old home had the occasional vermin, bed bugs, mice, squirrels and even a raccoon lured through the window by a series of false promises. But these creatures never made it past breakfast and the only signs Timmy ever saw of their existence were fiercely picked over bones, cracked, gnawed and marrow sucked.

He couldn't even imagine what made him do it. That's probably what bothered him the most. Why rats? He tossed and turned through the deep comfort of his first bed. Rats had invaded his head. He was overwhelmed and feared his professor might mutate. He breathed lightly across his lips, awaiting the sound of screams that meant the jig was up and he'd have to flee to the sewers.

Why rats? He'd playfully run through these types of scenarios a thousand times in his head. Boy faces danger and in his mind he becomes a giant, brisling with muscle, dripping with vile or he'd be a gang of the chain type, swinging shovels and axe handles. He imagined ninjas, cops, marines, ghosts, goblins, dinosaurs and wizards. He imagined how the dirty hoodlums, about to deflower the fair maiden, would react when Godzilla, King Kong, Genghis Kahn or a fat guy with a giant donut of doom showed up to save the day. But he had never imagined rats.

It felt almost as if the rats were always inside him, waiting to bubble, to stream, to burst into the light of his new found life. It was the most horrifying thing he had ever witnessed and one of the happiest moments of his life. He could still hear the monster screaming as he ran into the shadows, leaving only a trail of uncomfortable dampness to point the way.

After a particularly brutal night of more tosses than winks and more turns than dreams, the rats chewing away at his brain, he snuck out of the house. His thoughts were stuck on a gang he had followed the previous night that had been dripping with plunder from fresh larceny. They trudged contently, skin under their fingernails and blood in their eyes, the screams of ruined lives still dancing in their ears. They smelled of crime without punishment. Rape and pillage lined their faces and still they were not content. They strutted and swaggered, busting up every bit of garbage they encountered on the way, high on destruction and very possibly some sort of meth amphetamine. The very sight of them made Timmy nauseas, dropping him to his knees as he melted into a puddle and began to vomit.

He couldn't get his mind away from what he saw in their eyes, a self-satisfied neo-contentment on fire, high-intensity flames licking their eyebrows with cold disdain. The very thought of that much evil made Timmy sweat ice. These were not good men fallen. These were the men who made the good men fall. Tragedy reverberated under every heavy boot that dropped on the sad, salted earth.

He was drawn back to that alley with a compulsion he could not fight, didn't want to fight, changing as he slipped into shadows so thick that even those who hid in the dark could not see within them.

The spot commanded him. These creatures were made of things he did not know, could not understand. What made such beasts? Where did they go? Were there places darker still? Places dark enough to contain so much concentrated cold? If he found such a place would he find a way to stop them? If he found such a place would he ever return?

Waiting in the alleyway of an alley's alley that led into emptiness, Timmy found few places he felt comfortable. There were few spots where one could hide from men who destroyed even those things that were already ruined.

He climbed a dumpster that led him to a fence that allowed him to grasp onto a fire escape where he imagined he was the railing. Not because he felt he had to be anything more than night itself, but because he'd learned that railings were for safety and the idea of safety was all he had to hold onto as he waited in bad places for people who were worse.

They came. After an hour of waiting they came, bodies of stone marching. The only things about them that seemed alive were their eyes. They were alight with the flames of a civilization in ruins.

But something was different. Their lips curled with hunger, their jowls stringy and tense as molten saliva ran down their chests, filled their pants, leaving soggy footprints on the asphalt. Timmy saw evil, something so bad that even the fringes of humanity, the tattered shred with little decency but still a drop of shame, would have quivered at how the blackness laughed.

Timmy's blood curdled then hid. His limbs drained and became opaque. His safety railing nearly fell away when he saw what it was that made malice giddy.

Slung over the shoulders of a boulder-shaped man and dragged in a sack behind another, were the clear forms of two young girls, too scared to fight, too tortured by fear to cry out, a slight shudder the only thing showing they were alive. They couldn't have been any older than Timmy and the odds of them ageing further were bleak.

Timmy's heart leaped into his ears. He could hear his blood. His blood was angry. Fear and disgust dropped into the dumpster below as safety fell from the rail. Timmy felt his bicuspids forming into fangs, his nails turning into claws and flaccid limbs throbbing uncontrollably from the vast pressures of fast pumping blood. He hissed, pointy teeth gnashing. Crooked wings sprouted from his back as a screech flew from his forked tongue.

The gang halted cruelly. Tongues licked lips, searching for any sent of salt or blood. The sacks dropped hard as they turned and echoed the screech with a fury that tells any nearby rabbit exactly that will be done to them before it is over. Fear makes the juices taste that much more alive.

Legs spread so balls would have room as knives and chains, pipes, mallets and bones, weasels, chainsaws, porcupines, axes and cleavers played among eager fingers. Iniquity never looked more pleased. It was enough to turn the bravest man to stone.

Timmy wasn't running. He was beyond fear. Maybe it was the haunting of the rats. Maybe it was lack of sleep. But seeing eager savagery only made him boil faster. It sharpened his teeth and razored his claws. He howled and flew from the fire escape.

He did not make it very far. Timmy cannot fly. He has no wings. He has no pointy teeth or razor sharp nails. He fell, missing the side of the dumpster by inches, landing softly upon years of unrelenting filth, unscaved from a fall that should have broken a small boy in two.

His outrage was not as frail. His outrage could fly. It had taken flight as if launched from cannon coerced into such a rancorous rage that it made its firings fail to fall. Pairs of teeth became scores. A fist of claws became a sky full. An army of wings beat the air into a gale. A demonic choir screeched pitiless cords. Upon the gang descended a night sky full of howling, packed with clamoring wickedness, sharpened to a glistening point.

The fire in evil's eyes turned yellow with sogginess. Their weapons fell useless. Their balls recoiled into baby places. First they said it, then they did it.

Shit! They yelled as one and fled from descending death in every direction. Some disappeared back down the alleyway; some vanished into unknown voids. Still others ran into each other, into walls, into each other and then walls and into walls and then each other. Three died on the spot from pure terror, another four from repeatedly ramming their heads into anything as stupid as they were. But none remained long enough to see a small boy hit the ground or the demons vanish harmlessly into the shadows.

The two girls, squirming from their bags, saw little of the descending demons. Their eyes were on a small boy who fell as the gang fled. He didn't fool them for a moment. They heard him scream with pre-pubescent rage and they saw him drop from far too high. They knew there was more to the story. But it was nothing their eyes would see. It was not for them. Even so, they knew who had saved them. They rushed to Timmy's side and pulled him from the mire of deep ghetto filth and held him tightly till his little eyes fluttered.

Are you all right? He whispered.

We were just about to ask you the same thing.

Are you hurt? Did they hurt you?

Not enough to matter.

Not enough that seeing them cower and run in terror won't make things feel a whole lot better.

We'd better get out of here. They could be close and there's more like them on every block.

We may be in too deep to ever get out.

Even if the sun were to rise, it doesn't shine here.

You just tell me where you are meant to be and trust that I can get you there.

We trust.

To the end of the world.

Hopefully we won't need to go that far. Now, help me up.

The girls took Timmy's hands and he covered them in shadow until they emerge from the alley's alley, alley's alley into the blinding light of morning. It was beautiful enough for tears and sappy lip shuddering smiles.

Girls, there's only one thing better than not dying at the hands of malicious thugs.

I can't imagine what that could be.

Is it the sunrise on our faces?

Close. Very close. Timmy's smile grew bold and confident. It's a little thing I like to call eggs and toast. After a night like that, nothing could be finer. His smile turned coy. Will you ladies join me?

We'd be delighted.

Lead the way.

Good. Eggs and toast will go a long way toward making things all right. But we have to hurry. I've got a class to teach in just over an hour.

Timmy and His Wife

You've changed.

Noticeably?

Very.

I've been trying real hard to be the same every day.

Well, it's not working.

Is it the nose?

What do you mean?

Is my nose different? Sometimes I can't remember what I'm supposed to look like, so I just try to imagine I'm what I was before.

Well, you're not.

It's not a good plan. Which part is wrong?

You're more like you were when we first met.

Well a lot of pictures you have around here are kind of dated.

That's what I mean. You're so funny now.

Funny?

You know you're always playing games and you feel so much lighter than you used to.

I'm still growing.

And I'm glad, don't get me wrong. I missed you while you were gone. But before you left I missed you while you were here.

Where did I go?

I don't know. You were so serious all the time, so focused and cold. You know, first you had to get tenure and then it was one project after another. I thought you had forgotten me or didn't care anymore.

You're the greatest woman I've ever known. Except maybe my Mom, but I'm not sure I really knew her.

I love you too. It was just, for a while, I didn't know.

Didn't know what?

If you still cared, if we were still happy.

All I need is eggs and toast to make me happy.

You know what I mean... happy with me.

How could anyone not be happy with you?

You're so sweet.

She took Timmy by the hand and brought him back to her bedroom. She switched off the lights and started undressing parts of him that didn't exist, parts he had no picture of. He didn't know what was supposed to be under the suit. It never came up. Some things came up, but nothing that had ever been up before.

Timmy feared something was wrong with his body. Fortunately, whatever she was doing was far enough away from whatever was wrong with him that Timmy felt she might not notice. Still he had nothing underneath what she was fiddling with and wasn't sure what she was expecting, but he was sure he didn't have it and probably couldn't get it. He did the only thing he could think of.

Timmy screamed.

What's the matter?

What you're looking for isn't there.

Is it me?

No, no, it's me. I'm just not there.

Is it us?

No, no, I just don't go that far.

What happened to you in that house?

For the amount of people there, it was very lonely. I spent years pretending I was a coin purse just to keep off the floor.

Oh baby, I didn't realize. I always thought it was me, that you didn't want to come home.

Coming here is the best thing that ever happened to me. If I had known I would end up here, I would have come sooner.

That's so sweet and I understand. We'll take it slow, at least until we understand what's missing.

Deal!

She laid Timmy down on the bed and wrapped herself around him. It's the most he'd ever been touched. The most body he'd ever had against his. It was warm and he imagined that was how yokes felt, cradled by silky white. She kissed his forehead and whispered love in his ear. He wanted to stay awake in that embrace forever, but could not resist the warm comfort. He slept and that too was better than anything he'd ever experienced. He was the yoke, always hot, never runny and no toast could ever deplete him.

Timmy Meets God

Timmy's life hadn't been the same since he found God. He was hiding in his closet. He claimed he was lost. But that didn't explain why he was stealing his pants. God mentioned something about how his mother had burned his only khakis years ago in Hell, but Timmy tried not to listen. Family problems should be kept among family, but far be it for Timmy to lecture God.

Timmy asked God what he was doing with his pants.

God said they were his pants. He had after all created them.

Timmy said they were made in China.

God said he made China.

Timmy shook his head. It was too late to argue glaciers and tectonics. Besides, as God told it, he had big things to tell him.

So you're not just here to steal pants. This is some kind of burning bush moment.

I told you they're my pants.

I'm sure we could argue that for an eternity.

You don't have that long.

I guess I shouldn't argue that one.

Now you're learning.

Besides those pants are dirty.

I created dirt and several cleaning products.

And they belong to my wife.

So you're saying they're too tight?

I'm not sure what the fashion is in Heaven. But in New York City if you wear those, someone's gonna kick your ass.

42

Heaven ain't that different.

God shimmied out of the painted on jeans, revealing a little too much of his glory for Timmy's liking, but still, despite himself, he couldn't help thinking how the line 'he's got the whole world in his hands' was one hell of an exaggeration.

So what are you doing in my wife's closet anyway? It's not exactly what I'd consider a house of God.

God works in mysterious ways.

You're stealing women's pants.

Not anymore! Besides, I thought they were your pants.

What do you want?

Where's your closet?

I don't think I should tell you.

I'm God, I already know.

Jesus Christ!

He doesn't wear pants. Of course his robe is a lot younger than mine.

Why don't you just create a pair?

Everything I create chafes me horribly. Except the velvet ones, but I only wear those when I'm feeling smooth.

Like when you sneak into people's closets!

I was waiting for you.

In my wife's closet!

You showed up didn't you.

It's my house! Of course I showed up.

You spend a lot of time in your wife's closet?

Not as much as you.

But you came here today.

Well, I, um, needed…

Tada! It's a miracle!

Oh you're just a laugh riot aren't you.

I created laughter.

Bet it chafes you though.

Everything does, which is kind of why I'm here.

To get pants?

Not exactly, but it all starts with pants.

Over what felt like a death, a resurrection and then death again, God recounted to Timmy the afternoon he spent in Hell with his mother, how she had demeaned him, insulted him, spilled coffee on his new khakis and eventually set him on fire.

God said it was just like any other outing with his mother, except for the pants. That part really hurt. So much so that he chucked a perfectly good

43

orb of fertility at the earth and had nearly forgotten about it, till some dead guy told him the story of a small town with large hallucinations and a world's record for babies delivered to a single woman. That's when it became clear to him what had happened.

So we're an act of God!

All children are an act of God.

But we were a direct act, an intervention.

I threw some fertility away while crying like a baby. I wouldn't exactly call that a miraculous inception.

That makes my mom some kind of modern-day Virgin Mary.

Virgin, please, the only thing that kept her from mounting every man in sight was that her vagina was too busy blowing out babies to slip one in.

Yes but…

I mean Christ, that woman knew her way around an aircraft carrier.

She was an instrument of God!

They all say she was heaven till the burning started.

You're talking about my mother!

You thought she was just a nipple till you were five.

She's a good woman.

You left home when you were six.

Well, maybe if you hadn't fertilized her I could have stayed longer.

Yeah, well, let me tell you, if I hadn't fertilized her you'd never been born. Egg number ninety-eight thousand thirty-four hardly ever drops. Not to mention that if she had kept going the way she was going, you would have dropped out of a cesspool.

What are you saying!

I made you.

That's what you always say.

There has never been a woman in all of creation that was promiscuous enough to deserve the Orb of Fertility, but one.

I ought to kick your ass!

Now you sound like my mother.

What the hell are you doing here anyway?

I've come to enlist your aid.

Well you have a hell of a way of doing it!

Thank you. That's just the kind of thing I'd like you to tell my mother.

What?

You may be the first super hero I ever created.

I teach economics.

You're six.

Okay, I pretend to teach economics.

That is what makes you super. You can be anything.

And what is it you want me to be?

Well I haven't gotten that far yet.

What do you want me to do?

I want you to impress my mother. And I want pants.

Pants?

Yes pants, lots and lots of pants.

Lots of pants?

So if some get ruined I still got a sweet stash.

You're afraid of ruining your pants?

My mother hates pants.

The mother I need to impress by becoming a super hero.

You will defeat the forces of evil.

And where are these evil forces?

I haven't contacted them directly. Not yet, but I've got some people in mind.

I'm supposed to fight evil you haven't made yet.

That's pretty much the gist of it.

And what do I get out of this?

All the pants you could ever want.

Aren't you God?

God damn right!

And all you can offer me is pants?

Good pants. The best pants.

Some kind of magical heavenly slack?

God no, I'm talking about really great pants, like the pair I bought at Macy's.

The ones your mother burned up?

And spilled coffee on!

The same mother you need me to impress.

Not so much impress as depress.

I gotta push down your mother?

No, just show her that good can triumph over evil.

The evil you have yet to create.

What am I stupid? You really think I'd create evil before making sure I had enough good to defeat it!

If you'd done that you'd never show your mother anything.

Exactly, but that's not it. I want you to not only defeat evil, I want you to ruin their pants.

And why should I do any of this?

I'm God.

You're some weird guy in my closet.

I'm God in your wife's closet.

Why would I believe anyone in my wife's closet?

I could turn you into a squirrel.

You could turn me into a squirrel.

Timmy rather enjoyed being a squirrel. It was much more fun than he ever would have expected. He liked the tail. He liked the teeth. He could climb straight up a wall and leap like he was flying. He was light and fluffy. His claws dug deep and he could smell everything. He saw the world more clearly than his human body ever had. He knew it by smell; every nut, every egg and all the toast. He could describe in detail anything around completely by smell, down to the number of socks stuffed under the bed in the small bedroom (seventeen) and he knew intrinsically which ones were good eating and which were made out of low-grade synthetics not suitable for ingestion.

Timmy had just begun nibbling on a cotton-wool blend when poof, he was once again a young boy pretending to be a man, on his back, on the floor, nibbling at the air.

Do that again!

Not until you've defeated evil.

You haven't even created evil yet.

Then you're willing to fight them.

Maybe, if it means I can be a squirrel again.

You are the greatest impersonator ever. You can be anything you want.

I can pretend to be anything I want, but I can't feel any of it.

That's for the best. But if you do all I want, I'll make you a squirrel.

I don't want to be a squirrel.

You just said…

I want squirrel control.

You want to control squirrels.

No, I want to be a squirrel only when I want to be a squirrel.

If you defeat evil, I'll let you be a squirrel anytime you want.

And pants?

As many as you can handle.

You might just have yourself a deal!

Shake on it!

Hold on! Hold on! We gotta slow down. I'm still thinking a little squirrelly.

I thought that's what you wanted.

I want happiness without pain.

But without pain, how do you know happiness?

I'll take my chances on that one.

But without pain, how do I know happiness?

What do you mean?

If I wanted to watch a nice game of chess, I would have made smart people more attractive and brutal people less virile.

So our happiness depends on violence?

That's how good crushes evil. It's also how evil crushes good, but I don't think you need to know that.

I don't want to hurt people.

Of course you do. Remember the rats and the vampire things.

That was different.

Everything is different. But now you can justify it by saying it's God's will.

It's only different when it's my will.

Evil's coming for you, God on your side or not.

I'm gonna have to take my chances.

Fine, no pants for you. And no squirrels either! Now you're gonna do what I want simply because I want it. You have no other choice.

There's always another choice.

That's what they all say.

Johnny Paul and Paul Johnny

If you were to ask Paul Johnny about his son Johnny Paul, he would tell you that he was born backwards. Everything Paul Johnny was, Johnny Paul was not, or rather, he was the opposite. They were like two sides of the same consciousness, one was guided by whispers from angels, while the other received loaded advice from a maniacal jerk.

To further make the point, let us consider that Johnny Paul was a vegetarian, while his father only ate meat. But Johnny Paul wasn't a vegetarian because he cared about animals any more than his father ate only meat out of some savage yearning.

Johnny Paul, fruit of Paul Johnny's loins, had stopped eating meat at the tender age of three, but it wasn't to save the world. He stopped eating meat to destroy it. He was a vegetarian in an attempt to nip the food chain at its source. Every time he ate a carrot he pictured a rabbit starving, leaving no food for the fox and the snake, thinning the herds of coyote, bear and cougar and from there it was only a small step to the weakest of men, i.e. the pizza delivery man and once they're gone the rent-a-cops won't be far behind.

Conversely, Paul Johnny felt that vegetables were the source of all power and meat was simply vegetable concentrate. By condensing the vegetables he gained greater power from every bite. That was why he ate only meat-eaters. They are the most concentrated vegetables on the planet. Paul Johnny preferred gamey meats like lion, otter, cat, ant-eater, killer whale and Mongolian.

This is almost everything you need to know to understand JP and this father PJ, this and that they were both evil. One was an evil messenger of God and the other was one of Satan's angels. Despite the difference of Heaven and Hell, they both had the same goal, they each wanted to bring the world to its knees. Only their mutual ambition followed contradictory paths.

JP's plan for world domination started at the end. He wanted the finality created by the world of machines. He sought complete control of the used ends of production; he wanted the diamond rings after the diamonds had fallen out; the cars on their way to the crusher; toasters that didn't toast; chickens already consumed; worn out Astroturf, broken plastics, spent fuselages, the rusty shells of tanker trucks, spam cans, Twinkie wrappers, sludge, industrial wasted, refinery bi-products, the shit dripping into our rivers and billowing into our air. PJ wanted control over all the waste products and ultimately the nation's garbage.

JP thought himself a seer. In his mind he had seen into a future where the beginning had ended and all that was left were the ends. Once pre-production goes the way of the Truffula Trees, trash will become the only world resource and he who controls the trash controls that world.

JP stock piled trash, lived for trash and fantasized about trash to the point of mysophilia. Garbage was all that JP believed in. It is the final final. Unless you consider recycling, but recycling was too Buddhist for JP who received his directions from a quant retirement community on the edge of the Lake of Fire.

In mission PJ was a lot like his son, but as far as tactics went, none could be more different. PJ went right to the source. Money controlled the world. Energy interests controlled the money. Energy was ruled by oil. Oil came from the ground and the ground was made of rock. So PJ went directly to the source and determined to rule the world of rock.

If it was made of rock, PJ wanted it. Starting at the tender age of two, PJ stole rocks by hiding them in his diaper. By four he was chipping away at the asphalt street in front of his house. By six he had figured a way to bring his sandcastles home from the beach.

PJ didn't stop there. He soon gained control of every sand box within two miles of his house and had stolen every sculpture, every stonewall and every rock garden in the community. While he was a suspect in many of these robberies, the police could never pin so much as a grain on him. It was as if the stone had vanished and by the time he grew his first nut hairs he was making gravel pits, highway overpasses, coalmines and large section of New Jersey disappeared as easily as if he were stuffing stones in his diaper.

PJ and JP loved each other very much, just in very different ways. JP believed that love was the beginning and PJ believed it was the end. Since that was not what either of them wanted, believed in, or could accept, they no longer talked. They hadn't stood face to face since the day PJ caught JP squirreling a barge full of McDonald's waste under his bed. He wasn't proud of it, but PJ lost his temper and hit his son with the Washington Monument (which he had acquired only moments before and much to his chagrin it broke over JP's head, damaging it so severely he nearly returned it. But rock was rock).

Being mistakenly evil and rather upset about the size of the monument his father hit him with, JP had vengefully kept his father as far from garbage as his growing empire would allow, believing that garbage deprivation would eventually show his father the error of his ways. His father has not been within ten miles of a garbage scrap in over two years. For unrelated reasons, JP also took his toaster.

The Mamma God Defense

He goes and creates a universe and suddenly he thinks he's God! Does he give the woman who created him any credit? No! Does his Bible acknowledge my efforts? No! There's not even a dedication! Like I didn't carry him! Like his giant head didn't stretch my hips beyond ever snapping back! Like I wasn't in labor with him for three-quarters of an eternity! And it's not like he was an easy child, constantly creating things he couldn't control, then calling them evil just so he could smite them, the little Devil! That's what he was too, a little Devil, giving his poor mamma no rest!

And it wasn't like I got any help from his father! Damn celestial anomaly. Every time I even bridged the subject of his bastard child he would start down the whole I'm unstable. I'm an anomaly. Space and time don't really exist; how could something that doesn't exist even have a child? And Jesus Christ, get that damn kid a robe or something, he's streaking all over the cosmos!

So what do I do? Being a good and loving mother I did exactly that! I made him a robe and it wasn't easy. Most of the materials I needed didn't even exist when I started stitching. And now what's this! Not only does he toss me out of Heaven! Not only does he rip me from my rightful place as matriarch of all! But he ships me to a rat hole on the Lake of Fire, then dares to show up in pants. Pants!

Mommy isn't good enough and neither are her clothes. And to make it worse he spent my money on it! Like the nursing home hasn't seized all my property! Like the only possessions I have left aren't squirreled deep inside my anal cavity! And still I tried, digging out enough money for a nice gift certificate, leaving myself with only five dollars in Canadian pennies, a few rings, two and a half pieces of French toast, a canned ham, two towels from the Holiday Inn and a Christmas wreath. Hardly anything considering my son seems to think he's king of the world! Where do you think he got all the omnipotence, omnipresent and all that other Omni shit of which he's so damn proud?

He's got nothing I didn't create first and I'm at least twice as almighty. And he comes to my house! Drinks my Café Oley! Eats my canned ham! All the while flaunting his new pants, shoving them in my face every chance he gets!

And all that talk about how crappy his old robes were, barely befitting a God of his stature, please... Oh and when he spills my only coffee all over his precious store-bought pants, who does he go and blame? Not God, no he's infallible. It must be Mom's fault. After all, she's the one that lives in Hell. Little bastard, storms out the door, dropping my ham on the floor, all the while crying like some little pussy-ass-bitch, swearing that I'll get what I deserve…

What I deserve is a son that cares for his aging mother and appreciates all my sacrifices, not a little fuck that cries over spilled tea! It's time someone taught him a lesson.

He may be a God, but he didn't create being God. And as far as Gods go, he's far from the best I've seen. It's time he understood his true place. We'll see who's visiting who in Hell when this is all over! We'll see who's hoarding Canadian coins in their butt when all this is finished! I can guarantee you one thing. When all this is said and done, I know of at least one woman's son who's ass will still be far too tight to ever keep a canned ham stowed away for company.

Timmy Breathes Ants

Timmy was excited. He was excited about being excited. It was a new sensation. In his short life he'd had little opportunity to experience hopeful expectations. From what he'd seen so far, he figured that first time you did something was probably the best, though he wasn't sure, having done precious few things twice.

Timmy had a lot of firsts to look forward to, ike tonight. Tonight would be the very first time he'd battle evil for the third time and the very first time he'd do it on purpose.

He could hardly wait till dark. He sat anxiously in front of the television trying to watch the news, but his attention kept drifted out the window, where he'd wish the sun to set. When it didn't, he'd return his gaze to the news, in case it knew of the night's arrival before the window did.

He thought about wearing a costume. All the best crime fighters wear costumes. But if you're going to appear as something, and you're not sure exactly what that something might be, till you get to where you're not sure you're going, then there really isn't much sense in dressing up. Besides, anything he could put on, he could pretend to wear. But somehow pretending wasn't as much fun. So he figured he could wear a costume and pretend he wasn't, that way no one would know that his outfit made no sense and everyone could be happy.

In the end he went as a cowboy. He'd never been a cowboy before and this was the perfect opportunity. It was also the only costume in the house, that and Frankenstein, which happened to be two sizes too big, at least according to the tag. But it fit better than two sizes. You wouldn't know it by looking at him, but deep down Timmy was becoming a little big for six, not a lot big, but a little, big enough for a size eight Frankenstein maybe next year. Right now, the cowboy suit fit great and better than that, it felt right.

He'd thought about making his own costume, but knew he wasn't gonna get much better than a sheet with jaggedly cut eyeholes and a Mardi-Gras mask. Even if no one else was going to see, he didn't want to know he looked stupid.

As he left the apartment, he imagined himself Wyatt Earp, tall upon his steed, six guns dangling. But he had to stop for fear someone would see him and call the cops to report a cowboy riding through the hallways. It was the kind of thing that might even give someone a heart attack, which was no way to start a night of crime fighting.

When one seems to be anything he imagines, one must really be careful what he imagines himself to be. He learned that lesson one day in the park, playing in the sand box with some kids he'd just met. He was pretending to be a bulldozer. He pushed the sand around with the flats of his palms and was revving his engine into higher and higher gears as the pile got bigger and bigger. He was feeling pretty good and even a little bit normal, when he noticed his new friends running, police raising an alarm and mother's screaming as they scooping up their children.

He sat in that sandbox, shocked, a sad little boy who felt he couldn't even be normal as himself, when he realized what he'd been doing. He'd been pretending too hard and everyone around him thought he really was a bulldozer. They weren't running from him, but from an out of control machine that somehow appeared in the middle of the sand box.

After that, Timmy tried not to pretend too hard around others, not unless he really meant it. He let go of Wyatt Earp and walked down the hallway as a professor, six guns silently firing at the ceiling as he moseyed his way out the door.

In the new dark of night, his spurs rang against the concrete, his silver star sparkled under the street lamps and his guns clung closely to his hips. He sniffed the air, then pulled it deep inside his lungs. It's a good night for laying low the bad guys, he thought as his mosey became a bowlegged strut.

Three blocks into the shadows, he decided his cause would be best served as a young girl, immature in a tiny blue dress that was a little too little for her, adding to her innocence and vulnerability. It was a good disguise. Perhaps he showed too much knee, maybe his pigtails bounced a little too much and the sweater twisted about his shoulders could have fit his mother, but other than that he was a dead ringer.

He felt creepy, like he was doing something wrong. He could nearly feel the skirt billowing about his lower thigh. It tickled and he giggled in a way that disgusted him. But to battle evil, sometimes you must do despicable things. Girls were not his enemy. They were just not what he ever imagined himself becoming.

No one would ever expect it. No one would see this coming. Not that they could have. But he determined to be at his best, just in case, cause maybe someday, someone would see through the imperfections and then he'd be in a real fix. It was even possible that God might rat him out and he'd find himself ambushed if not careful enough.

He added a nervous skip to the routine. He thought it added wiggle to the worm. Not that it mattered. It didn't take long for the bait to get a bite.

It started as no more than a hiss, but gained momentum into a beckoning call.

Little girl… You look lost little girl.

I am a little sir. It sure got dark fast.

It does do that. Are you far from home?

A dark form, a shadow, moved forward through a pitch darkness that the dark form was still somehow darker than. He was nearly an apparition, apparent only as a hovering variation in the blackness.

Come closer. It said. I have been here a long time and know many ways to many homes. I'm sure one of the ways will lead to yours.

I've been told horrible things about strangers and the tricks they play on little girls.

Ah, but I have no tricks. I have no candy. I have no van. I have no false messages from your mother. But I may have better bearings than you and that should be enough for a little lost girl to start considering me a friend.

Timmy turned cold, trying desperately to control his imagination, fighting the shivers that ran up and down his body. He waited, inching closer, waited some more, looking for the first sign that showed what he already knew: this man was no friend to little girls, but a fiend.

Timmy had been planning a Tyrannosaurus Rex, a monster with hunger dripping teeth and razor sharp claws. He kept it in the back of his mind, comforted by its distant roar. He could barely hold it back. He could feel the tail starting to grow, but managed to pull it back in as he approached the shadow, watching its features darken as he drew near.

Child, do not fear me. Listen to my voice. I am too old and too frail to hurt anyone and I've seen too much pain in this long, long life to cause any myself, let alone to a little girl.

The darkness of his face seemed to wrinkle before Timmy's eyes. The black that was his head turned sparsely silver atop. To Timmy's astonishment, limbs appeared from the shadowed torso and from somewhere beneath what Timmy couldn't see, the old man produced a map that unfolded in shinning brilliance.

Timmy's jaw dropped, the dinosaur fading from his mind. A gentle warmth rose in his chest, gladness trembling on his little girl lips as an arm tightened around his neck.

Timmy never saw the other man, but the bicep crushing against his cheek was large enough to fully eclipse his head. He gasped, but only a gurgle, a soda bubble drizzles through. He kicked at what felt like a wall. His sight grew blurry. His little arms clawed behind him, finding nothing and no one.

Every vein in his body tested its walls. Explosions were imminent. He was going to burst or maybe pop. He was not sure... He was no longer certain... Darkness was entering his mind. The schoolgirl fell away.

Timmy became himself, a limp, struggling, getting smaller by the second self. His soul sucked desperately at the tiny bubbles his lungs were able to pull through. His throat was being crushed. The air passage was too small. He began to fall away. He became smaller and smaller, till the air that could still bubble through filled his lungs with blackness.

Timmy had no idea where they came from. Maybe it was all he could afford. When the hole is too small, send something smaller. Or maybe the darkness had only left enough of his mind to conjure the tinniest of aids, but call them into being he did, again and again and again.

He didn't know. He didn't remember, not all of it. But certain sensations are not easily erased. He had to imagine. No not imagine, that would be dangerous, but he almost believed that if something foul enough happened to the dead, even they would never forget it.

He could not have had much life left. He was dangling over the edge, when he felt the bubbles he so desperately sucked upon, reverse and one by one the ants began to march. They squeezed through the tiny hole afforded his throat, marching across his tongue, over his teeth and lips, attacking the arm that was nearly four times thicker than his Raggedy Andy body.

He didn't know how many ants it took, but the single file line seemed to march on forever. One by one, marching, climbing, attacking that arm. One after another, after another, after another, after another...

They may have marched for hours or maybe it was a flood. But when the grip loosened and the air returned like a tornado down his esophagus, he exploded. He burst into tiny bits, black ants covering the night, raining, itty, bitty, black. They fell upon their backs, squirming. Timmy expecting a sneaker to come down and change his religion.

He was broken, dashed, his abdomen dragging near useless upon the asphalt, when the tiny bits, the single file army and the blanketing flood from the darkness of his mind, returned to him. His tattered bits of imagination, the fury that what was left of him could muster, returned, dragging him to safety, huddling around his body, guarding him through the night. It turned away would-be adversaries and blanketed him against the cold of the night.

He spent the wee hours as the darkest of the dark, cocooned behind a dumpster. He would never remember how the little pinchers and little feet dragged him there. He would never be sure if they were him or if he was them. He did not know who was saving whom or how he could be resurrected from certain death. He did not know that, behind the dumpster, he neither tossed nor turned.

Alone, in the cold, he would surely have died, had his pieces not taken such great care of his whole. He saved himself, a power arising from within in his time of need, to warm, shelter and guard him. It made no sense, neither did his dreams.

He dreamed he was a volcano, kept from hurling fiery devastation only by throwing himself again and again into the burning pit that was in itself himself.

In the morning Timmy was reconstituted, hurt and slow and happy to be so. His cowboy suit was tattered and soiled, but he was alive enough to worry for it, to worry about his son and how he would feel when he found his best costume ruined.

He limped home, grateful for an empty house and the eggs and toast that allowed him to muster a diseased-looking professor. He was worn thin and certain that the next time he decided to attack pure evil, he should do it as Frankenstein. Wyatt Earp never stood a chance moseying down the forbidden alleys in the big city.

PJ Meets God

Good ends in evil.
Evil ends at midnight.
Evil is born again after every twelfth strike,
While good is slow to rise.

This was why PJ, JP's father, believed he was working for God. He was, to be truthful, very slow to rise. He thought himself an extension of God's arm, his bad arm, the one draped in black and dripping with vile. There were also times when PJ believed that he represents one of God's feet, the one wearing the steal-toed boot. PJ loved his assumed relationship with God, for God was the ultimate rock (one which PJ someday hoped to steal).

PJ dedicated his nights to God. At night he pursued the devastation of mankind in his own way, which meant steel-toed boots and jackhammer fists. He was therefore not at all surprised when he received a long overdue visit from his boss and mentor (at least he respected his old testament work, though he considered much of his recent Goding to be far to new-agey for his liking).

What did surprise PJ was seeing God at night, at a time he considered well past God's bedtime. Compared to this shock, finding him half naked, rummaging through his closet, barely caused him to bat an eye.

PJ was feeling good. He had just acquired the Great Barrier Reef, replacing it flawlessly with a Polly-urethane reproduction. PJ felt there was something special about living rock. He was captivated by the very idea and felt it was some of the most important rock he had ever stolen. He felt connected to it even after he had sufficiently killed it. In his life, he had tried reproduction only once and felt very uncertain as to its results.

To get to the beginning you have to start before procreation. In fact, if PJ believed that God had any true defects, besides his recent new-age hippie attitudes toward the meek, it would have to be that he had wasted so much time creating. PJ felt God missed the boat when he didn't stop after he'd created rock. He couldn't understand why he covered so much glorious rock with inexplicable and disruptive creations, leading to problems which need never have arose and was much of what he wanted to talk to God about, had he not walked in and found God making such a mess of his stone-washed jeans.

You know those don't fold themselves.

They would if I had created them.

Haven't you done enough already?

Depends on what day you talk to my mother.

Leave your mother out of this.

Believe me I'd like to.

Good, then that's settled.

You're not the boss of me.

Well it sounds like you ain't either.

Slow down buddy. Don't forget I created you.

Bet you're regretting that about now.

And your pants suck!

They cover my junk, which is something I'd like to suggest for you.

Really, your clothes are complete crap! The whole pile is fit for the trash.

If they were trash my son would already own then.

That's why I never had a son.

What about Jesus?

Well sure him, but I'm talking about people who wear pants.

Mind if we move out of the closet?

God kicked off the jeans that were dangling around his ankles and headed for the closet door.

Aren't we forgetting something?

56

I'm God.

Play that card all you like, it still don't fold my pants.

You're getting on my nerves.

I didn't leave my pants that way.

Really, you shouldn't push me.

Ain't creation a bitch!

You don't have to stay created.

I can't imagine that you've been spending time in my closet just to smite me.

If you like I can smite you and bring you back till you learn how to talk nice to your creator.

Or we could leave the pants where they are and go someplace more comfortable.

God smiled smugly as they proceeded into the kitchen where PJ offered him a stool and a Tab.

I've been expecting you for some time. I'm a little surprised you didn't come sooner.

I didn't know about you till yesterday.

I've been working for you my whole life!

That's what the Mormons say too, still I didn't find about them till last week.

I thought you knew everything.

Knowing and boring yourself with the details are very different.

Then what do you do with your time?

Lately I've been trying on pants.

So you're here to try on my pants.

Don't be stupid, you know as well as I the shape of your pants.

Then you've come for me.

That depends what you mean.

You've seen my work.

Yes, yes, the rock snatcher.

That's me!

Very impressive.

I knew you would think so!

Well, it's time we took things to the next level.

If I could tap into the Earth's core, then we could get all them bastards in one fell swoop!

Yes, get them all. That sounds all right for you I guess.

With your help it will be easy to destroy them!

That's exactly the kind of thing I need you to try on your own.

But with your powers we can't fail!

57

That's just the thing, I'm kinda busy right now.

But this is what I've been waiting for. This is what we need! Your powers and my mind. We can reduce this planet to gravel.

That sounds great and all and really I'm completely behind you, it's just I've got other things on my plate.

You're God! You can't have too much on your plate! You're fuckin' omnipotent!

You obviously haven't tried to find pants worthy of God.

Pants! I'm talking a complete reordering of the world as we know it and you're talking pants!

To each his own.

If you not here to help me, then what the hell are you doing here?

God helps those who help themselves.

So you came here to preach shit to me.

Hey, don't blame me, I didn't write that shit. And what I'm here for is to get you to completely overhaul your operation.

I stole the Great Barrier Reef!

We can do better.

That's just what I did tonight!

But no one knows.

Exactly!

But people have to know.

If they know then I can't steal.

If they don't know then they won't realize that you're a super villain.

I'm not a super villain.

But you could be.

I work for God! I work for you!

And this is what I need from you. You are my evil enforcer, the man who sets the stage.

I pictured us as co-rulers.

I'm offering you greatness and you're talking stupid.

I didn't come here to be insulted.

This is your house.

Damn straight! You came to me! You need me and you're calling me a villain!

I'm calling you a hero, a warrior for God. It's the world that will call you a villain.

A warrior for God huh.

You betcha.

And I can still take rock.

All you want.

Alright, it's a deal.

Like you had any choice.

Hey, God or no God I'm my own man.

I could turn you into a squirrel.

Then who'd be your supper-villain?

Being a squirrel was much different than PJ expected. Usually he was a rock kind of guy, but suddenly his world became consumed by nuts. He had grand and furious ideas. The world was full of nuts, nuts he could steal and horde. If he had all the nuts, he could bring the world to its knees! It couldn't possibly survive, though his little squirrel mind couldn't focus on why. His tail twitched wildly as he imagined how the world would crumble. He clawed at the floor, leaped from counter to cabinet to God to the window, which looked like it was open…

He landed, quivered on the floor dazed. He twitched for several seconds, when, like he was made of rubber, bound to his feet and made a dash for the window, which looked like it was open…

He landed, quivered on the floor dazed and twitched for several seconds, when, like he was made of rubber, bound to his feet and made a dash for the window, which looked like it was open…

PJ could never be sure how long this went on, his squirrel mind seemed to hold no time. Outside of a desperate need for nuts and 'look an open window,' the only intelligible thought he had was 'hey, I'm a man again,' as he crashed through the window, that for a split second he was sure was open.

He felt excited by the sunshine, recharged and ready to ravage the world and make its nuts his own… only, as he lay bleeding on the concrete slab below his kitchen window, wedged between a retaining wall and the foundation, he couldn't imagine what world domination and nuts had in common. Instead, he felt overwhelmed with the strange and inexplicable desire to find God the perfect pants.

After the Ants

Timmy crawled to work, or maybe he armied, thousands of bits of him scurrying together like a tidal wave of insignificant proportions, hell bent on ravaging every egg and each toast from home to campus. Sixteen eggs and their counterpart in toast left him far from a man, but nearly a boy.

In the bathroom, before his first class, he couldn't muster a full size professor, which may have had something to do with the fact that he was laying down. He was carried on legs that had grown from ant, to rat, to beaver and a smear of yoke following him everywhere he went.

The students didn't notice anything unusual. Students are not known for being acute observers and Timmy's teaching style discouraged them from looking directly at him. He demanded answers from them and counter views, until he reached a consensus. It's the best he could do teaching things he didn't know. The administration loved it. They said that he was really making them think, that it was within the fervor of debate that real learning took place.

Well, Timmy figured, if someone had to make them think, it might as well be him. Besides he had far too much on his plate just dealing with the wife and kids (never mind achieving actual size) to spend his precious time learning facts and teaching figures. Just listening to the zombie-toned liveliness of the debate made his brain retract and nearly collapse within it's self. If it weren't for the eggs and toast he wouldn't do it at all.

Timmy could be anything. He could go anywhere. But he lucked into what had to be the egg and toast capital of the world. And if what he needed to do, to keep the yolk flowing, was to satisfy a wife, be a role model to children and teach immature adults, all of which were too dumb to see that he wasn't even seven, then God damn it he would do it in any condition the fates had left him. He would do it from the floor if he had to! For one day he would no longer be a child wandering from diner to diner, taking an egg here and dipping a toast there. Someday, he would be the one with the toast and the world would be crawling to him on the legs of rats, begging for salty, peppery, yolk-dripping toast. That is how life would be when all the eggs were his.

It could all be his. He felt it. He just had to learn to never again be where he appeared to be. To survive, he would always need to be at least slightly offset from his appearance. And while he was thankful for the ants within, he hoped they never again needed to come marching to his rescue. He hated to wake up in pieces behind a dumpster.

His final lesson was the hardest for him to accept. He knew he could teach from the floor. He'd always known size didn't matter. He understood that position was everything. He had seen first hand that second impressions aren't impressive to anyone. But laying on the floor of the auditorium, he knew acutely that smell does matter and no amount of yoke can cover up a trashcan.

Long Way Home

Timmy carried himself home on ant legs. He never realized how far things were for the tiny. Exhausted, he moved at the speed of urban decay. He travelled the hundred years from mansion to crack house on tiny legs, taking tiny steps that gave most the impression of standing still. The road ran on ahead for an eternity. Street crossings were a death trap. Stairs took an army. It took every ant he had to make it home.

Inside, safe again, his ants gave him back his legs. His limbs returned reluctantly, crashing him into every wall and door jamb as he struggled to the shower. He pulled back the curtain and fell in.

Under the hot spout he nearly melted. Bathing as someone thrice his size, he hoped to dilute the smell. He scrubbed with the stuff his wife used to dissolve soap scum. He really needed to learn how to read. Still, even in his broken state, he wouldn't soon forget the look of that container. He feared the burning would last forever. It was the best he'd felt all day, only surpassed by when the burning stopped, costing him two layers of skin.

Inside his scrambled head, Timmy thought dimly how he would have to talk with God and convince him to put the end of burning high on his list of things to make the world a better place. It was his new number one, right above eggs and toast for everyone.

He wobbled damply across his apartment, the image of a soft bed burned into his expectations. Numb, he drifted into his room, dropped his towel and reached into his closet for an extra long pair of fleece pajamas. Their softness and warmth just worth the effort of reaching.

God you stink!

Who asked you?

Awful sensitive today ain't we?

What are you doing in my closet?

I found you someone to battle.

Why are you in my closet?

He's a rock man from New Jersey.

Why are you telling me in here?

I thought you'd be excited.

Why wouldn't you just meet me in the hallway or kitchen or anywhere normal?

I like it in here.

Listen, if you're gonna be hanging round my closet, you're gonna have to do something for me.

I'm God.

Would you do something for me?

The burning?

Yes, the burning!

As soon as I start making the world a better place, I'll take care of that first thing. Now onto our villain.

No one should ever burn.

You haven't met my mother.

I like anyone who isn't keeping me from my bed.

It's gotten a little weird in here since you barged in. And before you start, yes, I know all about the ants and the whole trash dumpster thing.

You could have helped.

Ain't my job.

What is your job! Lord of pants?

Careful kid, I can damn every one of you to Hell.

Timmy Meets Mother

You're probably not surprised to find me here.

I really wish I was.

I'm sorry we had to meet this way.

Someone had to burn those pants. An uninvited guest slipped his bare butt in and out of every pair.

So I did you a favor.

I would consider it a favor had you burned them somewhere other than my closet.

I get a bit caught up in the moment.

Now I'm not real clear on normal behavior, but do people usually meet for the first time in closets?

In some places they do.

I'd rather this not be one of those places.

Don't blame you, though it's smoky enough to be one of those places.

That's not exactly how I planned it.

No kidding, you don't even have a smoke detector in here. This place is a death trap.

And still we live. Umm, I usually invite people I meet in my closet to the kitchen for a drink.

I'd love a cup of something really hot.

Now that the fire's died down it's getting a bit nippy huh.

Kid, you're reading my mind.

Timmy led Mother God to the kitchen and put on a kettle. She was a hard woman to look at, not to look at, but to focus on. She looked like nothing and everything all at once and none of the time, both sequentially and all together. She smelled and looked like she was burnt all the way through, or maybe she was made of flowers. Her black hair shone white. She was no particular size. Timmy couldn't tell her from her clothes, if she was wearing any, though it occurred to him that she may only be clothes, a thin layer veiling nothing. She was horribly beautiful and her eyes never left him. At least twice, he felt them in his ear.

I'm sure you're wondering why I'm here.

All I know lady is I'm staying out of closets from now on.

I tend to get a little agitated in them myself.

So I noticed, but really it's more a matter of occupancy than agitation.

You have quite a vocabulary for a child.

I've been spending a lot of time around universities.

Oh I know, a very impressive trick I must say Professor.

It keeps me in eggs and toast.

But you don't want eggs and toast do you?

Lady, you got some bum information.

What I mean is, you don't want to just get by, making barely enough to keep a little yoke on your plate do you?

Now you're getting closer to the truth.

You want all the eggs, all the time and a mountain of toast.

Make it all the eggs and all the toast and we're talking about the same thing.

Ambitious!

No lady, just hungry. I ain't nearly as big as I pretend to be and it takes a lot of smothered bread and salty whites to keep the whole thing going.

I think we can work something out.

Child Man and the Shrinking Woman

Timmy had seen a lot since he left the satchel. Big city, big university, God's junk, but nothing could compare to the room shared by his boys. That was what he considered them, his boys. Even though both kids were older than him, he still felt like their father. They looked up to him, which was always weird, because in reality, he wasn't where they were looking. And stranger still was that if there was anyone he envied in this world, it was those boys.

They were smart kids, kind and gentle, but tough enough to have survived life on the floor and they were rich beyond Timmy's wildest dreams. They had a room full of treasures the likes of which Timmy had never imagined.

They had cars and trucks in their room, big ones and little ones, some so small they could fit in the palm of your hand and tiny men, not alive, but plastic, some that bend with what they called action grip so they can hold guns, drive jeeps and fight, when necessary. They had blocks that snap together, pencils in a thousand colors, sparkly glue and a dozen colors of dough for molding, not eating, though they thought it funny when you ate some. Timmy made the youngest squirt soda through his nose twice doing this!

Don't eat the sparkly glue. If you do, you have to go see Timmy's wife and you feel great shame.

They had paints and crayons (you can eat the crayons, but it makes the kids angry), a dozen kinds of balls and board games where you rolled dice and tried to finish first and video games, where you pretended you're someone else, without having to change your physical features. It all happened on the TV screen and you had to play till your thumb hurt!

Timmy beat Ona at Super Mario Brothers twice already and almost beat Jack at Basketball, but Jack kept kicking him whenever he tried to shoot. And Timmy was apparently the best ever at Chutes and Ladders, which he even told his students so they would know that they're dealing with a climber and not just some shoot-sliding sucker.

Timmy was very impressed by the amount of loot his boys had collected; bears, swords, eye patches, silly putty, magnifying glasses, binoculars, puppets, plastic vegetables, rubber bands, petrified Cheetos, arrowheads, a bird's beak and nearly permanent tattoos (He put three on his arm in one day, went to class with his sleeves rolled up, wearing an eye patch and even though no one could tell, they still didn't bother him all day).

They seemed, to Timmy, to be the best at playing with all of them. They knew which doll (oh and never call them dolls) knew Kung Fu and which ones could fly. They knew how to make green out of two not greens. They knew when to put the video games down and get to the bathroom and how to clean up things they weren't supposed to be playing with in a way that Corrinna never knew.

They could build a log cabin, knew how to shoot things from straws through their noses and through straws in their noses. Ono once got a spitball stuck in his nose and almost died. They nearly had to tell Mom, but Jack said he had other ways to breathe and besides the spit ball would never get past the Tootsie Roll he'd stuffed up there last month, which he said was probably making its way to his brain and was gonna rot it like teeth. Timmy said it already had and Jack laughed, but Ono didn't and he felt kinda like a bad dad. So he told him that he put Tootsie Rolls in his nose all the time and he was a professor of something, so at the very least he wasn't rotting anything he needed for university work and Ono felt better.

When Timmy first found their room he couldn't think of anything else. They played and played and played and Corrinna would have to tell them all when it was time to go to school. Then after school they'd all rush back and play some more.

Timmy would catch his wife standing at the door, half hidden behind it, smiling, nearly glowing while watching them play. It was strange and it took Timmy a while to figure it out, but she looked different. Her smile had grown. The wrinkles seemed to fade and a new light shone in her eyes. Her skin went from dull grayish to a golden rosy. It was as if he'd never seen her before.

Then one day she left the doorway, picked up a rubber lizard and started to play. Again Timmy didn't know who she was. Her hair tossed back and forth. She giggled. She was radiant. That was when he understood what was happening. She was getting younger, bit-by-bit, day-by-day. It was only a matter of time before she became as young as he.

She even came home one day when he didn't expect her and caught him in the kid's room playing alone. There was no denying it. He'd made a real mess of the place. When she walked in Timmy was laying on his back making an angel in the middle of a pile of toys. He told her he'd come up with some new games and wanted to test them out before the boys came home. She just smiled and sat down, kissed him on the forehead and held his hand tight as she laid down next to him. They made the best toy angels ever. Timmy never felt so warm or so safe.

When the kids got home, they were still lying there. Timmy told them they'd come up with some new games he wanted to test out before they got home. They just smiled and jumped on their exposed bellies till Timmy and Corrinna yelled uncle, pinning the kids down with tickle monsters and kisses of fury.

It was then that Timmy really started looking at his kids. They were not the kids he met on his way out of the coin purse. They'd grown and not just older or taller. They appeared larger. The more they played together as a family the bigger they became, like corn being popped. They loomed where before they merely hunched. As happy as they seemed when their long lost daddy returned, they had been like seeds, ready to burst, but worried they may only burn.

Corrinna said she'd never seen him so involved before and it did things to her heart to see him giving them so much. She said that whatever had happened to him out there, he'd come back a better man. Where before he could only see himself, he now completed a family.

You can imagine how odd that made Timmy feel, but you might not realize how good. He had tens of thousands of relatives, but he never knew he wanted to be in a family. He had always assumed he wanted little more than shelter, eggs and toast. He never imagined how much more there was, how much more he was and could be, till he saw what his family was becoming.

They were less strangers to him and less strange to themselves every day. They transformed away from what they were pretending and Timmy felt the same thing happening inside his fraudulent form. He tried hard to keep the man strong and tall, but beyond the stature and appearance, he began to feel as if he too were becoming, not necessarily what he was meant to be, but who he actually was and never knew.

When you battle for scraps, when you cling for survival, you become nothing. Eggs and toast become everything because they ease the stress of a tomorrow always in question. Once tomorrow was secured, Timmy had the opportunity to become more than that nothing. Which could only mean, that before his arrival, his family was starving. It wasn't for food, but for something that, at least in part, he seemed to have been able to bring.

It made him think more and more about the world he saw around him. Like his wife, like his kids, like his students and even God and his mother, maybe everyone was starving. It could be that everyone was pretending to be someone else. Maybe he and his thousands were not the only ones spending their time impersonating what they believed others wanted them to be. They were starved into these forms and would stay hungry until they received proper nutrition.

Timmy didn't know what it all meant, not yet. But he understood that someday, if he did figure it out, the answer was going to be important. The answer was going to be important enough that maybe no one would have to go hungry ever again.

God's Revelation

Let's cut to the chase, your mom has offered me all the eggs and all the toast.

All the eggs and all the toast, now that's crazy. What I have to give you is so much greater than anything my mother could ever offer you.

I can't eat pants.

And the squirrel thing, don't forget the squirrel thing.

You already told me you weren't giving me anything.

Jesus kid, I'm God for Christ sake! She lives in Hell! And I don't know what she told you, but it's not even a good part of Hell! Eggs and toast is crazy! What kind of person wants all the eggs and toast? The whole idea is nuts.

You want all the pants.

Yes, but I don't really want all the pants. They are merely a symbol.

A symbol?

They're a declaration. They say I'm a big God, an independent God and mother can't push me around anymore!

She says you cast her into Hell.

Oh she exaggerates. I just thought it would be best if she lived in a structured community.

She's on the Lake of Fire.

Listen, I'm eternal, but she's even older than that. You just don't realize how cold old bones get.

Maybe it's just you.

What does she want?

I think you know.

God turned black as he smoldered, his hands bright with red and orange fire. He hurled scorching balls towards Timmy and disappeared.

Timmy dove, rolled, scurried and ran. Behind him, burned into the wall, was the crackling image of himself, the little boy, burning in a lake made of fire, despair howling in anguish through his every feature.

Timmy went to find some paint.

Invitation to Hell

It may have been red and it could have been black. Then again it could very well have been golden and the lettering upon it may have glowed, though he seemed to recall fire. Then again there may have been no writing at all. The words might have been seared deep into his mind. It read:

To John
Son of Paul
Son of Vincent
Son of Cornwallis
Son of Mud

JP wasn't sure if the letter had been open before he opened it or closed when he was through. The paper may have always been in his hands, but it was as likely as not that it never existed. Its message was clear.

Your attendance is required
Before herself
Mother God
One Half hour
Lake of Fire Retirement Village
Room 407
137 Lake View Lane
Deviants Hill, Hell

As soon as he read it, he never read it, it burned in his mind, or maybe it glowed. He doubted it would ever leave, if it was ever there. He felt as sure of these things as he was that he was wasn't anywhere and that the only thing his mind contained was the image of a gift certificate to Macy's and the strange desire to buy a skirt.

JP couldn't have been at Macy's for more than 20 minutes when he found the cutest little skirt that couldn't have ever existed. It had pinstripes that were neither there nor deniable. The colors seemed to flicker with every move, reflecting the world in a deep and ominous black. He admired the way it seemed to both slim and thicken. It was some kind of miracle.

He swayed seductively in front of a trilogy of mirrors. He had never noticed how nice his legs were. That's when the mirror jumped, swooped forward, engulfing his head, sucking at his shoulders and slurping him through like a berry several times too large for its straw.

Everything he knew about his life turned into pure heat. His screams melted before they left his lips. His teeth followed, oozing directly into vapor behind his inferno lips. He was too hot to move. He was too hot to stand. He would have collapsed had everything he was made of not already turned to melt. He dripped downward and steamed away to nothing.

Timmy Gives the Call

The flier read simply:

Breakfast at MSG
Free Eggs and Toast
All You Can Eat
To Any and All
"Cyclops"
Look-A-Likes
July 10th at 10:00am

The flier included a nearly impossible to achieve Photoshopped image of Timmy, with his eyes pushed so close together that they nearly touched under an eyebrow that spawned over his left eye and flowered above the right. Equally unattainable was the nose, which had been forced outward till it was so thin and sharp it could have shaved the unibrow. If that wasn't enough, his chin had been pulled into such a severe point it would make the Devil cry.

Timmy pinned his flier to a bulletin board inside the Café Fresh, a coffee shop and egg joint not far from school, then stepped back and admired his work. He nodded happily. The trap was set and all that was left was to prepare for the consequences. He imagined the news spreading like margarine on a hot summer day and worried how he would ever be able to get enough eggs and toast.

From that single, simple flier, Timmy expected thousands and figured he would need every egg and every loaf in the county and he had only two weeks to redirect them to a space he had yet to secure.

Fourteen days, that was how long Timmy had to feed an army. He expected an invasion by a numberless horde that would expect a buffet to be provided upon convergence. This was going to take everything he'd learned about the world. It would take more than just looks. It would take swagger. This was no simple rouse that Timmy intended to deliver upon. He had no other choice, the sign had been posted and this was a one shot deal. There was no room for error, which meant getting to the top and getting there quickly.

Timmy had to infiltrate eggs. He had to dominate toast. He had to get them to and sequester Madison Square Garden for the day and do it all well enough to put on the breakfast of the century.

If they were anything like him, they would show up hungry and if he didn't have each and every one of those bellies full by speech time, it would be for nothing. No matter how impressive the spread, regardless of the grandeur, no one is going to listen to someone who does not deliver on the first date. There would be no second chances. They would lose his number, never return his messages and tell all their friend how small it was.

Party's Over

PJ's particles retuned one by one. Creation hurt far worse than destruction. Fortunately, he hadn't yet the tongue to scream or the brain to remember. It was nearly a rebirth. When his synapses reconnected, he burst back into existence. Life had never been so frightening.

The heat had gone, as had the lovely skirt. The invitation was still burned into his brain. If there had ever been an invitation. If there had ever been a brain. He feared it had been replaced with an inexact replica. He could not remember what his brain was like, nor could he resist the searing upon his cortex, which seemed to read:

Next time
I'll come to you
Mother God

Timmy Gets the Goods

Timmy did many things he was not proud of to feed the expected hoards. Of which, everything he accomplished, he was very proud. He justified his means as being overshadowed by his ends. He didn't want anyone to suffer the burden of his plans. He didn't want to steal, didn't want to suck away the livelihood of little farmers. But he had no such issue with borrowing and felt, if the corporation was large enough, just about anything you could get from them was borrowing.

Wonder, Sunbeam and Hovis wouldn't miss a couple thousand loaves and eggs come into the city by the millions every day. If every New Yorker wanted eggs for breakfast on any given morning, every New Yorker could get eggs for breakfast. That meant millions and millions of eggs. So in a city that must stalk 20 million eggs at any given time, who was really going to complain if a couple dozen or say 80 thousand some odd eggs turned up missing?

Really, what are the odds that every New Yorker was going to want eggs for breakfast on the very same day? When you start to consider all the donut, bagel and pancake eaters and the short-sighted breakfast skippers, Timmy was really doing the city a favor. If New York didn't eat them, they'd go bad and bad eggs stink. At least that was what Timmy told himself as he began redirecting bread and eggs, along with the hundreds of gallons of orange juice that he thought would be a nice surprise.

Getting goods turned out to be easier than Timmy ever imagined. He started by collecting the profiles of every person he needed to be. It took him one afternoon, his first using the Internet. He'd go to a web site and download pictures and info on some high-ranking corporate officer from a distribution hub way out of the city. Then it was on to the next web page.

Once his folder was full, he spent two days dropping in to offices and redirecting special orders to Madison Square Garden. Stoves, plates, tables, salt, pepper, silverware, ovens, pans, chefs, butter, waiters, napkins, tablecloths, chairs, jelly, tobacco sauce and even Madison Square Garden itself went down the same way.

Four days, it took Timmy four days to set up an all-you-can eat breakfast for upwards of twenty thousand people. Hundreds of trucks, provisions and people were at his disposal and all he had to do was wear the right face and not ask for too much. Even MSG took little more than a smile and a nod.

He'd put on the proper body, someone high up enough to be recognized and respected but from far enough away to be personally unfamiliar and then he'd lay out his needs. Sure, they looked at him strangely for a second when he said that he needed the arena for the entire morning of the tenth of July. But as soon as he told them that they didn't have to do anything, that he had already handled all the details, that they didn't have to lift a finger and could even take that morning off, they handed the keys right over, danced a short jig and nearly kissed him goodbye.

Timmy thought of all the years he'd spent at the nipple and smiled fondly. He was sure that if he had known how willingly the world would give him anything he asked for, he would have spit that tit out years earlier and got right down to eggs and toast.

PJ in the Mirror

PJ had never looked so beautiful. His lips glistened like spring water. His cheeks beamed with a healthy red glow. His hair hung in long locks that pulsed with a life of their own, dramatizing his every movement with a bounce or a shimmer as if its entire job was to make him irresistible. And his skin, who would ever have expected someone who spent so much time brow deep in trash to have such smooth, supple and vibrant skin.

PJ looked so good that he began to think that maybe his fetish had been misdirected. Maybe instead of junk, he should be pursuing beauty or maybe some sort of compromise was in order. Maybe he should, at the very least, be collecting beautiful junk.

Don't go changing your lifestyle on account of me. His reflection scolded, flashing darkly.

Wha... wha....what did you say? PJ shivered as his bathroom began to overheat.

Honey, you are garbage through and through. Trash courses through your veins. To try and change that now would make you simply ordinary and you don't want to be ordinary do you? His image flashed scalding red.

You can't be talking? You can't be talking!

Did you really think you were suddenly this good looking? His reflection began to rot, layers of perfect skin peeling back, blossoming into puss-filled blemishes and green-blotched decomposition. His teeth chipped away into a fractured and broken smile that twinkled Tidy Bowl brown.

I know I don't look this bad. His bravery rose and fell.

Feel your face if you don't believe me.

He touched his face and his fingers stuck to the sticky clinging flesh.

He screamed through broken teeth, a skipping record of pure terror, before he crumbled into a heap of rotting garbage on a tattered bath mat. Make it stop! Make it stop! He whimpered through convulsive heaves.

God you humans are corny. The mirror scolded. How many of these ridiculous mirror sequences do you have to watch before you stop getting so freaked out? I mean Christ! It's not even original. I got the idea from daytime TV for God sake!

PJ looked up trembling and watched his wretched image turn golden, like a perfect apple stuffed with just enough poison to melt the masculine features away. It left behind a strong softness, scorched-white and dazzlingly repulsive. The woman pulled herself through the looking glass to recline gently in the sink with voluptuous maliciousness.

Don't tell me you weren't expecting me.

I... I...I...

Unadulterated fear is so trivial. Do you think we can bypass that and the hysterical frenzy and just get to acquiescence?

Who are you? His garbage lump unfurled as the surging heat made it unbearable for body parts to be touching body parts.

I invite you to my home and you still don't remember me.

Your home?

Granted you didn't last very long in Hell, but I can't believe it will ever leave your thoughts.

That was real!

How did it feel?

Like Hell!

There you go.

His last drop of moisture dripped from his chin and he began to crack, the furthest reaches of his extremities drifting away as a fine dust.

Mother God pointed a shower nozzle at PJ and monsooned his arid dust-bowl, sparking a frenzy of life. Flowers bloomed. Frogs mated wildly. Tiny creatures came out for a long desired drink. While snakes ate everything in sight.

What do you want with me?

Isn't it obvious? She winked.

I don't think I could handle that.

Please, I make something more alluring than you every time I sneeze.

Thank God.

He had nothing to do with it and if I start to think that you don't want me, I might just relieve you of those parts.

His gulp was dry and his esophagus shattered.

Not that I blame you, a girl comes through your mirror and props herself in your sink, how could you not think of sex? Her naughty parts sizzle and steamed luxuriously.

I'll do anything you ask.

Oh honey, I know you will.

Timmy Brings Them Home

Eggs were fried by the thousands. Loaves were dealt like cards to hungry toasters. The constant splitter-splash of orange juice roared like Niagara Falls. This was how Timmy always imagined Heaven, no matter what God said.

The sound of knives scrapping butter across toast filled his ears. The smell of hot oil ravaging eggs filled his nose. Timmy nearly forgot what he'd come for, what all the work was about. He was sure, if he locked the door, he could eat every embryo, mopping up each precious drop of thick oozing yellow with every piece of buttered toast.

But those uncontrolled desires were only in his dreams, in every dream he'd ever had. With eyes wide open, it would have taken tens of thousands of Timmys to consume what he'd created. As it turned out, there were just that many Timmys banging down the doors. Each with eyes pushed so close together they nearly touched, under an eyebrow that spawned on one side and flowered on the other, above a nose thin and sharp and a chin so pointy it would have made the Devil cry. Thousands of Photoshopped Timmys clamored at the gates for eggs and toast, oblivious to the orange juice surprise.

They had the place surrounded. They tore at the walls. They impersonated cooks, guards, deliverymen, stadium seating, retired jerseys, plates, glasses, railings and even toast to get to the promised booty.

Timmy needed to pacify them before the cops caught on.

There is no limit of eggs! He yelled over the PA.

There is no limit of toast! He hollered.

There is juice for a million! What should be hot will and refills are never ending! The fight for the front of the line quelled to a minor brawl.

If you eat me out of eggs and toast, I will supply them to you, free of charge, forever! The pushing stopped and the crowd lulled as if the bough had broken and baby was on its way down, cradle and all.

You will not eat me out of eggs and toast. But if you give me the opportunity, a moment to hum in your ear, I will tell you how you can still have eggs and toast forever. That is if you agree with me my brothers and my sisters! And you will! Just you wait and see!

They tried. Timmy had to give them credit. They really tried to eat all of it. After Timmy had waylaid their fears, they lined up so orderly you would hardly have believe their ability to devour, unless you shared their hunger. No one could have anticipated such a plague descending, except one who had once been part of the swarm.

Timmy manned the door, greeting his siblings one by one, slapping backs and shaking hands before whispering discretely, a tiny detail of who they really were and letting them pass.

Welcome sister.

Hello blue eyes.

Come in my squat nosed brother.

You have mom's tits.

Did you fly here on those ears?

I saw you catch that squirrel.

I remember when you lost that ear.

I didn't know we came in blonde.

You look just like mom.

You remind me of God.

They ate and ate and ate; nearly consuming Timmy's estimate for several thousand more. Nearly, but thankfully even the hunger that comes as a birthright must subside, if only momentarily. Over fifteen thousand of them had come and gorged themselves into submission. While only the most astute among them realized any family connections among the crowd.

Have you ever heard the sound of fifteen thousand yokes being broken simultaneously by the sharp end of an equal amount of dipping toast? Can you imagine thousands upon thousands of teeth gnashing and tearing as if they may never again know breakfast? Throats gulping, like they'd never known an egg? Glasses turned upside down, over parched holes that acted like they'd never felt the sweet touch of orange juice? If you were to accelerate every house ever consumed by termites into a thirty-minute clip, it would fail to compare to the noise of Timmy's family throwing down breakfast.

They consumed like piranha, with one exception. Timmy paced nervously about the arena, eyeing the stage he had constructed in the middle of the frenzy. On it sat a little podium adorned by a single microphone. It was small and black and Timmy didn't like the way it was looking at him.

He waited patiently for stomachs to fill. He watched for bodies to slump and recline, for bellies to bulge, belts loosening and that near pained, near blissful look of gluttonies victory over the glutton.

It didn't take long. Timmy was glad. He'd been waiting long enough already. He felt like he'd been waiting his whole life and that the rest of his life hinged upon what he did next. He climbed to the podium, tapping the microphone, turning every head till every eye rested upon him. Timmy dropped his guise with a smile and a wave.

My brothers and my sisters, see me as clearly as I am able to see you. This is not a simple buffet for thousands of unfortunate looking people. This is a family reunion! The Cyclops to your right and the Cyclops to your left are merely a rouse made possible by a common ovary. I ask all of you to drop your personas now. They do not become you. Not at a time like this, when we are about to become so much more!

A surprised mummer vibrated the arena as familiar faces appeared. Greetings passed from table to table and seat to seat. Screams of shock and awe rang through the crowd. Hugs and handshakes were exchanged. A brilliant glow covered every face, replacing the blush that came from being caught.

Since the day our mother hatched us, we have been lost, floundering, pursuing the next meal, like our lives exist only in our bellies. Our birth right until now has been our curse! All we have known, all we have ever been, is an imitation of other people's lives. Most of you are still existing in the shadows, providing for yourselves as I have provided for you today, by being someone you are not. And to that I say hurrah!

You are not merely leaches, you are gifted! You are the most talented artist in the world! Only you are using your gifts to chase the small, catching what must be admitted by everyone in this room to be pitiful. Pitiful! I'll be the first to admit it! But pitiful is not what we are! And pitiful is not who we are meant to be!

The very fact that you showed up here today, using your tremendous skills for something as small as eggs and toast, shows clearly how lost we have been. We thought nothing of coming here and perjuring ourselves for half-a-day's ration. And that's just today's mistake. We've been heading down the wrong paths. We've been going the wrong way! Our skills are great! Our rewards are small! Our lives are less then we deserve! Less than what we are capable of obtaining!

But even when you consider the minuscule size of our achievements, when we multiply them by our multitude, the effect of what we do becomes tremendous! If each of us were to live up to our enormous potential and we then multiply that by our numbers, we would rule not only our world, but the heavens and beyond!

I have been in contact with both the high and the low and neither makes any sense. But I believe, that together, we can build something greater than a simple accident of God. He made our mother a factory, but he never imagined how great its product could become!

He had no idea what he created. And until now, neither did we! But I can tell you from the shear size of this turn out, that what he made, accidental as we are, is greatness! If we bond together, if we join as only a family can, as only our family could possibly merge, our great talent and ability will prove greater than any that have come before or any that will come after! If we unite, we will not merely succeed, but we can and will determine the path that humanity takes from this time forth! Together, we have not only the power to change the world, we have the power to reshape it into anything we want it to be!

Big As God

God tried everything he could think of, but couldn't find any way to get into Gargantuan's pants. They were like walking into a circus tent during an earthquake. Several times he got lost. It didn't matter how large he became, the pants stretched with him. The Lycra was never ending and always two sizes too big. There was nothing survivable about the smell. God was lost inside those pants for weeks before he finally found a way out. He would never be the same God again. He had all new plans for damnation.

What the hell's wrong with you! God screamed as he burst celestially into Gargantuan's lair, rays of light and sparking smoke clouds punctuating his godly rage.

I feel as if I know where you're going with this. Gargantuan smiled.

Don't you ever change your pants!

It's sometimes difficult for an outsider to tell, but they are being changed even as we speak. A complete change takes several months and when the crew has finished, they have to start all over again.

I was waiting for you for weeks!

You were lost.

I was waiting! And you better start watching your tone.

You're in my house now.

You do realize I'm God.

I was about to ask you the same thing.

Blasphemy will get you no where.

Have you seen my wall?

I have and I gotta say it's great work!

Child's play.

I think it's more an offshoot of tanning, taxidermy and umm something pretty fucked up is as close as I'm gonna get to the last thing.

If you are going to barge in, at least be kind enough to not waste my time.

You are really missing what's going on here.

You keep making statements that are somewhat backwards. So to expedite things a little bit, let me tell you why you are here. There is something I want you to do for me.

I was about to say the same thing to you.

That goes back to the somewhat backwards thing I already mentioned, so let's start at the beginning. You, God, have been wandering through my discarded pants for weeks and somehow came out thinking you are in charge. Not only that but you're late.

What do you mean I'm late! God's eyes cracked electrically. I'm God! Don't you get what that means! Lightning flared.

You're gonna have to come up with a better argument than I'm God if you hope to get anything out of this negotiation and you are indeed late.

That's not even possible.

Gargantuan rolled a lumbering pinky against a buzzer.

Yes sir. A soft voice mused.

What time did I have God down for in the appointment book?

You had him down for 1:30 sir.

And what time is it now?

3:45 sir.

You see. Gargantuan turned to God. You are quite late.

I do not schedule meetings.

I never asked you too. But I do expect you to show up on time once you're scheduled.

You think you're better than me.

It is best not to think about it that way. What is important is that I'm going to overlook this tardiness as long as your services are professionally handled.

I can't even believe this shit! I'm God! I need no argument! I need no appointment! I need no forgiveness! I made Heaven and Hell!

I've never seen the difference between them.

Oh I can show you the difference.

I own half of Hell and the better part of Heaven. If I decide it should be so, I can burn up Heaven and freeze over Hell.

Yeah, well, so can I!

I really only had you scheduled for fifteen minutes and with the tardiness and all, I really must insist we move on with this. I hate running late.

That's it! God smoldered. I'm gonna make you a squirrel right now!

Gargantuan became hairy. His teeth grew. His ass had a nice fluffy tail to sit on. Very little had changed. He was still fat. He could still barely move. He was still eating a constant stream of food that arrived by conveyer belt from his kitchen to his tongue. The only thing that changed was that he was a little more comfortable. The fur and the tail really cushioned his bedsores and hemorrhoids.

Clearly, I'm not the one this prank has made to look stupid. Gargantuan squeaked.

God changed him back, dejected.

What do you want me to do? God pouted.

I want a planet. I need it shrunken and orbiting my back yard.

That's a big order. This isn't little God stuff.

Well you're a big God. I'm sure you're up to the challenge.

That's not the point is it?

I know where this is going. No, I don't have a lot of Gods on my Rolodex. But the very fact that you waited around in my closet for me, means there is at least one other God now interested in anything I have to say.

You wouldn't.

I bet she's listening now.

Fine, I'll work with you, but you gotta do something for me.

I don't have to do anything.

Ah come on. It would really mean a lot to me. I might even get you two planets.

I'd like Pluto.

Everyone would.

Timmy Gets One in the Bag

Timmy would never have confessed it to anyone, nor would he admit it to himself, but deep down, way beneath the surface, he liked being a little girl. And even though he needed only to imagine a fetching little creature for her to exist, he still liked walking the walk, swaying gently to and fro, his skirt sashaying ever so slightly as his hips rang the bell. And what was the harm? He wasn't hurting anyone. No one would even know about this strange fascination, as long as he did it away from knowing eyes.

He blamed it on the night. Daytime, he felt, was for men. Bright light didn't give proper respect to a gentle to and fro. But at night, the shadows made a delicate flower a little more precious, gentle features becoming distinct and exotic, revealing sultry details that the sun would blanch and burn under its unyielding inspections. But night made a female's details supple, luminous and radiant, which is exactly how Timmy felt.

Timmy lifted his face to the gentle evening breeze that blew cool and calm, stripping away the swelter of a long day. He felt alive and daring. These streets, through whose shadows he weaved, were dangerous even when the sun was dropping a hot bead upon his scalp. In the daytime, in these neighborhoods, the shadows were still so deep and dark they were almost sticky. In the night, they clung and groped, pawing at his sundress rabidly as he tried to flutter through night's fly-paper fingers.

A malignant chill blew straight from the inky darkness. His heart beat anxiously. He breathed deep to keep from hurrying, to keep her steps from clapping ever quicker against the pavement. Speed was pointless. If trouble was near, and trouble always was, speed meant little. Trouble would come when it came. It made no sense to run. You'd only get to it quicker or make it hurry, huffing and puffing. Trust me, you don't want to excite the bad ideas. Things go better when evil feels there is no rush, when it believes it has all the time in the world and can afford to be smooth and slick.

Time makes evil cocky. Cocky makes the bad man slip. It doesn't take that much to set them tumbling. These men are rarely that clever. A bad man lurking in the shadows of the darkest part of the city can be little more than dim. If he were smart, he'd be stealing from those with enough to barely notice the loss. Smart steals what won't be missed from those who have so much they can no longer see and have been raised with the kind of overflowing plentitude that makes them unable to appreciate any of it anyway.

That's what makes the shadows of darkness so exciting. Vulgarity lurks around every corner. In-bred abuse floats a regatta in every puddle. Ignorance, maliciousness and a vile disregard for the decent side of humanity blooms in every cigarette-filled flower box. These dark impulses move on swift legs and swing arms of deep forged iron. They are stupid, brutal and angry, yet they can track better than a thousand bloodhounds in a trash compactor. They can smell you coming while you are still out of state. They are ready, willing and able. But as much as they know and as much as they expect, there wasn't one of them that knew what this little girl was packing.

It didn't take long. It never does. The ones who take a long time never get there in time, like the grasshopper who played all day in the sun only to arrive well after the marrow had been sucked from the bones of the lion's kill.

Passing under a street lamp, Timmy admired the way he walked. He liked the way his skirt fluttered, always on the verge of showing too much, while never showing a thing. He liked the way his hair danced upon his shoulders, little ears flashing tiny sparkles, his shoes click clicking on the pavement, hypnotizing him as he eyed his ever taut calves.

Timmy knew it wasn't right, but he was beginning to develop warm feelings for himself. He tingled shamefully at his first attempt at lust. There was something about the way he looked from afar that gave him trepidations that rippling with green frothy foam while at the same time making him swoon in a deep comfortable warmth.

He wanted to run and tell himself that this was no place for something so sweet, that anything so lovely should stay always in the light, while he knew his heart could never bear being any closer to such perfection. He'd explode. He'd burst if he didn't meet her and he'd die if she even looked at him. He didn't know how he could go on existing, knowing that she lived always just next door in his imagination.

Which was probably why he became so angry, when what appeared to be two bags of trash leaning against an abandoned litter of pit bulls, turned out to be far less timid than he when it came to approaching fair-haired young ladies.

Imagine that garbage walking right up to her. To her! They weren't good enough to be gum upon her shoe! She should never even have gum upon her shoe! Her shoes touched her feet and even that which lies under what touched her feet was still precious. Anything stuck to her sole was good enough for Timmy. And these two, filthy, ill-mannered hooligans should never have stepped within a mile of where she would someday tread.

He bit his anger, chewing it, swallowing hard, squashing the giant that rose from his clogged throat. He dug his fingers into his arm just to keep from exploding out of his schoolgirl long enough to get what he had come for.

Hello little school girl. The men moved to block both advance and retreat.

Well, hello yourself. Timmy's girl twinkled, halting her forward momentum, while her side to side kept kicking up dust so seductively that Timmy nearly hated her for it.

Did you come all this way just to see us? They toyed, drool streaming from their overdeveloped jowls.

Why I didn't see you at all. Is it your habit to spend just part or all of your time amongst the trash? Timmy grinned rancidly at the flirty desertion.

You find the sweetest thing when you stop by the trash. They menace.

I suppose one who spends time with garbage should know. Timmy could have cried as her lips spoke humiliation threw perfect pouty lips.

There's a price to pay for being in the wrong spot and another to pay for insulting the owners of that spot. Hatred grew as fists clenched to strangle a neck too small and delicate for their furry.

I'm sorry, I thought you were merely by the trash, I didn't know you owned it. Timmy convulsed as she floated.

Steel flashed, fists curled and the men narrowed the gap between themselves and the girl. Timmy's heart leaped, but behaved, as roundhouse strikes encompassed her but failed to catch and metallic lunges lurched only to return spotless. She was a dish, ever sultry, but impossible to catch. They retreated ever so slightly and began to circle fast, yet cautiously, as if trying to capture light, arms wide in ever quickening rotations.

Light she was, radiating with every missed grasp and every gently dodged advance. They tightened the circle and she thinned, they dove hard with steal and swung heaters like hatchets. Timmy had taken all he could.

White light exploded from where there was once girl. The two men threw themselves into one and other, head cracking and steel piercing, their eyes locked on the light, despite metal dragging through their abdomens. They could not look away as sparking brilliance thrust upwards, soaring away from their empty grasps.

The light arched high and shimmered momentarily, a star of wonder, a star of light, bristling into claws that rained down. Long, jagged nails spiraled toward gutter trash that stumbled frantically. The claws arched low, forcing their faces into the cold concrete. The claws clenched into a fist that pounded the street in uncontrolled rage, moving the trash to their feet and into a desperate sprint.

Timmy was far from done. They had treaded vagrantly upon lands too holy for forgiveness, places that made his little heart palpitate, places love made him fear. While he remained unafraid of even the deepest and darkest of pits, he was afraid of her and now they would be too.

Fangs sliced through the air, pissing venom and crushing pavement at the heels of the fast moving refuse. Red-veined eyes glared at them as claws ripped through the walls of brick tenements, stone splinters tomahawking past their ears.

Running out of things to shit, the fleeing scum dropped organs: livers, kidneys and intestines. Vitals rained upon the street in an attempted to lighten the load as they took every turn into every alleyway, throwing down trashcans and hookers in their wake.

Teeth pierced the street before their feet, claws crashed at their heels. They turned hard into a narrow alley, grinding against dumpsters, their bodies teetering out of control as they propelled themselves into the deep dark hole.

The monster bit at the entry, chewing and slinking its way down through the corridor, pushing against the narrow, working its way into the crevice, forked tongue darting forward licking the air, nostrils a plume of purple vapor.

Cornered, the running made for a van with the back doors left wide. They slammed the doors shut and cowered. They didn't expect the van would protect them, but a final refuge is just that. We don't always get to choose where our last stand will be or if not standing, our final place of shivering in the fetal position.

Still, they hoped beyond hope that maybe the creature would only crush the metal box and they'd survive in some little bubble of metal. It seemed unlikely. They moved together, arms clinging tightly, prepared to die like mice.

A van is no match for tongue or for teeth, except if they don't exist. But few who have found themselves being chased by an enraged monster have taken the time to think about what lays beyond the only open door available. The cornered trash had no ideas except that they would soon die.

They were shaking nearly out of their cold, clammy skins when they heard the roar come from the front of the van. They waited for the teeth to pierce through the metal walls and the claws to pound them into mud. But they didn't come.

Seconds passed before they realized the van was moving. They leaped to their feet and threw themselves at a pile of boxes between them and the cab, digging till they hit a tiny window that peered into the driving chamber.

Drive! Drive! They shouted hysterically as the van pulled out of the alleyway with no claws and no teeth cutting them in two. Pure joy overtook them. Unfettered exuberance pounded through every cell in their bodies like each molecule contained a wild man with a drum, promised all the cocaine in the world, if only he maintained a ferocious beat.

Tears flowed, ecstatic screams of relief ricochet off the walls. The two men, once brave, then mice, now embraced, holding each other close.

They had never experienced happiness before. They had been raised maliciously. The streets were their mothers, living rooms and beds, the back of a hand as close as they'd ever come to a male role model. It was no wonder they were so surprised at how good happy felt. It felt so great that when the van doors flew open and they were handed over to the police, they could do nothing but smile, smile, smile.

Even when they understood that all their warrants were coming true, they smiled. They had been caught after being very, very bad for a very, very long time and they knew they were going to jail and not coming back. Even that knowledge was not enough to keep the two men from holding hands and skipping.

$50,000 in reward money was not such a bad night. Brothers and sisters everywhere were in need of some relief. Rents and mortgages would be paid and not just for those involved. If you were family and you needed help, it would come as soon as the family in greater need was no longer in greater need than you.

In such a large family there was always someone who needed something. This is not uncommon. Nearly everyone, everywhere, needs or believes they need something. That is just how it feels in this world, but Timmy refused to believe that was how it had to be.

There is not very much anyone can do for those that constantly believe in their own dire position. You cannot cure the lazy or the greedy of their woes. But Timmy felt he could do something for those that would never have enough if things didn't start getting better.

It had been agreed upon, that for good deeds to truly be good deeds, something more must be done, something more than mortgages and yokes. All were in agreement, the first priority would be to end any suffering within the family and the second priority would be to allow into the family anyone who was suffering and willing to work for something better.

The idea was as great as it was beautiful. The only problem was, that in a family of thousands, taking the first steps toward a new destiny, there was, right off the bat, plenty of need. Timmy had promised many eggs and many toasts and promises sometimes predispose greater good. That day the need amounted to $47,628 leaving just over two thousand dollars for purposeful improvement.

The family used the money to invest in the spot where garbage arose to harass a little girl. They took a small rental property on the ground floor and established a point of light, destroying a fraction of the darkness. It was a beacon, manned by a trusted family member in need, a rock in which to fasten a beginning, a flame of hope in one of the cities darkest spot. As far as two thousand dollar beginnings go, could you ever shed more light?

A Day For Eternity

What are you doing here? Timmy shrank despite every attempt to grow.

Do we really need to start this I am everywhere shit? Her smile simmered delightfully through a fearsome, blackened scowl.

I thought that was your son.

Where do you think the ingrate learned it? Her smile turned to death as her eyes beamed a constant joyous light.

You know he tried to kill me!

That would be very boring of him.

My death bores you?

Everything bores me.

So what are you doing here?

I just stopped by to tell you how lucky you were.

I used to think that was true.

If you've stopped, then you're a fool.

If I'm a fool, will you leave me alone?

No, I'll just finish with you quicker.

Maybe that's for the best.

You haven't even seen what I can do yet. I'm going slowly with you. If you knew what I've done to people I've handled quickly, you'd beg me never to finish.

Is that what makes me lucky?

In the long run, maybe, in the short run you're lucky just because I'm visiting you.

How does that make me lucky?

Change your tone or I'll show you what it is to be unlucky faster than you can flap that mouth. Remember, if I don't like the way this goes, next time you'll visit me.

And then I won't be lucky?

I live in Hell boy! When you come to me you burn as hot as I see fit.

Makes you sound a little like the Devil, don't it?

I see you've been talking to my son.

Only when I'm not lucky.

There you go. Today it's just me and if that ain't lucky I don't know what is.

I'm not gonna argue.

Then you might not burn.

Not many guarantees with you Gods.

Most kids your age don't have anything to say other than yes ma'am.

I've been old for my age since I was too young for any of this.

Riddles that don't need to be solved are boring.

Yes ma'am.

Don't be too smart.

I don't feel like I am.

Then don't act it.

Before I bite my tongue off, can you tell me why the visit?

I've come to offer you a deal.

I don't have anything you'd want.

You have my son's attention.

I'd be happy to give you any and all the attention I'm getting from your son right here, right now.

That sounds like Hell to me.

Then what do you want?

I want your attention.

You've got it.

I want you to tell God that you have joined with me. That we talked and you've decided you don't believe in him.

He'll kill me.

He can't do anything I don't want.

He put you in Hell.

I went to Hell.

Why would you go to Hell?

You try and live with him.

Point taken, still, I got a lot in this world that can suffer and you folk don't seem too keen on our well being.

You haven't taken sides yet.

I don't even understand the sides.

All you got to know is that you better be on mine.

Or I belly flop into Hell's reservoir?

It's a lake and I don't find it that interesting. It's such a predictable agony. I use it only when I need to make a point to the stupid.

Glad you don't think I'm stupid.

Don't be. It only means that I've got to be elaborate with my tortures if I'm to get your proper attention.

So if I don't join, you get creative?

I'm way past creative.

What does that mean?

It means welcome to the game!

That don't sound good.

It depends on your perspective.

I want to be left alone.

That ain't gonna happen.

So…

So, you wouldn't believe all I have to teach you.

I hate to ask.

I barely want to tell you.

Seems like we're coming to some kind of agreement.

I can't imagine that happening without your lips on my feet.

And if I grovel?

Then you're not as smart as I thought.

And I go to Hell.

You don't know what Hell is.

I've heard rumors.

You've heard wrong. Hell isn't a place you go when you die. Hell is where you stay when you can't stand being there any longer, when you've given everything you have, every last little thing and you're exhausted from carrying around the weight of a pointless and aggravating existence year after year after year after year and still you don't die and still you can't die even though tomorrow is gonna be just the same as every other yesterday.

Not dying is worse than burning?

What? You don't believe me?

Am I supposed too?

You will.

One in the Oven, the Other in the Freezer

Mother God flashed a revoltingly beautiful smile, her teeth shining a brilliant vacuous black. A cool breeze eased Timmy's hell fears as it licked away at his nervousness, drying the sweat accumulating upon his upper lip. He pulled at his collar to let the breeze in as the first snowflakes accumulated on his nose.

This is where I leave. Mother glistened heatedly. If you need me, I'll be in the oven. She winked watching him turn cold.

The wind bellowed and blew. The kitchen stool flaked away and Timmy landed in a pile, a drift, a dune of white. The air turned white, his sweat freezing over. A bitter arctic blast shriveled his lungs and raised his hair. He wrapped his arms around his body as the boogers in his nose turned crisp.

The kitchen was gone. Mother had disappeared, presumably into the oven of a kitchen no longer there. Shivers vibrated Timmy's body violently and he rolled down a drift of snow, head over tail over snow. Timmy thought briefly how much he preferred being a squirrel as his rolling catapulted him into a face-down snow angel at the bottom of the blow. He kicked and flailed, the snow too light and fluffy for him to grip well enough to pull himself out. All the while, the snow angel grew, becoming immaculate, ready to fly despite the storm, ready because of it.

Timmy dug down, burrowing, throwing a blizzard in his wake at the blizzard at his back till he reached something solid enough to grab onto. He feared it was a polar bear and hoped it was a penguin. It was the hard pack.

With nothing else, Timmy plunged forward, digging, plowing, scraping and sliding inch by foot by inch. He imagined himself a coal miner's daughter and laughed at the form as it appeared. It froze. No degree of imagining was going to get him out of this one. There was no one to be, no one to call. He was just a little boy in a white hole. The hole far brighter than one would expect of a hole, as if the snow wanted him to see how hopeless things were, how superior it was to a little boy in depth and boundless direction.

Timmy could have been tunneling in circles as much as it mattered. But giving up was choosing to die, choosing to die was going to Hell and no matter what Mother said, not dying beats burning. Burning is hopeless, he told himself, forcing himself further. Burning is boring. It's the same thing every day, which Timmy agreed may be what Hell is made of. Hell is never changing. Hell is an eternity of digging snow caves. Even if it was not death and his little cave was not endless fire, his mind was already burning.

But the hole, while tiresome, was not entirely unpleasant. Timmy liked the strange glow of the surrounding snow. He'd always wanted to dig a tunnel and he'd always wanted to play in snow, so it was almost like the freezing death he burrowed through was a poorly thought out gift. The surface had been worse, with its ice-laden wind smashing at newly formed frostbite and for a moment he was glad to dig and glad for his half bright hole, which was probably why the hole ended.

Timmy dropped off the edge of a high iced cliff, flailing, sliding, tumbling and crashing, bouncing and rolling down the jagged icy decline. A sharp, bitter wind pushed him down, propelling him faster, his helpless little limbs clutching at snowflakes as his screams froze in bubbles to his lips.

There is no contentment in a half-lit hole. The wind laughed at Timmy as he fell. Everything is endless. Everything is falling. The wind teased. The best we can hope for is that it comes to an end.

The bottom struck Timmy before he could hit it. It was too transparent for snow blind eyes. It snuck up on him, riffling him through a short slope and across a hard and jagged bottom. Sickles and spears of ice thrust upwards, around which the ice graveled and mounded, between which Timmy thankfully flew. It looked like the earth was angry and indecisive. An idea reinforced by the ever changing intensity and direction with which the wind blasted at Timmy's body.

He clutched himself tightly, narrowing his form to weave through the piercing juts of ice. He imaged himself a bobsledder, then a snowman, a polar bear, then a space heater and finally a bonfire. Nothing helped.

Timmy slowed and then stopped. His clothes were little more than fringe. His back was skinned and filleted. Again he was thankful. He was glad for the cold. He knew there were pieces of meat missing from his backside, but the blood froze and the nerves never had a chance to feel. He thanked the wind and pushed on.

Timmy pushed past the sharp, smoothed his way across the slippery, the storm whipping at his back, pushing him through the barbed and crumbled ice maze and still it was not Hell and still he did not believe that he'd prefer the constant burn.

Before him a mountain of slashed and fractured ice smiled heatedly.

Even a bottom as torn as tumultuous ice is better than a fall through the darkness. The mountain creaked.

The solid pack tearing you back is more reassuring than grasping at snowflakes no matter how hard you hit.

The cold began to win. But its victory lacked bite. As the cold wrapped its claws about Timmy, something wonderful happened. As the wind pushed his frozen body through the gale, the things that wanted him to believe that what he was given was rotten, stopped feeling and all that was horrible showed itself for what it really was, absolute beauty. Magic howled past his ears and marvels thrust toward a snow-white sky.

Timmy stopped fighting and let the wind blow, planting him into the garden of ice. He thought how lucky he was to have lived to see anything as perfect as this spotless vulgarity. Not that he said these words, being but a boy, but the relaxed ahhh that hummed through his mind told of his good fortune in ways that words will never experience.

Timmy hummed and touted an open sail to the wind as his parts began to fail, knees bucking, eyes icing over, lungs gasping but not holding. He slid on his belly into a snow bank, a smile leading him through contented dreams.

Timmy and the Sand Man

Quiet dreams were not in Timmy's horoscope for that particular Tuesday. If he'd bothered to read his horoscope before Mother arrived he would have know that some vivid, inspiring and intense dreams or visions would come his way. They could involve paranormal figures, such as angels. He would also have known that his higher self was trying to tell him something and if he listened he could come up with some profound insights about the world and himself.

But Timmy didn't read his horoscope. He didn't even know what a horoscope was and to be honest, as his eyes defrosted and hot air filled his lungs, he would never have suspected that his stars were aligned at all. He might even have believed it impossible when his lungs finally thawed enough to take the first deep breath of sand they'd ever known.

Timmy coughed near convulsion, blowing sand infused phlegm into the air as if from Roman Candles. His body melted and blood began to flow down his back as the pain made its way dramatically to his brain. He struggled to focus as the glaciers receded from his eyes. He could see nothing. He blinked and rubbed and still there was nothing. Pain from his back crippled his mind and he thought that the damage was making him blind. Only the hands he rubbed with were clear as day and he realized that nothing was exactly what there was to see. In all direction, pouring forth from his feet, were miles and miles of sandy desolation.

He pulled himself to his knees, rotating slowly. It appeared as if he was on the top of the world and the world had been buried eight leagues deep in sand. Dunes crowned nothing to his right and his left. Camel-hump hills ran in the distance before and behind him. It was still, quiet and burning. No sooner had he realized where he stood, his eyes trembled in the sun's blinding stare and his lungs withering in the crippling heat, that the sand began to blow.

It came fast and hard with a thickness that caught skin, eyes, throat and lungs in a single burst, grit burrowing deep into open wounds. In an instant Timmy could not see, could not breathe, he could only feel. And what he felt was his skin being ripped from his body, grain by gain. The sand tore deeper, each speck taking a bit of flesh before a million more followed behind, ready to bite and chew.

Timmy imagined a million moles and began to dig. He made a shallow grave and covered himself in a blanket of sand that saved the bits of meat his bones could still claim. He became a pig in a poke, a porker waiting only for sauce and the BBQ bell to ring. Under his sand blanket, everything frozen began to swelter, sweat spouting from ice nubs, until the ice departed, taking with it every drop of moisture his body contained. Jerkied, he pulled himself out of the dune to clear skies and a big white sun governing above.

Timmy shook the sand from his body and tumbled down the dune, thinking mockingly how it was better to burn while alive than forever dead, his pale, frostbitten skin blistering unanimously under the critical sun.

Blisters grew and blisters burst and Timmy felt uneasy relief from the pussy ooze that bubbled down his body. Conserving energy, he rolled down the dunes and crawled up, a snail trail made by his belly, the only marks of life to be seen. Sand worked its way into every pore, the sun so hot he pissed dust.

It could have been Hell. The sand might as well have been a Lake of Fire or maybe its beach, which could have been fun; making sandcastles, frolicking in the fire, if it weren't for the unrelenting sun that told him with no uncertainty that he was little and frail and could never stand up to its opalescence.

The sun was right, he couldn't stand. It was that clear-cut. He was weak. He had never disavowed that. He would never deny it. His entire gift was fictional. If you did not believe the story then he did not exist. It was his one trait that made him feel close to his father, without belief, he too was imaginary. It's probably why he felt compelled to interfere with people's happiness. People remember God most when things have gone from bad to worse, much like Timmy remembered him now as he tumbled down another dune, limbs on the verge of failure, his only hope of cresting the next mound was his boils filling with gas and ballooning him over.

Look around. The wind whispered. When you've seen as many suns as I, all is desert. Mine is an hourglass never empty.

Timmy's pain faded with the voice and the slightest notion of an idea began to occur, telling him that maybe life and Hell could have something in common. He began to see serendipity everywhere. His limbs fell limp, but he believed himself slowly rotating like a pig that enjoyed being on the spit. Smiling senselessly, his eyes latched upon the plushest, greenest plants he had ever seen. They sprang up about him, pushing a cool breeze that made his blisters tingle.

He smelled it first, the water, flowing only a short drag away. A trickling song filling his ears, swearing he would survive if only he could drag his belly but a little further.

His ravaged body was reassured. The pains of life led to plenty and even if there was no fruition, the beauty of illusion surely beat the certainty of burning.

Timmy summoned a final scrap of energy from a deep reserve he kept near his little toe and scratched his way to the pool's edge. He dropped his face into its reflection and was rewarded with the coolest water that had ever never been and Timmy knew that it was better to nearly be than to not.

There is something to be said for nearly. If death takes long enough, it brings you first to a golden place, a place where you can have what life never gave you, a place of a billion thoughts, a trillion feelings, that fill the spaces that come before death. A final gift that is designed to calm and to comfort, a phenomenon that Darwin could never explain with his survival of the species, yet Timmy had seen it, twice, and even now Timmy drank in its existence, at least until the tide turned the other way.

Timmy drank the reservoir down to the mud and still his thirst burned. On hands and knees he licked at the drying sand, his tongue swollen and cracked. He sucked at the sand till his mouth was a beach and his head simmered, puss drying to his burnt red face and cracks branching across his cheeks until his lips chipped and fell away.

Now maybe you see. The mud faced him, looking scornful and scorched. Imagine how it would be to drink forever and never feel refreshed even though your cup is infinitely deep. It's as if your throat has a hole in it just upstream of quenched.

The mud settled and Timmy's lids scraped across his eyes as he pushed them shut. He hoped for cool darkness, but there was only red. His arms shook, his knees quaked and he dropped his lipless smile into the sand.

Timmy of the Tide

Timmy's face plunged into the crest of a wave, the red behind his eyes replaced with the dark blues and greens of an uncertain sea.

His eyes scratched open to the hollering pain of salt filling his cracks and fissures. The protective puss washed away leaving hell filled wounds that felt infinitely larger than Timmy had ever pretended to be.

He screamed and the sea flooded his crusted mouth.

He drank with uncontrollable fever and choked his way down the backside of a sky pointed wave.

Timmy's overheated body went cold. Shivers bounced ripples against the giant, foam-crested waves that seemed angry with each other, battling for dominance while trying futilely to escape to the sky. Up they surged and down they crashed, throwing Timmy back and forth like beers at a redneck picnic.

He stretched his exhausted limbs wide and shook them like a turtle attempting flight. He sunk lower, his nose lifted high, tugging at salty mist. His mouth testing the water again and again, desperate to find a patch that was potable, but each sip proved worse than the one before. His tongue bled. His stomach pushed the brine water out through his nose as his tongue swelled exponentially, closing his mouth to both embrace and escape.

Slipping below the battling waves, Timmy began to thrash his arms and legs as wildly as exhaustion permitted, but it was never enough to make angles in the sea.

He floundered in the valley between two jousting waves, frothing with power. Smaller waves crashed from their path. The two bull waves charged for the right to call the ocean theirs. They rode fast and climbed high, rearing in the final moment, high above Timmy's head. He rolled on his stomach like a sick whale calf, lost from its herd, knowing all too well how a sea so full of life can be the loneliest place, a tortuous place, a place with no capacity to forgive even the most innocent of wayward wondering.

Being on top is no different than the bottom; both let you down in different ways if you wait long enough. The waves gargled as they fell. Given enough time, all attempts to breathe feel like you're drowning. The foaming crest winked and blew him a kiss as it crashed upon his head.

Timmy sank, was sunk, and filled with water below the shattered remnants of two mighty waves that tried to own what could never be.

The water rushed in and Timmy drifted downward. He was no longer thirsty and no longer cold. He was no longer aware of his limbs or how they ached, his wounds or how they howled.

He felt peace as he floated down, gentle as a feather. Back and forth the currents lulled him. He closed his eyes and rocked inside his mother's satchel, her hose of a breast filling him with sweat warm milk, her voice a gentle song. Her warmth filled him. His skin was smoothed by her gentle touch. Much, much better than an eternal burn he thought as the milk ran down his chin. He felt that this must be what Mother God was missing, that if she had something as warm and comforting as his mother's breast, she wouldn't mind the endless days so much. As Timmy opened his mouth for another drink, he was sure he could live that way for a long or short eternity.

You only enjoy it because you have not always been there, before long an endless drip will bore a hole straight through you.

I cannot imagine how joy ends.

Then I will show you.

God as Art

Contrary to popular belief, God does not know everything. At least not in the beginning anyway, but by the end he learned just about all there was worth learning. That is because he processes things at a rate that is unfathomable to the little minds of men. Compared to what we can conceive, he might as well have always known, though, amongst his God friends, he's considered a little dim.

One thing that God understands, that feeble fleshy heads can not fathom, is that in the big scheme, the universe is no more than a momentary glitch in the ever-expanding show of nothing that dominates vast planes of emptiness. Life is but a bit of static popping through a vacuume so fast that it could be easily argued to never have existed at all. Perhaps we are only a spec of dust, momentarily stuck in the corner of God's eye, before being wiped away. Many Gods argued exactly this with God, but he would just grin knowingly and say that they had been looking the wrong way.

God was glad he was one of the few to catch the brief glimmer of existence. It had given him something nearly interesting to do for a twitch of time. It became a happy memory within the eternity that is his curse to wade through. An endless time spent between games of Yahtzee with the God next door and the seemingly endless cleaning of his room that his mother demanded.

Another popular misconception is that God is everywhere. Nothing could be further from the truth. It would be more apt to say that God has been everywhere. He likes to travel and he likes to travel fast. He travels so quickly that no one has ever had the chance to miss him when he's gone, for even when he isn't there, he is rarely not there. God moves so fast that he regularly bumps into himself and sometimes wanders into himself as he is bumping into himself. Which is often very embarrassing, since he regularly catches himself doing things of which he really doesn't approve.

Sometimes God becomes tired of seeing himself everywhere and decided to give himself a little time to disperse. He filled his free time with crossword puzzles. I am sure you are thinking the same thing as I would be if I were thinking, and that is that crossword puzzles can't be much of a challenge for God and to be honest they aren't, if he were to fill them in conventionally, which he doesn't. He fills them in celestially. He likes looking at the puzzle voids and spaces and figuring out which cosmos fits best within the open cells. He then, in precisely 1:1x10^18 scale, plots the points, forming the words that answer the clues in such a way that the letters are identical to the stars, planets and cosmic debris in size, shape, luminosity and color, at the angle that God had chosen to depict it. Fortunately, in an ever-expanding universe there is always some time and angle in which some solar system or other happens to look like the answers to a *New York Time's* crossword puzzle. (The *New York Times* has full rights to the cosmos-crossword puzzle anomaly via a deal with the Devil.)

You see God is an artist. And no, I am not talking about Heaven or Earth and I'm certainly not referring to our selves. Any monkey could have made mankind. In fact, two monkeys made mankind and it took so little effort that they where able to mutate their kin into us while under the constraints of an artistic styling known as doggy. So don't go crazy with the wonders of creation bit. I mean Christ, some rocks get shoved around by wind, rain and ice, leaving a snail trail on pudding skin that bakes in the sun till things begin to grow and people who hate Jackson Pollock call it art. I can do the same thing with mayonnaise on a sidewalk, only difference between me and God is that in a billion years people won't be screaming miracle, and that's only because once the rot sets in, my universe gets eaten by pigeons. Honestly, do you think the universe we credit to God could ever stand up over time to a veracious pigeon? Not very likely. Yet so many believe that a God, who considers himself an artist, must be proud. Well, he is, but not of us. He had nothing to do with us other than using our existence as a bit of distraction during the blip that we registered in the great nothing.

What God is proud of is his art and I'm talking about way more than just crossword cosmoses here. God is the premiere God in the art of making nothing a little more beautiful. He has mastered layering the voids and the empty in ways that speak to the other God's souls. When they look at what God can do with nothing, they want that nothing for themselves, and he's not against giving nothing to them. Hell, he has forever to build with nothing and if he didn't start giving some of it away, his whole house would be filled from ceiling to shag rug with nothing and then boy would him mom be pissed. (It was a dispute over nothing that originally made him cast his mother into the retirement depths of Hell and that, he has since come to believe, was really something.)

So I guess what we are getting at is God is not the God that you might expect, but really who is? His entire affair with Timmy had little to do with Timmy and more to do with how he likes to confound people. Which I can find no fault in, cause hey, when the big empty gives you a blip, you better hustle your ass and get every bit of entertainment you can before that blip proves beyond a shadow of a doubt to have never really blipped at all and to have only been some static cling in the deep folds.

The problem God has with messing with people is that so few notice the true intricacies of his work. This problem stems from the speed at which he works, almost no one can focus on what he considers to be the important details.

It takes a brain of unusual dimensions and I don't mean giant, just unusual, for a person to see God and engage. Most people with this unusual style brain tend, for reasons unknown, to be evil. Which explains much of history. When only bad brains hear the provocative teasing of a restless God, what usually occurs in genocide, which isn't what God whispered to them at all. The real, real problem is that most of those that can engage with him only hear every ten thousandth word, which leads to a lot of confusion, bad assumptions and holes filled with corpses.

It was ten thousand years into humanity when God finally understood that he could never use the words eradicate, club, snake, supreme, kill, superior, take, celibacy, conquer, yours, right, given, chosen, sandwich, virgin or Jew in any conversation with any people ever. Even if these words did only occur every twenty thousand words or so, the evil minds seemed always to catch them and warp their meaning around their warped meaningless minds.

The list of words is continuously growing and by the time God met Timmy, contained most of the words used on Earth. That is what brought about the whole pants routine. He found the word innocuous, and it would be another two years before he'd realize how much damage he'd caused uttering that word to the wrong people and understood that pants too would have to join the no fly list.

Timmy understood God. Not in the you're making good sense kind of way, but in the I can hear all the words you are saying sort of way and that delighted God. It was probably that Timmy had so many God-like qualities that made him such a desirable companion.

God always assumed that what put Timmy over the top was his beautiful hair. God is a hair man. No, I don't mean he likes hairy men, if he did, he never would have used the unibrow to punish the Italians for crucifying (another word he had to stop saying) a nice young Hebrew that was able to catch nearly one out of every thousand words he threw at him. Oh and what he did with those one out of a thousand. Sometimes, when God thinks about it, he giggles for near a millennium. It's all that meek shall inherit the earth crap. Good luck on that one meek! I'm sure when your great uncle asshole dies, the earth will be waiting right there for you in his will.

Anyway, I think the idea is that God was really happy to find Timmy and was determined to make sure his life was the most interesting life any boy on any Earth had ever lived. He was so determined to show this kid a good time, an exciting time, where every moment was full of blood-pumping life, that he did not rule out killing him over and over and over again. To someone who can't seem to die, death seems like the greatest ride life has to offer, as long as it comes with enough pain.

Timmy Goes Beyond

Timmy gummed at a nipple no longer there. His eyes crumbled open, unsure if what he saw was nothing, or if nothing was what he saw.

He appeared to be nowhere or as close to it as he had ever been. He was in the void, the vast emptiness of space. Below him the Earth spiraled away. Before him the Moon grew bright. Space junk criss-crossed his path, satellites and their bits zoomed by at mind twisting speeds while appearing indifferent, bored as the universe tilted and twirled about them.

A fragment, a bit, a piece of something careened through his leg. It came too fast. Timmy was helpless, nearly hovering. He couldn't fly. He couldn't fall. He couldn't duck or dodge. All he could do was silently brace for the impact. He prepared a silent scream, but the pain didn't come. He looked down at his leg, surprised to see a gaping hole closing behind the fleeing shrapnel.

He nearly ventured a laugh when he thought how enraged God would be if he had seen what his mother had done to his pants. Tattered, he was in tatters or at least his clothes were. Upon closer inspection, his body was doing far better than the last time he had noticed it; no cuts, no burns, no bruises, frost bite, rashes, boils, puss, nothing. For a boy floating through space, he seemed to be in excellent health. He touched his face and found it smooth and soft. Smiling he let himself drift into a rocket, his eyes fixed on the craters of the moon, beautiful, luminous and tortured. Timmy could relate and did, for many hours as he drifted by.

On a whim, just for the littlest while, Timmy let there be two moons in the sky, subtly tweaking his so no one would ever believe there was an old man on his moon. On his there was clearly an old woman. Science made up many reasons for the phenomenon, but none of them included a little boy who felt like he'd been bombarded but still wanted to shine.

Timmy was amazed at the line between dark and bright, though he felt it was the truth. As he drifted past the line into darkness, he was amazed to see the vast emptiness behind it, as if the dark side of the moon was shinning upon the rest of existence.

Space was ecstasy for several thousand miles. The Earth shrank as steadily as the rest of universe stayed the same, making him feel always further away and never any closer.

Timmy marveled over the plentitude of tiny lights. All Timmy had previously known of the great beyond lay between skyscrapers above New York City. A city of enough light to dim the masses, a city where few things shone bright enough to be seen at all. Timmy saw how the dimming had its purpose, for if perceivable, the intensity at which all things wish to shine would surely scorch the retinas and reduce all onlookers to dust.

In the vast empty darkness of space, the tiny lights became unbearable, a billion-billion unblinking eyes, always staring condescendingly as if you were the one who was too small and too far away, you, cursed never to shine, forever unseen by the unblinking eyes. Sad and beautiful, beautiful and sad, Timmy felt only one of these as the exuberance of eternity diminished and the next several thousand miles passed with barely an interruption.

Specs flew by, sometimes rocks travelled with him and Venus started to grow in the distance, ever so slowly. The view never changing, like a slideshow of a boulder in the sand, snapped at the speed of light and shown by the neighbors over a hot cup of Moxie, accompanied by a brown-stained commentary of how they spent their vacation by the rock. Only the slideshow never ended and it had been ten thousand miles since Timmy cared enough to rocket or space walk or monkey in a suit.

Timmy laid lazy on a pool float and tried to ignore how unblinkingly the universe would not acknowledge him. He thought he'd be excited by Venus, being the first of his kind to approach it, but approaching it seemed to be all he was doing and all he had to look forward to since Earth had become a silly blue marble that disappeared, leaving him alone with the stars ever-present disdain.

He looked forward to Venus for so long that the very anticipation began to bore him more that the slowness in which it grew. But Venus is love and love sometimes takes time. For thousands of miles it had only been bright light, for millions more it was a glowing round cloud, veiled and closed off, shrouded but not mysterious.

Timmy was bored. He'd been bored for ten, twenty, thirty million miles. He closed his eyes, but the darkness within was no more settling than the darkness without. Unable to bare the stars, Timmy had no choice but to fixate on that slowly glowing swirl.

Timmy understood what it was to be alone as clearly as he understood despondency. He kicked his feet and swung his arms in an attempt to speed up. He spun, corkscrewed and twisted. It was the most fun he'd had in ten million miles. He orbited his best friend, a rock named Rocky that followed him everywhere he went. It didn't seem to matter.

Then Venus began to rapidly change. The white became clouds full of raging storms, the planet showed bits of red, glimpses of craters and endless smooth.

It was love, love arising from despondency, love blooming from dejection. He twisting in space erratically and could only see Venus every eighth rotation. So interesting. So difficult to obtain. He had to have it. He began to flail, kicking, contorting and swinging at nothing in an attempt to straighten, to propel himself toward love, but he could not get control. He wiggled and rolled, twisted and tossed, for a thousand miles he fought as if he'd been tossed into a bag with a thousand cats on their way to the river.

Venus was the love child of a grown up Moon that had taken the Earth in a passionate frenzy and spit out a smooth and shapely child that winked at you through swirling mystery. Timmy fought to keep her in sight, but nothing would let that happen. He drifted by dazed and unfocused, which is probably the best that love can ever be.

Venus, his love, disappeared and he set his sight on Mercury. Mercury the small, Mercury the silver, Mercury the moving away faster than he approached. Timmy had missed all planetarium lectures and felt the nervous excitement of a Quaker in Bangkok. Mercury was a mystery. No one was talking about it so no one had ruined the ending. It had flair. It had a personality that came on so slowly that at first it brought anxiety. What could it be? What would it be? What is it? The most interesting part of its personality coming from the fact that it was getting away.

Mercury orbited faster than he could arrive. It would never be closer than uncertainty. Timmy had so little that he felt the loss more than that he felt a longing. He was all alone.

Timmy turned his eyes on a Sun too intense to see, booming like fourth of July, erupting like a volcanic land, swirling with gorgeous rage, like a rainbow lollipop filled with evil, waiting to melt children and witches alike, an inferno to calm and placid to illicit proper fear and too volatile and sporadic to ever trust.

It was clearly the most intensely wondrous thing he's ever seen. And he stared until the white-hot over-rode his optics and the red-hot bright bleached through his brain and exited uninhibited through the back of his skull.

He closed his eyes but the white was there too. It permeated his eyelids like film melting over a bulb. It came out his ears. His pool float deflated and he gave himself inevitably to the Sun.

The miles passed. The temperature rose. It went on for so long that even burning became boring. There was no anticipation and no fear. A minute peak in his interest arose as he entered the bedlam of volatile hydrogen. The heat was vaporizing, but he no longer cared. He understood Hell. Hell was not the burning. Burning was at the very least interesting. Burning was at the very least intense. Call it what you will, but the moment in which you are burned alive, you are truly alive and as vibrant as the fire that engulfs you.

Sure, the burning is a horror, but Timmy understood how horror could trump mundane. The hell that made Hell Hell was the never-ending consistency of the burn. Once you knew what it was to be cast into Hell, lingering there became intolerable.

Timmy left the fiery center for cooler lands. For the first ten thousand miles, he knew only darkness and he appreciated the peace: nothing judging, nothing disappointing.

He was nothing and that was more than enough, it was Heaven. But even in the slow lane, when Heaven only lasts for a ten thousand miles, it is not enough. The blanched whiteness left his mind and leaking from his eyes, speckling the darkness with the never blinking eyes that made him feel naked.

He would in time know more than any other man had ever known, see more than any man had ever seen, but he would see it as a snail travels. He might get another glimpse of a planet, but then what? Some rocks? Some streaming ice? None of it made him feel lucky.

He had expectations of Saturn and its rings. He was sure that despite the approach it would be wonderful with all those moon things he's heard about. And he actually hoped to see Pluto, because they had made it a planet and then took it away. He wanted to tell it that it was okay, that he's had a lot of things given and taken away and if you stayed strong, neither one mattered. All that mattered was what you thought and how you felt and what Timmy felt was that even these little pleasures were far, far away.

The end of our solar system held so much nothing. Timmy was excited by asteroid belts, till asteroid belts became the norm. He missed, by a few thousand miles, several comets, but there was only so much staring at them a boy could take.

He floated on his back or maybe it was his stomach, it could have been his side. He wished that such things mattered. He had been through nothing for so long that he was nothing. Thoughts of Hell haunted his existence. He no longer thought himself better off. The more he travelled, the longer he travelled, the more he wished for death. Not death, but an end.

Mother God smiled. What you want is to no longer be?

What I want is to no longer be.

Because existence never ending is Hell?

Because existence that does not end is Hell.

Say it. Say if I must exist eternal, I do not want to be.

I do not want to be if I must always be.

Now you understand me.

Now I am you.

Not even close.

I don't want to get any closer.

Then tell God you're listening to me now.

Let me stop existing when it's my time.

No one ever does, everyone just suffers a different level of boredom.

Then I can't win.

No one ever has.

Then for as long as I can, I'd better live.

It will be more interesting that way.

Timmy Shuttlecock

There is a peace that comes with confession and a contentment that comes with understanding, but neither peace gained nor contentment made, makes mundane more bearable. If anything, Timmy felt a little less trepidation. If anything, Timmy felt a little less alive and alive is the only thing that makes life worth living. Pain and joy, hate and love, the extremes of feeling make life bearable. And extremes were exactly what Timmy was out of. He would have cried had he still those emotions to burn. He had nothing.

He felt long and thin, wide and stout, drawn and compressed, simultaneously in all direction and separately nowhere, like he were expanding and contracting in an incomprehensible stasis.

You are nothing.

I have always been nothing.

You have nothing.

I have never had anything.

There is nothing left for you to learn here.

I have learned nothing nearly everywhere.

A hand, smooth and stout, filled the void and Timmy drifted slowly into its soft, warm embrace, as comfortable as all had once been empty. It cupped him, cradled him, brought him back to the womb, where all was warm; all was soft and he was safe. The little finger bent inward and smoothed his hair, coochie-cooed his chin and gently pinched his cheek.

It is time for you to go home.

I don't want to go home. I want to stay here with you.

Then we would both be empty. Go and take the one gift given you, the chance to suffer joy and disappointment before you come back to nothing.

You are not nothing.

I am even less than nothing.

But I'm so happy here.

You will be back.

The little finger flicked him from his cradle. He tried to booger on, but nothing about him stuck. Instead he rolled, tucked tight into a ball, back into the empty. His heart broken, he glanced back at the hand that would not hold him in time to see it rushing toward him.

It struck him with a soundless crack that blasted him through the void, his speed so great that nothingness blew through his hair and stung his face. Within minutes he was exploding through the intolerable light of the sun, caught a glimpse of the Moon and surged past and into the Earth's scorching atmosphere.

The burning decent was the first thing he felt in an eternity. It was pig-roast wonderful. He closed his eyes to enjoy the unbearable pain, savoring it as it flared and then softened as he came to a stop.

When he opened his eyes, he was lying on the kitchen floor and Mother God was smiling with a vicious sweetness that shredded as it beamed down upon him.

Welcome back to suffering. She turned her head and moved toward the door.

What do you want from me? Timmy droned unmoving.

Everything you have, again and again and again and again... the voice dwindled but never really left.

When Timmy's family returned he was still upon the floor and barely bothered to become a man. He was nearly sure it hardly mattered, but equally sure that if he didn't, someone would want to know why and he was too happy with the way his lungs filled with air and how the floor pushed up against his back to convey any hows or whys.

Daddy! Ona sounded the alarm and the family rushed to his side.

My God! What's happened to you?

All of it or none of it and maybe both.

Are you okay?

Are you hurt?

Should we call an ambulance?

Noes and yeses all around. Timmy grinned, blinking long and soft. But really, don't worry about me. I'll be back up when I'm done with the ground.

After that all they could get from him was smiles. They would smile uncomfortably back, lost in worry. They left him there, eased and terrified by the depth of his cool grin. They brought him a blanket and a pillow and the hope that he would be fine in the morning.

A hope that was still in contention the next morning, when the family awoke to a kitchen bursting with eggs and toast and a father who seemed compelled by a need to touch, hold and smell them, often and with a reluctance to let them go. His smile beamed so bright it stung sleepy eyes.

The Trashing of JP

JP was a dick. He couldn't help it and it's almost difficult to blame him for it. He'd been through an awful lot in his too few years; his mother's death, his father's preference for rock over his own flesh and blood, being brought to Hell and melted. His life was shit, which may be what caused him to love garbage so dearly. Either way, it was hard to blame him for being a dick, but that doesn't mean anyone has to like him.

JP was angry. He hated most things, but beyond most things he hated socio-economic theory. He hated stealing it. He hated that it was categorized with his favorite things. He hated that something that sucked so much could be trash. But what else could it be? He'd already spent too much time transforming it from unacceptable trash to desirable garbage, using a little trick he liked to call burning. A little something he picked up on a quick visit to Hell that stayed permanently etched upon his mind.

He loved his old life of stealing when and what he wanted. He'd taken entire landfills and was the only thing on the planet keeping the oceans clean enough for life to survive. He loved ocean trash, after a few years of sitting on the bottom, it seemed like double trash and the shit floating on the surface was always pure gold.

He'd even set his sight on one day stealing Nauru, the little island known as the fattest place on earth. It was beautiful, abandoned phosphorous mines and junk food wrappers as far as the eye could see. The whole dang place was garbage including the rotten hulls of junked people. He could happily take the whole place and never even be bothered by how much of the place was rock. He saw it as a natural stepping stone for his eventual acquisition on New Jersey, the gold standard of trash.

Was he ever going to reach his goal? It really didn't look that way anymore. Not since the invitation, not since the melting and the mirror and oh god, he wasn't his own man any longer. He felt more like a dumpster diver than a young man on the path to world domination through resource reclamation.

The worst part was that Timmy and his family didn't even have any good shit. They ate a lot of whole foods, played a lot of educational games that involved family closeness. They didn't collect anything for no reason. Most of their garbage was either tied up in a bag or being prepared for class the next day. And he hated socio-economic trash.

The entire situation made him want to smash things. After a day of slim pickings at the Timmy household, he couldn't help but smash and tear at his vast collection of crap. He'd beat his garbage till he fell over exhausted and could do little more than curl up with his trash and make a nest.

He would have damned Mother God, but couldn't think of any place to damn her to. Where does one go after Hell? The best JP could think of was Arkansas. But luckily for him, even though he was a dick, he was not such a dick as to wish anyone be damned to Arkansas, for if he had even so much as though about damning Mother God, she would have let his puddle burn in her front yard for God knows how long.

Timmy Meets the Trash Man

Timmy had never seen any of his students. He couldn't see over the podium and besides, he had teaching assistants for anything that requires the breathing of similar air. He didn't grade. He didn't test. He didn't explain. He didn't acknowledge. He had tenure. His students never bothered him. Until today.

When he showed up today, his students were like a lost hive and he, their unwilling queen. They swarmed and hovered like so many homeless drones after rocks have pelted their hive. They buzzed about Timmy, repeating over and over that all they were supposed to know was gone. Each spewed the same story; their notebooks had been scavenged, their hard drives more or less eliminated and text books decimated.

The dumber the kid, the more that was lost. Their textbooks and handouts had all been meticulously plucked, each remained only as fragments. Of the text book, only pieces remained, sometimes paragraph were left untouched, other times only words, each book torn the same way. A strip of cardboard was all that remained of the front cover, branded deep, black and ashy with the word 'Son'.

Timmy told the smart to share with the dumb, knowing immediately the burden he had placed on the two of them. He promised them both A's, if they'd only divert attention from him till he figured out what was going on.

They told Timmy they already had A's and couldn't possibly get anything else, even if they never attended another class, turned in another assignment or took another test. They claimed they were the curve. Timmy explained quickly that he was the curve. Though, to be honest, he had no idea what they meant by curve. He told them he had final say on all grades, which, as far as he knew, was true. He'd have to ask his assistance if it was, though he knew he shouldn't be asking his assistants anything. His job was to tell and since they were on scholarship he didn't even need to be coherent.

He didn't need to be coherent with his students either. Do! He yelled as the building began to shake, bounce and crash. His upset hive ceased to fly as their bodies met uncertain ground. Riffs opened, plaster fell, the class above showered down, beams and wires cascaded, lights bursting, wires sparking, all in a pillow-dust fog.

Each breath felt like Timmy's last. His eyes burned. His bees screamed.

When the shaking finally stopped, the dust settled enough for pale light pushing through fractured windows to show educated people pushing and shoving their way towards doors that no longer existed, as those considered dumb headed for the pale window glow. The surest ones to survive were always the ones least likely to contribute, at least that was always the way in Timmy's house. The capable turned out to be strangely delicious and the dumb extremely resilient.

Taking his cue from the dumb, Timmy crawled out the window. He breathed deep, never knowing air could be so fresh or that a foundation could just disappear from underneath a building. The structure had turned in upon itself, limbs squirming out of holes like a millipede briefly up ended. Every brick was missing, every granite windowsill gone. Wood, wire and bodies lay in a pile that wiggled and kicked, gasped, yelled and continuously wet itself.

As his breath returned, Timmy regained his composure. He moved quickly away from the dust, the screams, the flailing limbs, scurrying bodies and urinal smells. His eyes cleared along with his head and he was able to see that the building had fallen linguistically. The travesty clearly spelled the word 'Father', before, in the midst of a final collapse, it briefly read 'Smoky Doom' as the buildings remnants descended into a basement that no longer existed.

Plywood, plaster, plastic and metal tangled among a student body that dispersed with a slow bewilderment, having experienced a collapse that carried not the weight to kill. Then in a flash, it was all gone, leaving shinning stupid students lingering as if bound to the spot.

Timmy moused away. This was not his problem. If this was anyone's problem it was the teaching assistant's. Timmy moved as an ant on roadrunner feet.

The world was flashing before his eyes. Prominent university buildings went and came in less time than it took to focus. The chapel was gone and back in a blink. The library disappeared and returned. The hall of science, over 200 years old, wasn't there as quickly as it was. Everything beautiful disappeared, only to come back, nearly before he knew it was gone. But it came back different. What was once old and refined, now appeared Disney, traditional replaced by Mickey Mouse, the transition noticeable only as a faint vapor trail that streaked skyward giving the impression that the souls of the dead, the ghosts of academia, had finally been released.

Everywhere he looked and everywhere he ran, the world transformed into a cheap imitation of itself, an impressive job of top notch knock-offing that looked no more like it should then it looked like it shouldn't. Timmy could barely believe the differences were not a dilution. Maybe he had taken a blow to the skull. He checked his head for blood.

If it weren't for the specter of ghosts left in the old building's wakes and the fact that he was never quite what he appeared either, he would never have known it was happening, neither would he have recognize how the switching stayed one step ahead of him as he ran. Clearly it was being done for his benefit.

Father, Son and Ghost, very funny! Timmy murmured. If God wanted something from him, he was headed the wrong way. He'd never had anything in his life. So if there was anything he appreciated, it was something, and God was destroying the somethings he had grown to love and was replacing it with kitsch. Being one of thousands of children, Timmy learned one thing and only one thing well and that was how to stand on heads to appear taller.

Timmy Corinthian Claws

Timmy followed the plasticization of the university, shadowing the shadows always one step behind the vapor. He gave up on the trail, moving instead toward the one building he was sure was not going to be left behind, the Low Memorial Library, the iconic emblem of the school, stamped on every piece of university paraphernalia for the last one hundred years. He bounding up its formidable front steps as the inky fingers of a shadow took it away.

Timmy was shocked that he was not leaving with it. They had taken the steps and left his feet, the doorknob replicated as his fingers twisted, the front hall passed right through him. Out of desperation, he ornated himself about the top of the last pillar still made of marble, a quick Corinthianing the mist must have believed.

Timmy was plucked into darkness by the shadow. He shot upwards like he was falling the wrong way, bounding into the sky, joining the rest of the university among the clouds like some part of a heavenly mobile for a baby of galactic proportions. He clung desperately, like a coin purse to a satchel with easy milk access, only this time the floor was a million miles away, though the drop was just as likely to kill him as falling from his mother's purse. He might as well have been eggs and toast, so ravenous was the ground for him.

It's cold in the sky, especially for a child molded around marble. Timmy's ears popped. His lungs expanded till he was full, still he had to search for even trace amounts of oxygen in the ever-thinning atmosphere. His veins popped and radiated purple. He was expanding as he fought unconsciousness, sure that the ants could not help him now. They'd be flicked off by the currents as surely as from a picnic basket. He'd be scatted far and wide. It would take years for his ants to rat together and more years for his rats to dog and who knows what his dogs would do, parts of his body could be lost forever, off sniffing the butts of the world.

He clung, becoming a thousand claws. They flew on, transported by what he could only assume to be nothing, a cable to nowhere that whipped what little atmosphere that still bothered to surround them into a wind that a million claws could barely hold against. Timmy held on long past what he felt he could reasonably bare, anyone could reasonably bare, and then he held on some more, each second adding years to his suffering, every minute he lived a lifetime of pain.

He thought about kites and parachutes. He considered butterflies, but had no proof that he could fall like anything other than a rock, or at least a small boy. He clung, wrapping himself around parts of himself that were already wrapped around other parts till he was knotted.

The building began to descend as the last bits of Timmy failed to stick or grapple. He fell imperceivable faster than the building, decorating the bottom on the pillar by the time they settled once again on solid ground. He peered through ravaged eyes upon a land of colossal icons, from Pantheons to pyramids from aqueducts to real ducks, giant ducks, ducks, ducks, honk, flap, flap…

His eyes melted into his brain and the darkness became bittersweet. He was exhausted several lifetimes worth. He fell asleep, lost to his dreams where everything had become ducks.

Timmy Puddles

He awoke gently rippling; a light breeze quaking the puddle remains of his body and spirit. His every drop hurt. He could barely bear just sloshing there. He may have wet himself, but there was no way of knowing.

The steps were cold in the warm sun. His top was browning, but his insides were runny. He tried hard to yoke, that at least he understood.

He had never imagined that water could hurt. It seemed impossible, which made Timmy believe that he must be mud. He could imagine the pain that mud must know. He could feel the pain that must be mud. Everyone loves water while no one wishes to be mud and if this was what mud felt like, Timmy didn't want to be it either.

Timmy spent his day in and out of the puddle, till hunger drove his eyes open. He focused ravenously upon a scrape of unreal existence. About him spread a vast plain surrounded by a great wall that was tall, wide and lightly screaming. Timmy was proud to have recognized it as belonging to China and as having the most unoriginal name of Great Wall (which seemed to Timmy to lack any attempt at creativity so he decided to call it Harry).

The wall surrounded every iconic structure that Timmy had ever heard mentioned, as well as many that he hadn't. His university was dwarfed by castles that abutted palaces that intermingled with skyscrapers, modern stadiums and ancient coliseums. The archaic remnants of Stonehenge, Troy, the Acropolis and Constantinople were placed among museums like the Louvre and the Guggenheim as if they were the archival pieces on display.

But most exciting, for Timmy, interwoven between the Taj Mahal, Hayden's wall, Big Ben, the Brooklyn Bridge, the Washington Monument, Machu Picchu, the Eiffel Tower and the Alamo, were thousands of heavily laden fruit trees; apple, pears and oranges; stretching grape vines, tangles of raspberries, dangling bananas, trees dripping with mangoes, pineapples shooting up like sunflowers, elderberries, nectarines, cumquats, blue berries, cantaloupes, peaches, watermelon and Brussels-sprouts all covered the grounds.

A garden of the grandest scale was in full bloom, planted without regard between buildings that had been strewn like a child's play things. The space needle looked like it was going to fall down at any moment, while the leaning tower of Pisa had never stood straighter.

Timmy muddled his puddle into a small boy and headed into the land of opulent fruitopia, gorging his mud until only he remained. With his body still in disarray but now fattened, fatigue once again overcame him with enough force to make a prickle patch the softest bed he had ever known. His belly too fat, his muscles too meek, a hundred thorns were sufficient to hold him tight, the bristle of raspberry leaves, might as well have been velvet. Timmy fell fast asleep.

From Prickly Patches to Big Red Dogs

They didn't have to poke him like that. He was just a little boy, too tired for pretending. There was no emergency, he was already held captive by the prickers and thorns. He wasn't even asking them to let him sleep, just not to wake him with pain. He was already in pain and it took far too many pokes for Timmy to realize that some of it was external.

The fruit had done much to make Timmy feel better, but the poking had done just as much to make him feel worse. His eyes fluttered upon hundreds of pokers, held by hundreds of pokies.

Guns, there were men with guns, all aimed at a little boy, riffles and blunderbusses backed by machine guns backed by tanks. Enough munitions to stamp out every ant Timmy could muster, though he doubted they'd do so well with his dark or find him among a thousand-thousand claws. But tired is tired and Timmy didn't feel like not being himself, not after what felt like a lifetimes stuck in the sky. He hadn't the spirit to run and exhaustion can only take you so far.

Timmy hadn't ridden a library to deal with armies. He wasn't sure why he had hopped that pillar, but it certainly was not to battle rude people in camouflage. Besides, they were just pawns sent to show a kid a bad time, an attempt to make sure he was adequately impressed, like the grounds full on antiquity and modern marvels might have fallen flat on his too young eyes. He guessed that guns and poking was just the way the game was played here and accepted being captured and prodded. He ignored their caterwauling and let them take him from the prickles and push him around a bit, so they could all feel like big men.

Timmy sat down despite pokes and threats and told them simply to bring him wherever they wished, he wasn't going to fight about it, but he wasn't going to walk either.

A riffle butt rose menacingly and he was told of the countless things that happen to those that do not do what they are told.

Timmy disappeared, taking on all aspects of a gnat. He watched as mayhem ensued, orders screamed and men sent scurrying everywhere, despite how there was nowhere for a little boy to go. He would have been more amused if he hadn't had to dodge and duck the desperately moving feet. Too tired for hide and seek, Timmy climbed up onto the foot of a giant Buddha and reappeared.

Into the frantic crowd he yelled. I said I'll go wherever you want. Just don't make me walk.

The men turned as one, hundreds of riffled readied.

Don't make me disappear again. Not when all I'm asking for is a ride.

It was a drag being dragged, but at least Timmy got to sleep at the expense of his back and his ass. He told his captors that if the dragging continued he'd be less than half by the time they got to wherever they were headed and that given the size of the welcoming party, someone on the other end probably wanted him in one piece.

The men scoffed and spat and Timmy allowed his image to wear away till he was paper-thin and fear started shaking through the officers. Next thing he knew he was riding comfortably on something, but he couldn't keep his eyes open long enough to determine what that something was. In his dreams, he rode astride Clifford, the Big Red Dog on his way to a water-bowl swimming party. The day was to be grand and full of expectation, but even in his dreams he couldn't stay awake and soon stretched and yawned, pulling an ear across his body and was off to sleep.

Timmy Meets Monumental

Timmy awoke on the floor. It was cold and hard and he thought for a moment that he had never quit being a puddle; that his stomach had dreamed of gardens full of fruit, till the emptiness left him dragged and then carried. Only it made no sense. If he was in such tatters then why did Clifford show him such a good time? If he was truly ravenous, why hadn't he eaten that big, scrumptious dog?

His belly was full and so were his pants. Sitting up, he tried to focus. His eyes didn't seem to work. All he could see, jiggling before him, was a squishy looking mound, massive and gray, like Jell-O gone bad. When the mound spoke, Timmy screamed.

How did you get here? It belched.

You've gone bad!

Tell me something I don't know.

I spent several years as a purse.

Paying out or paying in?

Clamoring for nipple.

If I had a dollar for every time I've heard that story.

You've got way more than that.

You're underestimating how often I hear of nipples.

I'm not prepared to underestimate any part of you.

In that we are the same.

You like eggs and toast?

Of course.

Two for two.

You still haven't told me how you arrived in my land.

I rode the university.

No one has ever held onto what I steal.

I was part of a pillar.

How do you mean?

Corinthian.

How do you mean?

I don't know Doric.

Doric is simple. What's complex is your arrival, which you have yet to explain. How did you manage it?

No one has ever asked how and I'm not sure I should tell you.

Everyone eventually tells me.

You don't know me.

But I'm guessing you know God.

Does anyone really know God?

I do, enough to know he hates his mother and loves pants.

Who doesn't?

Do you even understand the position you're in?

Do you know anything of my last escape?

No, I don't.

I'm a little hazy on that one too... So God made you steal my university?

No one makes me do anything.

So it was his mother.

She's one scary bitch.

She just needs love. Just like the rest of us.

I don't. I need only more.

Well, all I know is more love is better than none and having a wife and kids around sure beats hanging around in a purse.

How are you married?

I'm older than I am sometimes.

That's ridiculous.

So are you.

You seem to believe this is a discussion.

Don't you like to talk?

I talk. You listen.

That's silly.

You won't think so after you've been stretched and tanned in my dungeon.

Done both already thanks. But at least tell me who sent you. God or Mother?

They both asked me for the same thing.

Makes choosing sides a bit easier.

Take what he loves and your kingdom shall grow beyond all earthly limits. That is what they whispered to me.

Be careful with that beyond earthly limits stuff. It's probably not what you're thinking. Anyway, what do you mean take what I love?

You didn't have much worth my while, so I took the school. I'm not about to lower myself to taking that so called building in which you live. God, can you even picture it on my grounds!

What about my wife and my kids?

Not my problem. If it's not iconic, I don't want it. But I'll keep you.

That may take more skill than you've been able to steal.

You need to realize that you've already been stolen. You are mine and you are going to love what I have planned for you.

Thanks, but I already have plans for me.

Timmy made himself into a million and let the decoys fly. They ran in a million directions, gaining speed toward the horizon. Only Timmy remained, he needed to find a way home and blind running wasn't going to get him there. He needed a ride.

Monumental Moment

Tens of thousands turned out to chase a million Timmys. The walls disintegrated into men. The ceiling paratrooped, the floor heaved, bodies scattering, grasping at what wasn't, chasing bits of Timmy nowhere.

Timmy sent himselves away, far and fast. Guns fired, smoke rose, anyone near his imposters fell dead, holes in their aortas. Timmy felt terrible, things never turned out as fun as he imagined, not since God.

He gave the flock of Timmys greater speed and they put distance between themselves and the bodies in the way. They reached the horizon as an army gasped and grunted behind.

The inner working of the building had dissipated and Timmy found himself alone with a man the size of a monument. A megalithic man and a tiny boy in a grassy field that was trampled in all directions by a running ambush that never saw Timmy coming or at least never saw him stay.

The army's cleared, Timmy found himself in the courtyard of an even greater building, full of gardens and fountains. The fat man sat fuming just within the doorway of a great white palace with a domed roof and towering white columns. Timmy rose out of what a moment before had seemed only trample and made himself as large as his would-be captor. He became a thousand elephants, bound, cinched tight with a million yards of duct-tape and stuffed in a laundry bag. He smiled.

They never told me you were so good looking! The fat-man jiggled with a deep bellowing laugh that could only come from a live whale lunch.

Timmy blimped beyond him and for the first time Gargantuan looked surprised. But pleasure and amusement quickly dissipated as it occurred to him that he was being mocked. If looks could kill, he still would have been looking in the wrong place.

Show off, he mouthed, unable to handle Timmy being more. A fire rose in his eyes. His lunch flipped, causing a final acid splash amidst digestion as the thrashing tail turned a mountain of fruit into a lake of wine.

Gargantuan's face flushed, anger intoxicating and warping his senses as Timmy ballooned above and beyond. He looked like he might blow, so Timmy beat him to it, bursting into a billion bits that bricked as they fell, rebuilding about Gargantuan the room he needed an army to form.

Timmy had him surrounded and Gargantuan didn't like it. He vibrated up and down, sending typhoons of fat against Timmy's walls. Tsunami-ing blubber pounded the foundations without causing in Timmy so much as a tremor.

Enough! Gargantuan thundered.

Timmy lowered his walls, returning once again to a boy before a behemoth, small and timid upon troop trampled land.

What is the meaning of this?

You are one to talk or meaning.

Are you trying to make a fool of me?

You stole my school and chased all I could muster with an army large enough to envelope you.

Do you even realize whom you taunt?

I'm only seven. Most of what I know is that I like friends better than enemies and eggs and toast better than either.

You've made a great foe here today.

You said you were gonna keep me.

When I'm through with you, you'll wish I had only kept you.

God would never allow it and neither would his mother.

They sent me!

They sent you to get me to work for them, as long as I work for neither, either one may smite you if anything happens to me.

They said I could keep you.

They knew you couldn't.

It's been a long time since I've taken anything personally, which means that the majority of my cruelty comes out of a personal sense of joy. My ruthlessness thus far has been with little bile and look at all I've amassed.

Why?

Why what?

Why have you amassed?

That is what greatness does.

Who told you that?

No one had too.

I wish someone would tell me something that didn't sound crazy.

Not everything is about pants.

Pants, iconic monuments, it seems most people I've met collect things they can wear.

I'm going to break you in ways you've never imagined.

I've never imagined any ways in which I'm broken.

Then it's bound to be a surprise.

I doubt it.

If I could roll, I would crush you now.

That I've already imagined.

I'm going to chip you apart slowly, bit by bit.

I doubt it.

Don't underestimate what money can buy.

No one loves you.

Money loves me.

Money's not worth its weight in eggs and toast, unless of course you're buying with pennies and nickels, then I bet the exchange rate is awesome. Timmy chuckled, imagining the egg for penny ratio.

You don't talk like you're seven.

I've died three times, travelled the universe and teach at what used to be an old American institution where all they use is four syllable words.

That doesn't quite explain it.

We could have this same discussion about you.

I'm gonna almost hate destroying you.

But you're gonna love trying.

I'm itching for a challenge. Conquest for me has become rather second nature. It is nice to have a little difficult after all these years of easy.

Funny, I'm kinda hoping for easy after all this difficult.

If only your plight wasn't so hopeless, I might almost enjoy this.

Would really like to say I care, but I don't, so just point me the quickest way home.

I don't think so.

Then I'll just have to take the easy way.

Timmy feathered, stretched his wings and with a mocking caw disappeared among the clouds in the sky. At least that is what Gargantuan was watching as Timmy wormed his way through the trample.

Timmy wormed along for hours before he felt safe enough to dare the swiftness of a rat. The rat carried him to a helicopter. The helicopter carried him nowhere. Timmy couldn't even imagine how to fly. He could look like a pilot, but with so many knobs and him hardly reading, he was earth bound.

What he needed was a brother or a sister that knew the means and the way. And he'd already seen a couple dozen of them. They were easy to spot by how they chased what wasn't Timmy with complete lackluster. One of them was bound to know how to get him home.

Forty Feet From Home

She said she always knew mom's purse was a fake, nothing else in that house ever lasted, but that purse hung around for years. She even claimed she'd noticed the purse feeding. She was so jealous, she almost pursed right there next to him, but she had never been able to get that small or that material.

Timmy told her that he'd seen her at the eggs and toast family reunion and was glad they were finally getting a chance to talk. Then, after a long ride that felt to Timmy like a short nap, she left him on the rooftop of his apartment. Timmy thanked her and said he regretted being too sleepy to talk about all the things he dreamed they had talked about, but assured her that his dreams had depicted her as a witty and charming woman. She smiled, waved goodbye and disappeared across the city skyline.

It was Timmy's first time on a roof, which he thought was really cool. He liked the view. He enjoyed the solitude. He felt a sense of power, like he had climbed a mighty mountain and was about to plant his flag. He liked everything about the roof, except for the door being locked and how it was far colder up there than he thought it right for a rooftop to be. He circled the building's square again and again, wishing over and over that he was that bird the fat man had watched fly chirpingly away, for his best bet down seemed to be a little ladder that led straight down the side of the building, to a fire escape below.

Timmy went to the bathroom on that roof, number one and number two, to keep it from coming out on its own volition upon the way down.

He swung a doubtful foot over the edge and froze, one leg over one leg back, with number one making its way to the surface despite an empty bladder. When he finally mustered the nerve to drop his second leg over, number two quickly followed, leaving him soggy and stinky, clinging to the edge of a building. His feet tried to wrap themselves around the ladder while the building's bricks felt impossibly slick beneath his clinging fingers as they searched each nook and every cranny, again and again for a better hold.

For hours he clung, the tremble in his legs only ceasing when an electric, piercing pain ran from the center of his foot to the middle of his neck, loosening his grip, rocketing his pulse and pulling more number one and two from deep reserves.

He ran through his options, wrestling thought from a brain that only wanted to scream. Fortunately, the list was short, go back up and cry for help in a city where no one looks up and eventually freeze to death or risk another rung and maybe the one after that.

Prying his fingers from the deep and narrow crevices he had dug with his nails hurt enough to stun his fear and unlocking his feet from where they had formed around the rung. He managed to slide down one more step, then two more, cautiously, carefully, till the sensation that he was being pulled backwards by a gravity full of little boy lust, triple twisted his arms around the ladder, his teeth biting in, his tongue wrapping round.

He was going to die, he knew that, though he tried to convince himself that if he slipped, he'd land safely on the fire escape below. And though he hovered only three steps above a platform, in his fear frozen mind the likelihood of landing safely on such a tiny strip, seemed frantically doubtful. He was bound to plummet. His bones cracking on the cars parked below. He clung tighter becoming one with the ladder.

When the morning sun broke through the skyscrapers, warming the ice that his limbs had become and the birds began their morning songs, fear began to dissipate from Timmy's mind. He imagined, maybe, he really was that bird. He thought that if he could stand against a man the size of a planet, then he could escape a simple ladder.

Invigorated, he broke his hold, untwisted his arms, unfolded his shoes, unwrapped his tongue and opened his jaws. He lowered himself against the pain of muscles stiffened into rock, forcing his frozen limb onto the next rung, sliding his fingers numbly down the ladder till they fell, with the rest of his body, down through the morning rays and right through the get-the-worm chirps of breakfasting birds.

He plummeted like frozen shit, his limbs too stiff to move. Nothing flailed, nothing shifted. His mind was too paralyzed to even summon the bird that could have at least saved his imagination. All he could muster was worms, crisp on the sidewalk after the sun has baked away a passing storm, dying without so much as a final scream.

Timmy fell the entire four feet to the fire escape landing. The cold grate seemed to burn into his back as his paralyzed limbs and cemented muscles spasmed like concrete in an earthquake in what Timmy would grow to consider the most painful joy of his life. He shattered, barely able to keep himself from hour glassing through the grate, as his mind emptied into blackness.

He awoke under the heat of a noonday sun, the birds pecking at his sweat spots. He shooed them away with a warm limb that flailed like a kite devoid of wind. Exhausted, he rested his head against the window, his forehead sliding down the glass till his mouth formed around the sill, his teeth clasping on, trying, with no help from the rest of his body to pull him back up.

He chewed his way across the windowsill, splinters porcupined his tongue, the sharp eclectic pain brought enough life to his fingers that they began to twist. He let them spider dance a long quiet knock on the pane of glass as his mouth spit away from the sill and suctioned onto the window. There were eyes blinking between the flaps of the blind.

Timmy and Grandma

It was less than three blackouts later that the wrinkled bag of feeble bones managed to pull him through the window while singing in his ear.

You poor thing! Don't you worry now. Grandma's gonna make it all better. She hummed, catching Timmy's head between the window and the radiator. Squeaking and tugging she pulled him through and over, dropping him heavily onto the carpet as her frail old bum crashed to the floor and broke into quarters. But she didn't mind. It happened all the time and within the hour she was back on her feet, dragging Timmy into tables and chairs before trying to push him onto a couch.

Timmy's body folded and flopped as the little old lady dropped him again and again upon the floor. She'd hoist him, pulling him toward the couch, then his head would bob forward breaking a few more of her ribs and he'd jelly his way back to the floor, pulling the old lady with him like a prize Bluefish after a long and bitter fight.

Determined and more resilient than her pantyhose, the ancient raised him to couch level a pillow at a time, lifting one side, stuffing, then the other and more stuffing, until she was able to roll him onto the cushions.

They slept for hours, Timmy on the couch, the little old lady on the pile of pillows. Snores sang, drool puddled, incontinence seemed to be agreed upon.

From then on, any time the two were awake at the same time, it was a barrage of juice and cookies, pudding and crackers, hot water bottles, heated blankets, Woody Guthrie albums, homemade pickles, broths made from cat food and Bugs Bunny Band Aids. (She's been saving the Band Aids for her own grandchildren, but since she didn't have any children of her own, she figured they wouldn't mind.)

Timmy wasn't sure if days had passed or if it had been just enough hours to make up several days, when he was finally able to sit up on his own, progressing from spoon-fed to a TV tray of his own. Still too weak to stand, he watched Ed Sullivan repeats, ate Saltines with tea and honey and drew with the fattest crayons he'd ever seen upon a seemingly endless supply of Chinese take-out menus.

The old lady told him stories. She said she'd been a stewardess all her life but never left the state. She told him that her children had grown up and left home so quickly, they hadn't even given her enough time to have them. She'd married a man that wasn't there and stayed with him even though he paid her no mind. She collected cats till she noticed how the news made cat collectors look crazy, so she had turned them into pillows, cause no one was going to call her crazy. As a young girl she'd starred in a silent-picture movie she'd found in a box of Cracker Jacks. And she'd been living in her apartment for so long, that when she moved in, the building had only one story, but oh how things had grown.

Timmy loved her stories and he loved her cat pillows, even if more than one of them was still alive. He was fascinated to learn that he was not the only person who seemed to be pretending. This old lady had seen Mongolia while looking down a well, had invented the T.V. dinner, but lost out on piles of money when she couldn't decide if the dinner was made in or of televisions. Timmy understood and told her that sometimes the important part was choosing and not the choice. She agreed and told him how she had once shut her front door just to see if the rest of the world would go away.

Timmy asked her if it had and she said yes, only it comes back whenever the door is reopened. She explained that the world was tricky that way. It's never not there when you're looking, but it's always not never there when you look away.

Timmy imagined himself into her stories and the old woman squealed and bounced like a much younger really old woman as she watched her scattered and tangled memories play themselves out on her couch. On that couch she had a family that loved her and collected dodge balls. On that couch her childhood was happy, filled with splashing streams, hide and seek, cow stacking and days spent sledding down Broadway. She nearly drowned in giggles when she watched her dog say his first words – I will fetch anytime, anywhere and all it will cost you is a bag of chipmunks. And she nearly fell down honking when she saw herself as a young college girl, getting felt up at a drive-in movie with her family.

When Timmy's mind was finally clear enough to draw a picture of his own family, using both circles and triangles, he knew it was time to give his thanks and get back to being a man.

He kissed that old woman sloppily on the cheek and told her he'd be back with hugs and kisses to spare, for he was her grandchild now.

She offered to bring him home. She wasn't ready to watch him go. She was happy playing granny. So he told her that he would come back to see her often. He knew she was lonely and was sure that somewhere in her muddled mind, finding him and getting to keep him may have crossed paths. But she didn't go all crazy. She just reached down and wiped spit across a smear of chocolate on his chin, patted him on the head and watched him go.

Timmy Finds Home

The door was unlocked and Timmy, fearing his family may still be asleep, tried to slink in without being noticed. He eased the door open, slunk in and tiptoeing down the hallway to the living room.

It was as glum and sad a place as Timmy had ever walked into. His wife sat silent, apart from their children, who somehow managed to look both older and younger. He saw swollen eyes and down cast heads. He had walked into sadness and his heart sunk as he entered the cloud of gloom. Something bad had happened and he didn't have a God or a God's mother to believe in. Timmy frowned and furrowed his brow deeper than any man his age could ever achieve.

My God! What's happened! Timmy cried in despair as his family turned to find him near tears, moving forward with arms outstretched.

In unison, his family's mouths dropped open, their limbs working faster than their brains as they propelled from their seats. Their mouths pumped out nonsense, tongues clamoring around emotions too bit to fit words past. Their fingers reached for him as if directed by a mad blind man.

They came at him quickly, erratic sounds that could have been joy, sorrow, fear or anger sirening from their throats. Timmy prepared to defend himself, but he wasn't sure he could take them all. They came so fast, teeth gnashing, lungs turned inside out and limbs flying. He crouched ready to turn. He imagined pythons. He thought of grizzly bears as his family's clawing limbs and pumping jaws reached his body.

The arms encircled him. It was like sunshine and birdcalls with all the donuts you can eat, forever. They fell upon him, hugging and kissing and squeezing him so tightly they nearly made him into sun-bird-nut juice.

Cries of Daddy! Daddy! Filled his ears. Oh my God where have you been? Thank God you're home. We were so afraid. Where have you been? Thank God! Thank God! Thank God! They latched on, holding as tightly as little arms could while his wife kissed every bit of his face, whispering, I thought you were dead, lost in the rubble. I don't even care where you've been. I'm so glad you're home.

For the first time in his life, Timmy knew he was home. He was where he belonged, where he was wanted and apparently needed to be. He could not be the injured little boy that parts of him needed, but he could be a happy man and that was more than enough for now.

Timmy Takes a Stand

They had just finished the greatest block castle of their lives. It had both towers and parapets. Timmy had just learned what parapets were and had been eager to get some built. They were better than he would ever have expected. He half felt he could make himself small enough to walk those ramparts, but he'd never been good enough at pretending to fool himself. He always knew what he was, even if no one else did. Fortunately, being seven, he could nearly feel what it must be like to be a knight wearing tin underwear. His little brain was already in them.

He imagined both armies under his control. He stormed the castle while leading his men in defense of the wall, bravely battled forward as he held himself at bay, fending himself off as he consistently pushed himself

121

back. It was a delicate dance, victory and defeat held evenly in opposing hands. His bravery on both the give and the take meant certain victory and a routing defeat. Battle noises drooled and spattered from his lips, his family's laughter shook the walls, threatening to explode as a storm rolled in. Timmy disappeared within the stacks of blocks as the battle raged upon the walls and parapets.

Timmy had to learn to be more careful with his imagination. He laughed himself into a smile, amazed at the level of detail he was able to obtain as the outer wall of his apartment building was torn away in a sheet that rolled like an anchovy tin all the way to the street. Lights flooded his fortress, both armies retreated, slinking all the way back to Timmy's imagination. His family quickly followed.

Timmy assumed the crouching attack of a crowded feline, a tabby cat, blood in his eyes, an eternal killer, always just a hair's breath away from hiss and claws, even when hiding. A thousand beams of lights searched the rooms for his shadow, making it look like a disco on fire, with hundreds of choppers dividing the air between countless spinning blades that left some places devoid of air and others overfull. Little tongues licked at his home, hungry enough to devour him like so much dim sum.

Bullets tickled the building, but seemed shy, as if they were only browsing, flipping through the racks to see if anything jumped out at them. Timmy didn't jump. He watched patiently, through cool, calm, cat eyes.

Gargantuan had wasted no time in coming for him. He had finally found something to take personally. Timmy purred. Gone was the slippery stealth of take and replace. This display was clearly meant to make Timmy shit something larger than himself, perhaps something so large that the fat man could add it to his iconic collection.

Timmy crept to the void to see what obesity had mustered. Gargantuan was holding nothing back. For miles in every direction, including up and inexplicably down, marched an army so vast that it could only be amassed by unadulterated greed.

They covered the city in numbers so great the rats began to complain and the pigeons had nowhere to land closer than Jersey, forcing every winged rats with even an ounce of self respect to fly all the way to Pennsylvania.

Timmy watched the machine guns teasing. Foreplay, Timmy thought but was too young to understand what he had meant by that. What he did know, could see clearly, was, as he'd expected, that Gargantuan didn't want him dead. All enormous men know that death is not a punishment, it's an end to punishment and the fat man was not about to give Timmy some sort of special reward. He wanted to make him suffer, so he could feel the kind of infinite superiority that was his drug of choice, well, that and frosting. Timmy smiled. For a large man, this was an enormous mistake.

Most of what Timmy knew of war was from watching the Three Stooges, playing video games and setting up army men. Still he knew there were enough toy solders pointing at him to blow the entire block to dust, if not the entire island.

Timmy's cat kittened and then moused as a wall of climbers scurried up like a blanket desperate to keep the building warm. They scaled up and dropped down, the strongest climbing over those who fell behind. They spidered their way toward Timmy's hole, a throng of darkness sent to sniff him out.

The streets were green with helmets, the sky black with men. More men jumped from planes and rappelling from copters, while some seemed to just be falling. Below him in the street, the soldiers were layering, one army building upon the shoulders of the one below, as more layers arrived, the bottom layers quickly faced extinction, massive weight pressing them into oil, used to fuel the next layer of army.

Timmy knew this was not what God or his mother wanted. What they did want was for him not to want this. He knew they were waiting for him to choose: Heaven or Hell or at least decide he needed help so they could compete for the rescue. He pictured God putting on his Velcro-laced sneakers and Mother sharpening her fire.

Rapelers from the roof converged with climbers from the ground. The weaker waterfalled away from the congested façade, the army below pilling up faster than some climbers could ascend. Buildings were removed to make room as the upper floors of his apartment building were ripped away.

Timmy slunk, little more than a rat trapped on a rooftop. But of all the creatures he did not wish to meet, a cornered rat was up there on the list.

He backed into the remaining corner as men gushed, in a tangle of limbs and guns, into what was left of his children's room. He bristled his fur and hit the panic button.

He decided rat was the way to go; three headed, razor teeth, serpent's tongue, big and mean enough to shit Godzilla.

It didn't matter how well the army was prepared. Timmy could smell the fear, as he reared the first of his monstrous heads. Terror flowed in a yellow wave that surged from his apartment, washing the climbers down upon the mounding army below. Timmy's creature reared high, a scratchy, mind-splintering half howl, half squeal exploded through the comparatively quiet sounds of war as Timmy made it appear as if bullets merely encrusted the monster's hide, armor plating the enraged vermin.

Men ran straight over the edge to get away, throwing brothers aside, running over and through comrades for a chance to plummet, rather than face a ragging pestilence.

Those that reached the bottom alive, dug into the battle lines, burrowing through a rising army that appeared from above to look less and less like a field of helmets and more and more like a valley of feet, kicking like a chorus line on meth as it attempted to dig through the ranks to safer ground.

The weight of so many men crumbled the streets. Charges were blown from within the sewers, causing the sea of men to boil and overflow. Thousands were jammed head first into the exploded gutters, infuriating the rats, which fought for every inch of dirty and dank.

Octopusing cables rained down upon the copters, scattering rappellers and tangling around the rotating blades. The copters rocked and weaved, engines smoking as men leaped, swan diving into the waiting pool of legs, all clamoring for a little piece of sewer they could call their own, further infuriating the rats, who had seen nothing like this since the Irish immigration over a hundred years before.

Timmy's apartment emptied. Bodies piled in the street, wedged together with no escape, heads wrapped between legs, twisted around torsos, wound about arms as the first of the copters started down, striking the edge of an old brown stone before rolling down its facade and into the street, mincing a battalion before bursting into flames and molten bits of metal.

Eight more choppers fell. There goes the neighborhood. There goes the fat man's army. What wasn't made into buttery spread from the out of control rotor blades, burned in cadaverous fires that filled Timmy's home with a thick black char broiled smoke.

The rats were enraged. They had armed themselves with their most viscous teeth in defense of family and home, chewing threw squadrons at an alarming rate. At least until the lower army's fresh pressed oil caught and the sewers were blown clean.

Twenty minutes and the army was as good as gone. Timmy now had an air force. Eighteen pilots, ten planes and three copters, courtesy of family members that had been part of Gargantuan's army. They had told him of the impending attack. They had said it was hopeless, that Timmy would never escape no matter how well he hid. They said resistance was suicide. They refused to save themselves. They stuck with him and fought beside him, dropping the cables that took out air support, setting the charges that blew manhole covers and platoons sky high. And they lowered the ropes that dropped brothers and sisters into the folds of suffocating black smoke to find and save him.

Timmy had started without so much as a bullet or a bomb, yet the enemy was gone. If the fat man had understood any of what had happened during Timmy's visit, he certainly hadn't expected that he was not alone. Those with no one seldom expect family.

Simple sabotage, espionage and one hell of an imaginary rat and the only thing left to show that the army had ever existed was total devastation. Buildings had been reduced to scorch for blocks. The stink would never go away. Neither would the spirits of the men too simple to say no when told to go and fight for nothing.

Timmy considered once again how foolish he'd been for staying close to the action. He never needed to be in his apartment. He'd underestimated how angry and powerful the fat man was. He had been warned, he'd seen his army's and his plunder, but still hadn't seen it coming.

He was lucky to be alive. He was glad he'd sent his loved ones away, not that there had ever been a choice. Still, all of this… It was too much for his mind to contain. There should have been a way of preventing it. He stared out of what was left of his home and couldn't believe any of it.

Maybe he should have fled, let them take the neighborhood, let them search the city. Maybe he should have given himself up, made the sacrifice. Was he really worth all this? If he couldn't come up with a plan that didn't end in total destruction, lives wasted and the city decimate, then maybe he had no right coming up with plans at all. Maybe the only plan he should have come up with was complete surrender.

Timmy knew Gargantuan would never attack him so carelessly again as surely as he knew that he would again attack. Everything had spiraled out of control. And what of his family? What if they were home next time? What if the network failed? What if he had to move them from place to place and they were still never safe? What kind of life would that be? Was this really all because of pants?

Thousands died, tens of thousands. Blocks, a whole neighborhood were blown into the next state (Landing, to its inhabitants chagrin, in Clifton NJ, making it overnight New Jersey's third largest city). How was any of this okay? Why should a seven year old have to go through this? As hard as he thought and as angry as he felt, all paths led to the same place; immortals, nothing but holocaust can result when Gods play God.

Timmy wondered what else was going to come his way. He was going to have to tell his family far more than he ever intended, at least more than he intended since God came into his life.

Oh God, he thought. What if I end up just like my father? What if all this death leaves me empty and I began to find pleasure in the games? It was more than he could take. He'd been crying and coughing for more than an hour when his brothers finally found him, reduced to droppings at the buildings edge. They scooped him up and helped him to the waiting chopper.

Timmy Tells

Timmy hadn't told his wife and kids why they had to leave their home and he wasn't ready to tell them when he called to say that they had no home left.

His wife said she'd been watching the news and was only relieved that he was safe, though she had to chew on the words a little before she could get them out, less they break into sobs of undirected fear and rage.

Timmy told her that he had saved the valuables, the costumes, video games, Legos, and most of the play dough.

She asked about the pictures and he told her he didn't know about all of them, but he'd saved the crayons and markers, so it wouldn't be hard to make more.

She cried a little. She does that when she's happy and when she's sad. It's hard for Timmy to tell which is which. Either way he knew it was best to say he loved her and that everything was going to be alright.

She choked on something and asked if he was ever going to tell her what this had all been about.

He told her it was news best served over eggs and toast.

They met at Timmy's favorite breakfast place where they call their eggs organic and have grains that are whole. Timmy was always impressed by the number of words they used to say eggs and toast, even the orange juice was a paragraph and judging by the price, customers were paying by the word. But there was a salty, creamy, voluptuousness to everything they served that was bound to make bad news and inconvenient truths a little easier to swallow.

Are you angry about the apartment?

It's more of a sad. It was our home. I'll miss it and the life we had there.

It was the best home I ever had.

Me too.

I'm sorry.

It wasn't the place. It was us! We were our best there and I'm afraid that this little breakfast may be the end of that.

You don't want me around anymore?

I'll always want you around. I'm just afraid that you're about to tell me something that's incompatible with that.

I'm not the man you married.

Tell me something I don't know.

He was devoured several years ago by my family. There are thousands of us, all uniquely talented and individually hungry. He never stood a chance.

Boy these eggs are....

I know it's a lot to handle.

It's a little more than a lot. It's a lot more than a lot. Am I supposed to believe any of this?

You watched the news. You saw the scorched pit that used to be our neighborhood.

You're not just exaggerating or maybe trying to let me down stupidly?

I'm understating everything and I'm afraid I've already let you down.

And this family of yours, are they responsible for what happened?

They are responsible for stopping what happened. We have come together.

What for? I mean, from the devastation I saw on the televisions, I can't imagine what they stopped.

It's a little hazy in my head too, but I can tell you there is one less evil army in the world.

And what does this have to do with you?

Someone has to fight.

Fight? Fight who?

God, his mother and all that is bad in this world.

That sounds like an awful lot of fighting.

I hope it won't be.

But you think it will.

I'm afraid it will.

And where does this leave us?

Wherever you need.

What am I supposed to say to that?

You also need to understand, that when your husband was consumed, I hadn't even been born.

You say it so matter-of-factly.

I'm just a kid. I'm afraid even to show you who I really am. You'd be so disappointed.

I saw through you a long time ago. I wasn't thrilled knowing, but I'm not disappointed exactly..

What exactly are you.

I'm worried.

I don't blame you. I'm worried too.

This family of yours and the violence that comes with it, how do I know this won't happen again?

It will.

Then we're in danger.

Yes and no.

It can't be yes and no!

It has to be, but people are watching out for us and we'll always have help.

How do you know that's enough?

I don't. But there are too many of us, hidden in too many places, so many places that when we finally pool our knowledge, we'll know nearly everything.

And when will that be?

Tuesday.

Tuesday?

That's when the cable guy comes.

What?

At the new place.

New place?

It's all set up. Bed's, towels, toast…

And I'm supposed to just forget all this and go back to happy.

You've been happy?

For the first time since our honeymoon.

You don't mind me being a child.

Honey, all men are children, but since you were consumed, you've been more of a man than you ever were before. You've been really good to me and great with the kids. You're not what I imagined I'd be growing old with when I said I do, but it's too late now. We're a family. So I guess I'm not in such a hurry for you to grow up.

It's gonna take a while.

I'll wait, so long as we're safe.

I have people watching after us that you've never even seen.

I'm not sure that makes me happier.

You want to see the new place?

Timmy and the Trash Man

Things were disappearing daily. Nothing great, though a seven year old would disagree. Timmy couldn't find the TV Guide. There were no Ding Dongs or Anne Rice novels to be found for miles. The Abba records had all disappeared along with the Toaster Strudel and the Disney channel. Ranch chips bought at the grocers never made it in the door. It was impossible to get home with anything from Wal-Mart or Target. Everything shitty had plain old disappeared. Old sox were gone, stained underwear missing, Twinkies would vanish from your hand, Miracle Whip could not be found, every Will Ferrel movies had left the house, along with the Crate and Barrel furniture, conservative rhetoric, Chinese take-out, Liberal ideals, fried chicken skin, dingle berries, Teflon pans, Chia Pets, Cheetos, sea monkeys, Southern Comfort, white jeans, Indian music, recycled toilet paper, pork rinds, Family Guy, salad shooters, conspiracy theories, soccer, Steely Dan, unsalted potato chips, ring worm, flip flops, pit stains, relish, reality TV, curling, Canadian whiskey, peppermint schnapps, back hair, haikus, parsnips, Vogue, hamsters, Nutella, pigs feet, black mold and John Updike.

On the plus side Timmy never had to dump the coffee grounds and hadn't taken out the garbage since they moved in. Junk mail stopped coming, toilets plunged themselves, drains flowed clear, expired food saw itself to the door, toenails could be clipped anywhere without fear and no one cared what you did with your tissues.

The family had PJ's number. They called him the Trash Man, the apparent son of a man named JP who seemed to have a thing for stone. Together, with the fat man, they had attacked Timmy's university. PJ had taken away nearly all signs of socio-economic theory (as well as several of Timmy's students) and then emptying the trash cans, before the father stole every piece of stone in his building, from the decorative door jams to the gypsum powder in the drywall. The father had caused all the damage, risking the lives of hundreds in the process and when it was all over, PJ cleaned up the mess.

While PJ hadn't orchestrated anything powerful or awe inspiring, not even contributing to the destruction of his classroom, he was become a little bit annoying, down right pesky in fact. It was hard having someone ghosting around with such discriminant tastes and it had become impossible for him to prepare anything for class (not that he understood anything about the socio economics, but he sure did enjoy pretending to be prepared).

Who had named PJ God of Trash anyway? Timmy had a good idea and he was grateful it was only junk that went missing. Still, one person's treasure is another's trash and Timmy could really have gone for a Ring Ding.

But as annoying as it was, there was something nice about the attention, creepy, but still nice. Timmy didn't even have to flush and the toilet always sparkled. He didn't sweep or vacuum, but not a spec of dirt was anywhere in sight. The family even lost large amounts of unsightly fat without effort and all they had to do to keep life flowing normally was to redecorate with objects of presumed merit, objects that were made to last, antiques mostly, quality from a bygone age. Timmy and his family became extremely fond of Victorian goods, partly because they never had to dust them.

Finally a break! It brought a long lost smile to Timmy's face. Instead of doom, God had sent a maid.

Timmy Tackles Stone

Timmy opened the door to a yard full of brothers and sisters all packing wood, two by fours, four by eights and yards of crown molding. Word had leaked out, as word tends to do when you have an army of ears, that the stone man was coming and he wanted not only the decorative, but also the foundation of where Timmy lived.

From what the family could figure, he cared only for stone. He could steal a pebble from your intestines or a 20,000-ton embellishment of Abraham Lincoln, if that is what you had laying about. And he did it with no army and no guns. He was like a pool of acid, able to dissolve a brick in less than a blink.

By all reports, a trail of rock stripped land was on a collision course with Timmy's home. JP was headed their way; leaving in his wake not a single upturned and unpocketed stone (along with a hint of acid, a touch of diesel fumes and some kind of thick acrid smoke that spoke of demolition).

Timmy's family came full of planks and plans. Coffee was put on and sandwiches were made. The house rocked and rattled under a storm of flailing hammers, buzzing saws and thundering jackhammers. Materials came in and rock went out at speeds that were nearly a blur.

The foundation was removed and replaced with railroad ties and split lumber. The sheet rock all had to go, along with the countertops and the bathroom floor. The brick steps leading to the front door were replaced with cast iron and the chimney was redone in chocolate colored glass tiles (why melted sand and forged metals didn't count as the rock they had once been was beyond the family, but rumor had it that JP hated industrialized products and would never lower himself to taking them).

It was impossible for the average person to get an accurate count of how many people worked on Timmy's house, since so many of his brothers and sisters still couldn't shake the habit of looking like someone else, but Timmy had hundreds of carpenters in his family and hundreds more that pretended to be carpenters and most of them came to his rescue. In the end, every bit of rock in Timmy's home was replaced with either wood, metal or a high quality synthetic that could never be considered junk, leaving the house looking better than ever. And it was all done well before sunset and comfortably ahead of the rock lifting twister headed their way.

They left nothing plain or ordinary. The wood was beveled and planed, carved wood ran up the banisters and around the doors, crown molding fringed every wall and the floors had all been done in hardwood. Even places where no rock had lain were redone in heavily detailed wood, giving the place a log cabin / Swiss chalet feel.

Once again, Timmy had been the one in need and they came. They came without asking and they came without any motives other than helping the one helping them. Timmy and his family thanked each brother and every sister. For the first time in what seemed like ages, Timmy and his family felt safe.

Stains and shellac dried as the family enjoyed a party on Timmy's new deck. The entertainment was simple yet magical. They enjoyed cool beers and lemonade as they watched the construction debris vanish, bit by bit. Then as eggs began to cook and dusk began to twinkle, a cool wind picked up the street as a vague mist stole all the stones in Timmy's yard, then like it was being erased, the driveway and walkways left in haste.

By the time the hash browns were browned and cozied up against eggs and toast, the fog had passed, the stones were gone and Timmy's home looked even more beautiful amongst its new rustic appearing surroundings.

God. Timmy called home. Life if good when you're out of armies. If you have to keep coming at me, please do it through the hands of the inept. Amen.

Timmy Gives God Hell

Nice place you got here.
Oh hell no!
Oh hell yes!
Haven't you done enough damage already?
Earth's still young baby.
I don't want you coming here.
Can't help it, omnipresent ya know.
Then where were you when they were trying to kill me?
I watched the whole thing.
Didn't even bother to help.
You're not dead are you?
I could have been.
There's no such thing.
And lots of people died.
Lots of people who made bad decisions.
That shouldn't matter.
Live by the sword die by the sword. I made that one up myself.
It's not right.
I know. And it's not even what I told the guy. It was just what he
heard. But I think it's catchy.
It's not.
Been around for thousands of years.
I don't care.
Well that's no fun.
I'm not here to amuse you.
Of course you are. That's the only reason you're here.
I hate you.
Flip side of love is what that is.
What do you want?
I'll ask the questions here. And the first question is what's up with
the closets?
I had them removed.
I know that.
Because of you.
I know that.
Then why are you asking?

Isn't it a pain in the ass keeping your pants under the bed?

It keeps the vermin out.

They're God's creatures.

It's not his creatures I'm worried about.

Kid, I've been in and out of your pants a thousand times without so much as an unfold.

I'll be sure to fumigate.

You can't keep God out of your pants.

Well, maybe it will keep your mother from burning them.

You'd think by now you'd understand mother better.

What do you want?

I want to know if you're ready to start working for me.

You tried to kill me!

If I wanted to kill you I wouldn't have sent them.

You destroyed my home!

Material possessions are nothing compared to the riches that can only be found when you devote yourself to God.

Should I bow to you or your pants?

If you see my pants without me, assume I'm not far behind.

I'm not gonna work for you.

That's what Jonah said.

Are you threatening me with a whale?

I don't need to threaten.

You do it all the time.

I don't need to; I just like it a lot. Keeps things interesting. Unless you'd rather I go the way of boils and locus, then up and kill your whole family.

Please don't do that to me.

I hate repeating myself.

Thank God for that.

You're welcome.

Get out!

Not so fast. You've only momentarily defeated one of my boys. I've got another that's just itching to go.

I think I've already finished with him?

Cocky aren't we. I decide when my envoys are defeated.

And when you're done with him?

I'll make three more.

And if I don't want to play.

It's your life.

Meaning?

You'll defend it.

Maybe I'll join your mother.

Oh she can destroy you, but she can't protect you.

And if she makes the same proposition?

Then you're damned if you do and damned if you don't.

Can't burn the pants, can't wear them.

You're pretty good at pant analogies.

Why don't you two just get along?

If we did that, in all likelihood it would be far worse for you.

And since you don't get along, I won't be here long.

I have a plan to defeat her.

Does it involve me living?

At the very least eternally in Heaven.

Is that what you promised your mother.

No, that was my dad.

And where is he?

Jersey Shore.

So both your parents are in Hell.

At least during the tourist season.

I gotta think my best bet is keeping to myself.

Ain't ready to join up?

There's just no benefit to it.

Desperation will change that mind of yours.

I destroyed an army pretending I was a giant three-headed rat. Don't tell me I'm not desperate.

I loved that part!

I hated it.

Flip side of love.

I thought you hated repeating yourself.

If once was always enough, I'd have run out of things to do on day one.

Would have been better for us all.

There wouldn't be an us all.

You gotta treat your toys better.

Not when the shelves are stocked I don't.

Trash Man Overhaul

It was the mother load! The article first appeared during a particularly slow week for news, but PJ never needed to check these sources. There were certain stories he knew before they happen. Such was the record being set for the world's largest bag of garbage, rumored to have already broken all records for height, width, volume and weight. PJ could nearly taste the trash and the pile had grown so large that traces of the smell had reached his discerning nostrils as it drifted putridly from a small town well outside Boise, Idaho.

The town was called Durken, after the original settlers to whom everyone in town could trace their roots, by following a rather straight line. The town had been preparing for this day for years, selling wide-open spaces and rich prairies to the mountain builders that included over 800 municipalities nationwide. Hundreds of towns and cities that had nowhere, within their own borders, they were willing to tarnish with such a thing as their own refuse, sent their waste, as quickly as it could be loaded, to little Durken.

They paid by the ton and through the nose, truckload after truckload, piling up the largest mountain east of the Rockies, a mountain that had made the entire town rich, rich enough that they didn't have to be as dirty or as inbred as they were. They had money for maids, money for groomers and more than enough to afford brides from any country they pleased, but none of that seemed to matter to the Durkenites.

It wasn't until one particularly drunk town meeting /family reunion/orgy that they decided what to do with their money. They would put themselves on the map, honoring the very dirt that had made them so rich in the first place. They would do it in what they considered style, using the one thing they all agreed was better than money. The next afternoon, when the hangovers had not yet begun to ebb, the first calls were made to Glad.

Finally, the day for which PJ had been waiting, for what felt like his whole life, was about to arrive. Eight years and thousands and thousands of tons later, on the anniversary of that drunken meeting/reunion/orgy epiphany, it was finally time to close the bag in what was dubbed The Great Zip Tie Ceremony.

The surrounding towns half joked, half wished for Durken to be airlifted to New Jersey, but PJ wasn't laughing. It had taken all of his willpower to let that much garbage collect in one place for so long. He'd been uncharacteristically patient, deciding to wait until the tie was twisted to be certain that it was the largest ever and therefore a necessary addition to any serious garbage aficionado's collection. He wanted it on the books before he hauled away, but he wouldn't wait much past dark. He had his route. He had his plan. And the mother-load was sure to be his, minutes after the custodians called it a day.

The Great Zip Tie Ceremony

PJ had front row seat for the Great Zip as it was being called. He'd been sitting in the front row since before there had been a front row. He'd been there all week, squatting and smiling, needing neither food nor facilities. All he needed was the sweet, sweet smell of mankind's final contribution and the occasional wayward fly.

As the crowds arrived, he could nearly chew upon the overflowing excitement. Everyone that came looked like they belonged in that rancid oversized bag. They had come from under rocks and out of gullies. If smell was an indicator they had traveled by sewer, and if looks told the tail, they'd been inbreeding in those same sewers for generations. Their clothes were shit colored. Their food was shit colored and deep-fried. Their children were shit-colored members of the Arian race, whose only knowledge of whiteness came from folk tales told around burning tire. The few who's mobile homes were still truly mobile invited the rest in, apparently to spit, sleep, defecate, fornicate and fry Twinkies.

PJ was so happy he could have cried. It was like he had come home, like he always imagined home could be, if he'd ever imagined that garbage could walk and talk nearly coherently. If this were his home, he'd tie all these people to stakes so they could never get away, allowing them only enough chain to fry the foods they seemed to thrive upon. That way the trash could grow naturally, organically so to speak, some of it alive, some not so much, but all of it wonderful, like an unsanitary geyser blowing below a festering garbage falls. Trash is trash, is trash, is trash and just because it blows in the wind doesn't make it any less beautiful than when it plays the harmonica.

As the first few words of the keynote address reached PJ's ears, he wondered how long he'd been crying. It might've been for days.

Brothers, sisters, those who just look like us and those who are strangely clean and probably sent from some metropolis despite your desperate pleadings, I welcome you to the greatest day in the history of trash…

PJ would like to have heard more, wished to absorb every word like some sort of rabid e-coli, but his sobs had grown to such an intensity that even the 'Ye Haws' and the 'Sure diggiddies' of the crowd were drowned like so many rats in so many sewers. He hoped they were going to sell DVDs or preferably beta tapes, since trash to be relived is best preserved on trash.

The rest of the ceremony was a blur, garbled sounds and tears stained pageantry. He tried to imprint the tying of the bag forever upon his brain, but it too had become soggy and remained such well past the time that the living, breathing trash had left.

It was as if he were a prisoner of his own ecstatic glee. They cleaned up around him. They took his chair. His eyes always on the prize, his brain was wiped clean and for once the cleanliness didn't bother him. He was dripping wet. He had cried his was through three layers of second-hand clothes, at least through the upper half; the lower half was most likely number one and to be honest, a good bit of number two, but none of that mattered.

The crowds had all gone home. The stars arrived and PJ's eyes dried enough to focus upon his cherished prize. The bulging black plastic-wrapped tower contained everything he cared about. It was his greatest love and for the first time, they were alone.

He wanted to hold it, to caress it. He wished he could grow as large as a water tower so he could wrap his arms around it, embracing it, pulling it closer. He wished it had ears that he could whisper sweet nothings into, before nibbling them off. He had professed his love to garbage a thousand-thousand times, always longing for it to confess that it too loved him, even though he knew better, knew that his love would always be unrequited.

Unless, maybe, maybe if the garbage were large enough, maybe this time. Surely such a pile was more alive than dead. Maybe, just maybe, this time the trash he loved would love him back. He peered up at the massive dark form that the moon was beginning, with some difficulty, to rise above and made his wish upon the North Star.

Star light, star bright, first star I've seen tonight, I wish I may, I wish I might, have this wish I wish tonight and I wish with all my might, that which I love will love me tonight.

His thoughts strayed briefly to his father. If only he had loved him more than stone, things may not have come to this. But after his mom had passed, it had been nothing but stone for his old man, which is probably what led him to trash. He was searching for all he had lost in the one place where all things eventually belong, becoming the thing he deep down believed himself to be.

He shook the ugly thoughts from him mind. Today was to be joyous. The past was just that, you can't change it any more than PJ felt he could change his destiny. All of creation belonged in a bag, a giant bag, the likes of which would make a baby out of the monstrosity that sat waiting before him. He smiled despite himself, then smiled because of himself, stepping forward to caress the thick, dark, bulging plastic.

He grabbed the first nodule his hand ran over, it was firm with just enough give. He reached higher and found another. His fingers tightened and his arms flexed. He drew closer, pressing his body against the hefty sack. He lifted himself, grinding into the bag as his feet left the ground, his hands searching for higher bulges and greater protuberances, his eyes on the stars, his cheeks sticking and peeling.

He was halfway up the bag before he even realized. He was a vine, a cat burglar, a rat, scurrying, clamoring, climbing, inch by inch, higher and higher. He was Jack of the beanstalk on his way to take home the giant. Effortlessly, he slithered his way, groping and mounting up the bag, till he reached the summit and finally stood above.

Flat-footed, on top of the bag, on top of the world, believing in miracles, believing in love, PJ knew he was not meant to be alone. If anything was ever going to understand him, it would have to be garbage itself. He felt sure, the only thing that could ever love him might just be the very mountain he had so recently crested.

He untied the super-thick plastic straps as if they were the most delicate lace, smoothing out any bumps and wrinkles, running its length between his fingers, tugging, massaging out the kinks until it was factory smooth. All that stood between him and love was but a little pull. He breathed deep and let the plastic unfold with a tiny whimper. He worked his fingers in slowly, eyes closed, clenching the bag's collar lovingly. He took another deep breath in, opened his eyes and pulled the bag opening wide...

White light burned through his eyes, setting his brain on fire. Laughter ruptured his ears. His nasal passage opened. His sweat glands exploded. His bladder released.

Honey, you got to be careful what you wish for. It might come true. The words permeated his mind, echoing from lobe to lobe till his poor brain vibrated itself into mush. Long dark nails, pretty and piercing entered his chest and pulled him, scream first, into the bag.

No What But Win

Just shut up about the damn pants for a minute!

Now you sound like my mother.

I'm a little tired of that topic too.

On that much we agree.

So why don't you drop it.

Hell's as far down as I could get her.

Not her, the pants!

You want me to drop my pants?

Forget about pants!

But it's a good icebreaker. Boring, insipid Gods talk about the weather, while fun, interesting Gods talk about pants.

You know as well as I do that none of this is about any pants.

I know better than you do about everything. I made everything.

So you keep telling me.

You better start listening. I could destroy you then replace you with a cat and no one would be the wiser.

But you're not going to.

And why not?

I don't know.

But you're so smart.

Yeah, well, this is all stupid.

Then try being smarter about being stupid or is it vise versa, stupid about being smart? Either way you know enough to have figured this has nothing to do with pants.

The pants thing was just crazy. It didn't go anywhere. No one needs a little boy to help them rule over pants.

Then why do I need you at all?

You don't.

True. So why do I let you exist? You resist me at every turn, yet you walk around without so much as a boil on your ass. Historically speaking, that kind of shit just don't happen.

You tried to kill me.

I don't try anything. I either do or I don't. Even when you know the outcome, sometimes you still deal the cards just to stay in the game. It's like watching a movie you've already seen long after you wrote the script.

So you weren't trying to kill me or my family?

Try is such a vague term. It's hard to pay attention to the little things.

Our lives and deaths are not little.

They are when you're bigger than the universe.

But I'm still alive.

Can you tell me why?

I can't.

You already said it really.

Because it's not about pants?

Exactly.

I'm not dead because of pants.

You're not dead despite pants.

Because only I can defeat your mother.

You can't defeat my mother! God laughed. Christ kid, who put something so stupid in your head? She could turn you into a venereal disease without bothering to wake up.

But she hasn't killed me either, even though I oppose her at every turn.

Ah, a common thread.

It's not about pants. It's about me. I'm the pants!

You're as precious as you are fragile.

I can be anything and project anywhere. I'm the best, which makes me interesting to you.

I could make a billion better than you in less time than it takes for me to say time.

I haven't given into either one of you.

Precious and fragile.

If I give in someone wins.

And if you don't, we continue to play.

If I crack someone wins.

Said like a true egg.

You're a God. What could you win?

Christ kid, sometimes I forget how much of a child you are. There is no such thing as what.

What do you mean? You said that if I crack because of you, then you win.

Correct.

What I want to know is what you think you win?

I don't think I win what.

What?

There is no what.

What do you win?

There is no what. There is only winning. The only prize is that I pretend I win.

Then what you win is thinking you win?

I don't even win that.

Why not?

I know better.

If you know better, than why are you doing this?

I gotta do something. Eternity is a long, long time.

So you pursue things that don't exist?

Winning exists, even if the what that you win doesn't.

Winning can't exist without a what.

Maybe you can't exist.

What do you mean by that?

Oh you'll find out.

Hell Hath No Trash

PJ was nothing more than a boiling puddle. He bubbled and burned, his agony sounding like 'bloop'. His pain existed in the vapors that surrounded even as it suffocated. He breathed himself in and asphyxiated.

You pathetic trash monger! You were supposed to be one of my son's secret weapons, his mighty human ally in the quest to teach me what is what! But you are nothing but a weak little boy and I am enrage that I have wasted time upon you!

PJ bubbled helplessly. He wanted to plead. He wanted to explain. He had no ideas.

Save your vapor. Here you are less than refuse. So listen closely. I am going to tell you how it will be. I've been watching you attack the mere boy Timmy…Don't you dare bubbling at me!.. You were told to harass and intimidate, to lure the boy to my bidding and what do you do?.. I said save those bubbles for someone who cares…you took out his garbage! You cleaned his house! You made certain he never encountered so much as a speck of litter anywhere he went! Oh and of course, the topper must have been taking his TV Guide. That must have really hurt him. Poor boy, had everything worthless removed from his life. Mother God hissed enchantingly at the puddle and picked a bit of nasty from her spotless teeth.

Now I can see how that kind of dismal performance might be fine for my son, but what I can't figure is if you're completely stupid or just unbearably pathetic!... No, don't try to explain. Here all the trash ends up in the same place. It's called the Lake of Fire, which you are a short, slippery slope above, so I am more than certain that you are going to agree to anything I suggest. Am I right? Mother God glared.

No, don't vent toward me!... The question was rhetorical. You do my bidding or you burn in ways far, far worse than the simply boiling puddle you are now.

Even evil and threatening PJ loved her, his puddle swooning inpercievably.

Listen closely and understand me, I will only tell you this once. The boy will be mine along with anything else my son believes is his.

Her smile tightened the bubbles around PJ's puddle, both in horror and appreciation.

You see, and not that I need to explain myself, but this burning hole that you would do anything, literally anything, including damning yourself to a hapless eternity in this very pit, just to get out of for even a moment, just for so much as a drop of water, is where my son felt fit to deposit me as soon as he had his own world to play with. Which I forgave him for till he found new ways to antagonize me. Well enough is enough, a concept I'm sure you are bubbling through right now and as certain as I am that I've had enough. I am equally certain that you have now joined my side whole heartedly. The worse he can do is send you here, while I control here. Bubble once if you understand. Just kidding boil boy. I control that too.

PJ boiled in beautiful concentric rings that popped and danced, skipping across his surface before plunging deep, only to reappear as a center fountain that bubbled like some gorgeous bag of trash he once knew.

So let me tell you what you are going to do and because I'm feeling generous, I'll even make this pleasant for you. I'll play by the rules of mythology. Since you are so fond of garbage, back on earth you will be given a golden sledgehammer with which you will turn everything in Timmy's life into garbage. Really a win-win for you don't you think?.. Whoa, hold the bubbles, again rhetorical... But think of it, you'll get more trash and spend less time as boiling goo. Boil twice if you understand. Just kidding. God damn I love that one. Oh and you have one week.

World's Largest Yard Sale

God threatened him with eternal damnation. He'd felt that way before. God's mother boiled him down to a thick paste. He'd felt worse. Most days he weighed nearly five tons. He hadn't stop shitting in nearly eight years. His home had its own Pepto Bismol factory. It was a major ingredient in everything he ate. He'd been on diets worse than damnation. He'd been on binges worth an eternity of burning.

There was no toilet paper soft enough, strong enough or wide enough. There were no lotions able to soothe all the places he overlapped. Hell bubbled up from his intestines daily. If he were to search for God's mother, looking for the tributaries to the Lake of Fire, he would start with a spotlight aimed down his stretched beyond-capacity esophagus. His ass hurt like the holocaust and his back was all ass.

He hadn't seen his penis in years, though the river flowed eternal. He had places where natural yellow springs sprung, irritating and infecting till puss damn bursts.

Cocaine was just a laxative. Heroin didn't exist in the quantities he needed. He hadn't slept since he was eleven. He belched with every breath. Vomit burned coming up and going down. Acid was dissolving his stomach and stomach was the only thing left inside him.

Hell was nothing less than a vacation. He had been longing for it for years. He feared nothing more than his life and collected the world merely as a distraction from his gluttonous pain. Most of his collection he'd only seen once, during the initial fly-by. He knew he owned the pyramids, but they were hidden from view, somewhere behind Parliament. He used to have things flown over on a continuous rotation, but looking up had become such a bother and he couldn't bare the noise since even his eardrums had become completely engorged. He couldn't remember the last time he tilted his head or tried to move his morbidly obese eyes.

Gargantuan's life was misery and there were never enough distractions. But for the first time since he suspected his father of plotting to enlist him in t-ball, he finally had something to latch onto, that for seconds on end, made him forget how much he hurt, by focusing his attention on how much he wanted to hurt. He would use his empire to take down the boy who threatened his empire. He wasn't going to just kill Timmy; he was going to make him feel what pain was.

He had lost much in the failed attempt to take Timmy. The financial costs were pennies compared to what he was worth, but most of that was tied up in architectural wonders. His operation was down and you can't steal an army without an army. You can't hijack an air force without pilots and well-trained personnel were harder to steal than Denmark and rarer than attractive English women.

He had no real choice. He had to have a yard sale. The only problem, how do you sell illicit national treasures that no one knows are missing? E-bay wasn't going to cut it. He'd need more than an ad in the local shopper.

He'd have to contact not the original owners, but the one's who hated them most.

Iran would love to own the Wailing Wall. The Mongols could yell into China if they had the Great Wall. He could sell his Washington, DC collection by the piece to the highest bidder, the same with Big Ben and the Tower of London. He'd give discounts for trades, a pyramid for a thousand good pilots, your pick of cathedrals for a shit load of heavy arms. It would take Gargantuan no more time to make these trades then it would to steal the treasures back once his army was trained. But for the first time in his life he had no interest in collecting.

He had no interest even in food. His doctors warned him that he was on the verge of the world's largest shit through a door that was threatening to fuse shut from years of neglect and too much traffic. They weren't even sure where the back hatch originated from anymore. But he didn't care; not about shit; not about money. Not about stuff. His vague and overwhelming ambition had finally found a focus.

He felt nearly light and giddy, like a perky little school girl. Apparently in his agitated state he had moved his neck and his brain wasn't getting enough oxygen. So they brought in the crane for a quick adjustment and the lightness went away and all that was left was a giddy child. The biggest, meanest, most straight-up evil child the world had ever seen. And he just picked out his new playmate. Make no mistake; on their next play date he would bring all his toys.

Family in Disguise

There were new rules in Timmy's home or maybe there were just new games. He was training the children and coaching his wife in the one subject in which he was totally proficient; how to never appear as yourself to anyone watching, while making sure they knew that someone was always watching.

Honestly, Timmy was surprised he still had a family. They were still removing planes and rubble, guns and bodies from what had been their neighborhood. They were obviously scared. The World Wars had nothing on what showed up at their front door.

The authorities didn't know how it happened, the politicians couldn't explain and the police were mystified, not only by the death and destruction, but by how all the residents within a square mile, through the most inexplicable and improbable array of coincidences, had all been away from home during the attack, along with every pet in over 1,000 multistory buildings.

Cars had broken down, vet visits changed, free massages were offered and fumigations forced out residents. Every restaurant in the city that laid outside the doomed square mile had at least two of the families from within dining there. Old friends had come into town, job interviews were being conducted; cabs got lost; lights wouldn't change and fire alarms malfunctioned. There were even three men mistakenly abducted by the mob and later released. The police recorded thousands and thousands of easy to explain coincidences that, when taken together, no one could explain, except for Timmy.

Not wanting to sound crazier than necessary, Timmy had told his family that special agents had contacted him due to his in-depth understanding of personal behavioral traits. They had asked him to help fight rising evil and even though he had yet to give them an answer, bad people had gotten his name and decided to take him out preemptively. When his family asked why they sent thousands of men with bombs and planes to destroy anything even remotely near him, Timmy could only reply that the Gods must be crazy and that he completely understood if they wanted to leave and start over without him, since he felt certain the bad men would come again.

What Timmy couldn't understand was his family's willingness to stay. He didn't understand it any more than his overwhelming need for them not to go. Not only did they fall upon him with hugs, kisses and promises of a life spent together or not at all, they cheered his fight against an unexplained but obviously dangerous enemy.

Timmy could have been happier, but not much. Love in times of war feels like all the juice from a big plump love has been concentrated and injected directly into the veins of the neck. For a boy who had only recently discovered love, to get it pumped straight into his veins, showed him clearly how close Heaven was to Hell. To save his family he would have to stop more than just his enemies, he would have to put a stop to the whole enemy making machine.

But before any of that could happen, there were changes that had to occur at home. His family had to change. They had to become everyone and anyone. No one could follow them home. Their names could not be mouthed audibly or inaudibly. They would not be allowed to recognize themselves. At least not on the outside.

Timmy started simply with haircuts, dye jobs and name changes. But before he was through, he would need them to be able to be everything or nothing at a seconds notice. No one unwanted would ever find them again.

At least as long as he could keep God's and his mother's mouths closed. One of them had already nearly gotten him killed and in all likelihood it was both of them that done it.

What do you do about God and his mom? They didn't seem concerned about life. You couldn't fool them or hide from them. Not taking sides was going to see him dead. And choosing sides was suicide. His only hope was to appeal to another power. Fortunately for Timmy there was another power.

God liked to ramble endlessly and had told Timmy where to find the only other immortal on the planet. Apparently the God line goes way back. But millennia upon millennia of Godding around had left most of them straight up despondent. Being everywhere, all the time, able to do anything, is only an exciting proposition to those that can do little, hardly anywhere, sometimes. The truth about how tiresome it is to be immortal comes nearly as quickly as eternity is long. And if it weren't for the distraction created by inner squabbles, nearly none of them would do it hardly at all. But there was still one other nearly active entity out there. God's father was living on the Jersey Shore, kept from hapless oblivion only by the never-ending drama of his ex-wife and son.

God had never gotten into details, but he apparently lived near Egg Harbor, spending part of his time influencing the outcomes of barbecues, alternating orgasmic chicken and botulism beef and part of his time determining the fate of bikini tops. If a bikini top stayed up against an overwhelming wave blame Old Man God, but when it comes down you better give thanks. Which is strange, because according to God, his dad never approved of tits and had actually thought holes that go straight through the body so people could scratch their backs would have been a much better idea.

God's dad also spent a lot of time pretending to be a lobster and wandering into traps. Seems he felt there was something very spiritual that could only be experienced when one was eaten, digested, shat and then reformed in the toilet; Old Man God would reach up and bite the ass of the person who consumed him. He called it ass for an ass and declared it to be the only justice in all creation. That was the first thing Timmy ever heard God say that made any sense.

Timmy hoped Old Man God would help control his family. If anyone could help, he might be the only one.

The Misunderstanding of JP

Things were not turning out the way PJ had imagined. His imagination was full of rocks and all he was getting was pebbles. He couldn't help but think God didn't understand him. Where once he'd been stealing the great stones of the world without leaving a single tell-tale sign, now he'd been reduced to foundation work and he was expected to tell the world.

Clearly he was embarrassed. He hadn't managed any big announcements about the pebbles he'd been finding around Timmy's home. Oh he'd written a few cryptic messages that he hoped no one would see, just so he could say he was complying, but nothing clearer than "This rock taken by PJ" written in clear plastic wrap and left in a field on a windy day.

God must have made a mistake. He was worth so much more. Maybe he had misunderstood, or God had. He was sure they were supposed to rule the world together, taking things back to the days of the heaven and the earth, before things got complicated by organic matter. He didn't even care if that meant he had to become rock. He had always secretly wanted to. He felt close to rock and felt that it felt close to him, and any sentence that uses the word felt in it three times must convey the truth damn it!

Rocks, pebbles, what was the point? His talents were being wasted. He'd been working on a plan to steal the bedrock out from underneath Timmy's home (the only real rock anywhere near the boy), but bedrock is unfortunately continental.

He'd managed some large capers in his time, going so far as redirecting lava flows. It made him feel like he was stealing from the center of the Earth. He even had a game he liked to play, where after stealing a flow he'd pretend the next eruptions were out to get him, only to run blindly into his diabolical trap and end up his captives as well, further infuriating the molten core.

But stealing boiling rock and cutting away a tectonic plate were different matters. It would be easier to lower the Himalayas by a thousand feet than to cut down to the mantle and survive. Besides, even if he did make it to the mantle, there was no way of being sure that it really wasn't angry with him for kidnapping its envoys. Even to a rock man, molten retaliation is not a desirable way to go.

Which left the rock man picking up pebbles. He had them all, leaving only sifting dirt for sand. He hadn't stolen sand since he was in diapers and he wasn't going back to it now. Damn God, damn him straight to Hell if he didn't like it!

Night of the Living Timmy

Timmy had seen a lot of crazy shit. He'd ventured into the dark places where no one should go. He'd skipped through evil and curtsied to pure malevolence. But he'd never felt as scared, had his nerves stretched as far, as when he watched the undead eating brains.

Every time the suspenseful music started, his children's eyes would turn towards him. Then they'd laugh all the way to the floor when the monster struck. Timmy squeal changed form and fled. He would flee from the monsters spontaneously, outwardly meek and literally running. Once he'd squirreled up the grandfather clock, another time he locused through the air and more than once he moused under the carpet, always to reappear again just behind the couch, his eyes peeking above the cushions, his sons rolling across the floor, a smile stretched taunt between pretty little wifey's ears. The family would barely have time to recover before a head would be ripped off and Timmy would become dust in the wind or jingle his change into the deepest recesses of the couch. Timmy was better to watch than the movie and laughter was more common than popcorn.

Tonight, they had enjoyed the zombie classic Night of the Living Dead. It was almost as good as watching Timmy flee from the zombies time and time again. There were lots of jokes and popcorn fights and soda squirting out noses. On nights like this, it was easy to forget that trouble seemed to loom high and heavy about them.

Afterwards, Timmy gave each boy a kiss on the forehead, told them a story about a bullfrog that thought he was big, till he was confronted with true enormity and the revelation made his tiny little head explode. He then sang them a short but sweat medley of TV show themes and advertisement jingles. The kids fell fast asleep, just like they always did, though Timmy was still shook up enough to think he'd never sleep again; which was fine. He still had a full night's work ahead of him.

Leaving the kids nodding in dreamland, Timmy opened his closet and pulled out his cowboy suit. He was sitting on a trunk, pulling on his boots when his wife smoothed forward to give his cheek a kiss.

Is everything ready?

Ready and waiting. He kicked his boot heels together as he rose and tipped his hat.

You better mosey on then.

Yes Ma'am. He winked.

She hugged him. She didn't tell him to be careful or to stay out of trouble; she didn't want to think about trouble. She wanted to think of the nice things, about the good that would be done in the world, anything but the dangers of the night and the man that she loved being a little boy in a cowboy suit. She let him go with a heavy smile.

On the street, Timmy wasted no time. He pointed his guns to the dark side of the street and followed them into deeper and deeper shadows, till it was dark enough that he dare not walk alone, but preferred someone else to do that for him.

Timmy slipped into darkness as a figure swayed into the light of the street's only lamp: a man wearing his bola hat crooked, like he'd had trouble finding his head. His suit was tailored and obstinate as if it defied dirt. It looked arrogant as if it were the only offspring of a wild night spent between Rockefeller and a fleece of virgin wool. Watching the man, it appeared as if it were only the finesse of the suit that kept him from falling face first into the trash ridden street.

The suit propelled him forward, dodging filth, making him stagger forward, despite his side-to-side intentions. Failure loomed with ever foot fall, yet he continued upright despite the odds, the only sign of rebellion coming from his tie, which slithered slowly down his neck, hoping to find a cab it could hail or a patch of clean it could escape to. The man's fingers were constantly at the knot. They understood that to lose the tie meant the rest of the suit was bound to follow and then there would be nothing left to keep him from the gutter.

The blackness about him rose up menacingly and he halted, his arms flailing blindly as they grasped for reassurances.

Nice shoes. The darkness hissed.

The shoes smiled, the suit glared and the man threw up, covering the shoes in what had once been caviar, hundred-year-old scotch and a call-girl. The suit sneered, sure the shoes had it coming, sure that if necessary it could prevent the same fate from besmirching its fine tailoring.

Ah that's a shame. The darkness hissed again. I hope you're carrying enough cash to make up for the loss of those wonderful shoes.

Think nothing of it. The man managed. I have a closet full.

I wasn't worried about you. The darkness slithered. Those shoes were mine before you ever put them on this morning. Now you owe me a new pair of shoes.

How impertinary, Bola slurred. How impertuary... How imparticulary... very rude.

It's rude to come into my home wearing my shoes and ruining them before my very eyes. Darkness blew like a freight train urging - get off the bridge.

Of course... shoes... never should have happened. He tried to fall backwards but the suit refused, keeping him aloft at a precarious angle, safely above streetly garbage.

The darkness, a thick and oily pitch that eyes cannot penetrate and few, once incorporated, can find their way out of, surrounded the man, slowly slithering, faster by a margin, than the dapper man was not falling.

The darkness differentiated. Smoky voids coalesced into storms that solidified into men so blackened, their very scars radiated the darkness of burdens and deeds too vicious to describe. They wore flowers of black leather, spikes of iron and steel and were covered in wounds that glimmered around splintered blades and imbedded bullets. Weapons dangling from their sides like seeds soon to be sewn. They demanded the darkness of their surrounds. Their surroundings demanded the darkness in them. What had haplessly wandered into their terrarium was little more than well-dressed fertilizer.

We will now take everything that already belongs to us. Darkness crackled, the circle tightening, inciting the dapper man's adrenalin so he nearly straightened up. He put up a cute little fist, covered in frail skin that had never seen a scuff, rings shinning as brightly as his manicure.

Timmy watched silently, glad he had hidden in time. A group like that was just as likely to pounce for an immediate kill as play with their intended victim.

The dapper man swung at the nearest blackness, sissy fist barely assaulting the air. Darkness grimaced and laughed so hard it nearly tumbled. Then, thinking better of it, stepped closer and sneered. Chains hissed; clubs gained downward momentum; and pipes whistled through the air. The suit could not believe it. Never had it known such atrociousness. It screamed. It split. It frayed. It soiled. Chains rained; clubs plummeted; and pipes arced.

The dapper man ruptured into tiny pieces. Shocked, the darkness stepped back, dismayed by the loss of what should have been plunder, enraged at the disappearance of shiny treasures, leaving only bloody splatter and meaty chunks to show for their effort. They stepped back again and pointed accusingly around a chain of daisies.

Little bits grew into chunks. Blood puddles coalesced. Flesh tremored and expanded. Chunks became mounds. Mounds became piles.

The little piles contorted, twisted and formed into little men that grew dapper and sophisticated despite their unquenchable hunger.

Dapper became a dozen; a dozen became a dozen-dozen of dirty dapper dead.

The circle of darkness took a step back, but the dapper dead were already behind the darkness. Surrounded, darkness flailed; chain, clubs and pipes reducing the Dappers back to broken pieces.

Steam rose thick, darkening the shadows so darkness could no longer see, cloaking an army that grew out of bits of dismembered dapper. The army muttered brains as it hissed and sizzled. From broken bits to rising dark blossoms, a thousand evil flowers rose up into an empty eyed, drop jawed, sullen-cheeked army that could take a crowbar to the head. Arms grasped and fingers grouped at throats with the slow determination of cripples on ice. Tongues wagged, metal swung and hit, leaving ripped faces with sidebar smiles as hatchets chopped, knives slashed and the army grew.

The gang grouped tightly together, back to back, legs straining as the fingers drew closer, carried on cooked limbs that lurched always just short of their targets. The undead hovered within an arm's length of the embattled thugs who pressed desperately together, keeping the fiends the few necessary inches away by slashing desperately at arms and smashing crooked yellow teeth.

Ghouls climbed ghouls. Walking corpses scaling the undead, forming a siege tower that demanded brains through floppy tongued, saliva-dripping mouths. The blood lust reaching a fevered pitch as the dapper dead scaled the walls, arms stretched, bodies swaying as dangerous men screaming like little girls in a blender.

Crooked brown and yellow fingers, with dirty cracked nails, splintered sharply. They were fused with thick brown blood and scratched within inches of hardened terrified faces. Every second there were more. The gang swatted and screamed, huddling together, holding each other, their legs shaking, strength failing and sweat streaming. When the tower broke and imbecilic faces came crashing to the ground, their limbs never ceasing their brain-ward stretch.

The bad men never hesitated. They broke through the hole, tails between their legs, pushing and shoving each other like the last tickle me Elmo had just been spotted in a Target outside of Philly.

They ran the only way they could, scared and oblivious. They headed down an alley, the brain-hungry horde stumbling idiotically behind. The horde, the mass, plugged the street, forming a grappling cork behind the fleeing men, the toughest men in the city, running like stooges to get away. Their eyes so fixated behind them, on the advancing undead, that they plunged helter skelter down the alley and ran blindly through the open doors of the moving van.

The door slammed shut as the engine revved to life. The van chimed happily through the night like the bells of St. Peter's on ecstasy. Weapons pounded against its reinforced walls till they sounded like a symphony.

The zombies vanished as the van backed through the alley, rejoined the street and headed to jail.

Timmy couldn't help but laugh. Imagine falling for cheap horror. But what did he know? He had no idea how he would react if the man he had beaten to pieces came back as a dilapidated crowd. He'd probably turn into a puddle, just like he did when he watched it at home.

The captured gang was at the very least notorious and their rap sheet was worth their weight in shiny pennies.

Timmy took care of his own, as he'd always promised. Then he bought the building at the corner where the dapper man was clubbed. Ten stories and half a block long. After a little paint and plaster he moved some of the struggling bits of his family into the top nine floors. They were charged with repairing the decades of neglect and building a home out of a soulless disparity full of rats, graffiti and crack heads.

Timmy supplied all the materials as well as the eggs and toast. And when things got near comfy enough for family, they opened the first floor to the community.

A vegetable market, a teen center, a savings and loan, an animal shelter and a dojo, all built on a pay what you can idealism, not a take what you want system, but a give us value and you will get it back morality.

Timmy accepted time and effort. Time and effort could always buy some apples. Wash two dogs and get a cat vaccinated. You want to hang at the teen center, well parkay doesn't lay itself.

It seemed like a crazy risk, except that in a city so dirty there was always enough money to finance the risk. All it took was a little late night cleaning. And if all worked out, Timmy would put himself out of business. He aimed to stop the cycle by giving bad places back to the good while shipping the bad to what he assumed was still Australia. If things went well, Timmy hoped to put to rest the terrible things inside himself, the things he didn't even know were there until the rats boiled over, space went on forever and he lost his will to sleep.

PJ Cleared

God apparently doesn't care for being damned. It also seems he really does know what you're thinking. Word to the wise, don't think God should be damned, at least not while you're under orders.

PJ apologized over and over and over. He was wrong, God should not be damned and he didn't want to be rock. Not anymore. Being rock feels bad. It feels like everything you are has gone to sleep at the same time. Not the peaceful place of dreams and startling erotica, but the near numb yet painful tingling sensation that makes you cringe and slap at your limbs.

PJ had always imagined that rock would feel like the world, even though he had no idea what that meant. He assumed it meant greatness and power, but he was so very wrong. Rock feels queasy, like it wants to hurl but can't even get as close as a dry heave. He'd expected Heaven, but as near as he could describe the feeling was New Jersey. As everyone knows, nothing feels right in New Jersey.

I'm sorry God! I'm sorry! I'm sorry God! I'm sorry! You should never be damned! You should be the opposite of damned! You should be revered! He thought unclearly over and over and over, until a voice he knew cracked through his hard head.

Until I know exactly what to do with you, you will do inexactly what I don't know what to do with you! Am I making myself clear?

No, God. I'm afraid it's not clear at all.

You think all the wrong things.

The voice went away and the rock that was PJ hardened till the tingling became a hive of sleeping limbs bombarded with itching powder and the frenzy nearly crumbled the rock man into sand. He felt tiny stuck inside largeness, large with nothing inside, pain ready to explode and exploded beyond redemption. He cried through his mind.

I'm sorry God! I'm so sorry! So sorry! Everything is glass to me! Everything is glass! Please God! I'm so sorry! His mind stormed, skipping beats and beating itself into rock pudding, which in neither mud nor lava but something that makes a man feel like passed gas.

Rocks have no way to measure time. Every moment a rock feels an eternity. Every eternity a rock feels only that it wishes to escape. PJ had no idea how much time elapsed before the voice returned.

You will do what I have not yet determined to bid you to do until the time I tell you what you should have been doing. Do you understand?

153

Like a window.

When I come again with instructions, I will expect the job to have been completed. Can I count on you?

Better than I can with my fingers.

PJ began sifting the sand around Timmy's house that evening, separating the organic from the stone, hauling his cleaned grains away every morning in a wheel barrel, careful to think only how wonderful it was to be working under the every watchful eye of God.

Mother No Win

I know this isn't about pants.

Of course you do.

God told me.

Of course he did. But I bet he didn't have to.

He said it was all about winning.

Oh child, there's no such thing as winning.

God says there is, there's just no such thing as what you win.

That boy thinks he can create anything.

He created me.

Did he tell you that?

Me, the earth, all the people, animals, trees...

You poor thing, you really think you exist. If you think that, you must believe us Gods to be extremely callous.

I don't know what that means.

You must think we cause you pain out of some sort of deranged pleasure.

Yes, I mean, I don't know what callous means.

That's what callous means.

The deranged thing.

Yes.

What does deranged mean?

It's a kind of sick evil.

Yes, that is what Gods are.

Only if you exist.

I feel pain.

You're an illusion with a very strong imagination.

You're saying my pain is imaginary.

If you don't exist, how can your pain?

You're trying to confuse me. Either that or you're lying to me.

Yes. I'm wasting my time messing with the mind of a child that only exists in the Gods' collective minds.

When you put it that way. That does sound like something you'd do.

Timmy Law Man

New York had lost a square block and life had never been better. Crime was on the decline from Canada to as far away as Brazil. Many crimes where stopped before they began. Insiders were inside of everything. Outsiders hadn't a clue. All they knew was they could once again walk the streets, stroll the avenues and even skip down the boulevards if that is what they had in mind.

There was a lot of talk on the news about prisons, overcrowding and the cost of retention on the American public. There were many discussions about the need for new prisons and how it had become common place to release career criminals early. There was also a lot of strange talk about a supposed decrease in some re-offenders, of how a certain sect of convicts, captured by mysterious means, seemed scared straight or as the guards like to call it scared timid by whomever or whatever had brought them in.

There were great debates. Was prison reform finally working? Were the police, FBI and CIA using new and/or unconstitutional tactics in pursuit of the new breed of vicious man, criminals who wouldn't think twice before eating a woman and her child, criminals that had previously been so tough that any officer who attempted to arrest them would have been compressed into diamonds and their badges melted into a lovely art deco belt-buckle. And if illegal means were being employed, were there any law-abiding citizens that would frown on these measures? Such were the continuous debates raging on every channel that wasn't Fox, which remained in full support of prison and any stabbing and raping therein.

Fortunately, Timmy watched only cartoons, where the debates were always held between mice and cats. But he was not immune to the arrival of a cleaner, gentler street. He wasn't just aware; he was proud. He had cleaned those streets and more importantly he had kept one of the few big promises he had ever made. He was feeding his family, which with nieces and nephews, wives and leeches, had swelled to well over 70,000. This made for lots of eggs and toast, truck loads daily and there was not a single mouth in his family not dripping in yolk.

All were well. All were housed. More than sheltered, they had homes. Within six months of his first if-you-look-like-me-you-get-free-eggs-and-toast brunch, he had established a network of do-gooders who were doing very well for themselves.

Money earned by turning in the worst society had to offer was reinvested in the communities that the worst had stripped society from. The family bought up property and started businesses. They established the very image of what survival should be, for everyone, by giving lives back to those that had lost everything again and again, year after year. The bastard children of God had turned legit by day and become savior by night.

Timmy was wearing his sheriff outfit fulltime. Not that most people knew. Though more often than ever before, people did know. With more streets secured, Timmy felt more comfortable being himself. He didn't need to be smaller or large. Most of the time he didn't need to hide. Such are the gifts brought by pride and the love of a good family and he had the biggest, lovingest family anyone ever had and his personal collection of two kids and a woman were warmer than his momma's titty on a hot summer day.

His family was doing well. They were beyond recognition. He'd taught them that and much, much more. They could be anyone or nearly anything. They just couldn't be themselves too often and in too many places.

Timmy's pride cried nightly despite the daily praises his efforts had awoken. His wife comforted him continually, freely and willingly. She was a bright, kind and nobody's fool. She gave the love that kept the child a man, or at least enough of a man for Timmy to be able to sacrifice more than most children have ever had. She did it for the good of her family and every other family that ever wanted to feel safe enough to enjoy the simple pleasures. The world owed her many thanks. Thankfully, Timmy thanked her daily with enough true love for everyone.

Yet Timmy's warmest place, the place where he kept his heart, was also his largest source of pain. His wife and sons were the ones in the greatest danger due to his accomplishments. He had fulfilled a promise no savior ever could. He had brought peace or at least the beginnings of a peace that showed all signs of spreading to everyone but himself and those he wanted most to protect.

God and his mother were full of constant threats. They spoke continually of enemies on their way and Timmy knew Gargantuan was still out there looking for him, waiting for him. It was never going to stop. Destruction was always looming no matter what he chose. His greatest accomplishments were marred, his greatest joys accompanied by eternal fear. Something had to give and all he knew was that it couldn't be him.

Timmy Talks to Lobsters

Timmy told his wife he had to go to the Jersey Shore to visit the home of a high-ranking agent. He'd seen enough movies to know how to give her the ol' I've already puts you in harm's way and one of us has to be here for the kids speech. And even if it hadn't been right to twist the truth, sometimes the ends have to be justified. Being crazy enough to stay with trouble is one thing, but following trouble when trouble is looking for trouble was just out of the question. His wife might have been driven crazy enough by love to dye her hair blond, answer to Marilyn and call her newly blond children Mark and Johansson, but Timmy wasn't looking to make her up the ante. And she was smart enough to know without asking that she wasn't invited.

Timmy had no way to explain to her what he had to do. He knew it was absurd. He knew that the words could only come out wrong. How could he tell her he was on his way to The Shore to search for either inexplicably terrific or confoundingly horrid meat, while debating the fate of bikini tops? And then there was the whole lobster business, having no ability to eat every lobster just to see if it would bite him in the ass on the way out, he planned to whisper to them, introduce himself and make his plea. That part would have been as hard to explain as anything.

Alone and determined he hit the beaches, walking sandy mile after sandy mile, stalking barbecues, ogling the ladies and whispering to the crustaceans.

Excuse me. You don't know me, but I know your son. I can prove it. I know for instance that if I were to bite you, you'd eventually bite me back and I don't blame you at all for leaving your wife. All I'm asking is a little bit of your time. Maybe we can figure some way of getting you out of this tank. I'm guessing you're hiding from them. If I could hide from them I'd have done it by now, but maybe you know a way. So if you're willing, maybe you can help me put an end to the problems your wife and son are causing me, my family and let's be honest, most of the world.

Over the days that followed, Timmy sniffed dozens of barbecues, walked hundreds of miles of beach, talked to thousands of lobsters climbing over each other in tiny tanks and learned many things.

First off, he learned that given waves of even improbable size and force, mostly bikinis stay on, unless they are being worn by women who want them off. These members of the set them free and shake them class were always easy to tell apart from the rest as they were always surrounded by man-boys, heaved their little tops against every wave and then turned in mock horror, covering part of a nipple while screaming loud enough to make every head turn, smiling all the while.

Second, a beach barbecue is no eggs and toast. While most revelers do not find the food so bad that they are left convulsing, Timmy found that on average, two pounds of trash bound attempts are generated for every pound of edible meat, made by men that grunt as they flip and burn, smothering the blackened meat in corn-syrup sauces. The best part about the BBQ seemed to be that most people in attendance aren't paying for it, instead showing up with a bottle of wine or six pack of beer, which they more than consume on their own.

Third, people don't like it when you talk to their lobsters. And while he hadn't attempted to talk to any barbecues, he felt it had more to do with the owner's intention of dropping the lobsters live into a boiling pot of water than any ownership issue. Restaurants and beach partiers alike took a similar attitude to lobster whispering. They acted like Timmy was a conspirator, like maybe he was passing on an escape plan or calling for a mutiny. Within the first day, he'd been threatened with police and met with enough strong-arm tactics that he stopped walking up to the tanks as a young boy, but approached instead as an old man of the sea, head to toe in fisher's garb, wearing a bib with a lobster on it tied around his neck and when anyone drew near, he quickly changed his introduction into a yummy, yummy, yum chant which seem to satisfy everyone, except for the most sensitive of the lobsters. It was these lobsters, which stared up at his yumming with a look that resembled pain, that he felt might be God. But after eating, they always failed to bite him on the ass. Leaving Timmy right where he started, with the added trauma of feeling terrible for eating the only lobster in the tank that seemed to understand.

For three days and three nights he searched, his feet burned and blistered from the hot sand, his sleep ravaged by creatures that though too small to see must have been comprised entirely of teeth. He was mostly salt and sand. The only parts of him not burnt were covered by his shorts, hair or some sea filth that had mercifully clung to him along the way.

He became smaller and less conspicuous at every barbecue and more desperate and boisterous at every tank. He hid from people and sought every lobster. He tired of every aspect of beach and ocean life, except, unexpectedly; he felt he could have scanned the waves indefinitely, hoping to see just one wayward boob bouncing in the current, shimmering with clinging wetness. He felt for them in ways he had only before felt when the eggs were sunny side up, bright and yellow with the toast was on its way. He had never before seen anything that had so much in common with perfectly cooked eggs as he had seen walking along the seashore watching young nymphs display their wares.

Despite the perks, Timmy had become despondent, ravaged by the coast. He felt dismal and hopeless. He felt like the rest of his life would be an endless burnt and itchy search along a barren land that would not bear its fruits, no matter how he stared and hoped.

Then he heard the scream. A scream of honest terror from a girl in true distress, her top floating away, her arms so desperate to keep too much under wraps that she was sinking. She bobbed in the shallow, launching herself toward a top that floated away faster than she sank. She flailed and coughed, too far adrift for even the worst intentions to see anything clearly, yet she seemed to believe it was better to drown.

That was when he smelled it. A gentle smoke, a hint of sweet in the air. Something divine. He pulled his eyes reluctantly from the girl, put his nose to the air and followed the breeze. He was bombarded by aromas he could barely connect to food. There was meat involved, but meat was nothing of it. There was a sweet, light brown candy smell that held his nose lovingly. He recognized the smell of garlic and pepper, but there was so much more, the smoke held a thickness that was neither air nor gravy, like the smoke had been smoked and then sauced into a gravy that was capable of flight.

Through the smoke came the sounds of yumming. Timmy followed the sultry smoke through a hedge to where the meat hit hot coals, was splashed by heaven and heaved to the awaiting sticky fingers of sauce-covered faces.

Flip a stake and it would become twenty. The bratwurst chains had no apparent end. Every time the ladle dipped into the sauce it came out double full and the charcoals were flaming like Timmy's son's second cousin. Timmy could and would have eaten anything this smell touched. The grill burned red hot and all he wanted was to lick it.

As his tongue wagged toward the grill, Timmy understood what he was seeing. He inhales deeply the barbecue of the Gods and cast a quick glance at the girl who never wanted to be bare at the beach and knew that somewhere nearby there was a lobster that wanted to bite him on the ass.

Pulling God's Dad From the Tank

Propped upon the dunes, looking as if it had barely escaped destruction by the waves that hated it for always taking and never giving back, sat a ragged shack disguised as a quant sea-side restaurant. The ocean hated that shack as much as it loved pushing bikini tops just out of reach. Someday the tide would win and the shack would give back all it had taken. Timmy could see it as clearly as he could see that the lobster he'd been searching for waited for him inside.

Sun burnt and blistered; sand coating the roof of his mouth, the inner lids of his eyes, his nasal passage and his rectum all the way to his colon, Timmy headed inland. His hair had been bleached the color of the sun and his eyes barked red from days of windblown salt and tiny bits of crab. But to see him you'd think he was any other fishermen, dedicated to the surf, the kind of man that regularly set half a dozen poles into PVC piping and ran translucent lines across twenty feet of the best beach, throttling runners, tangling walkers, causing romantic flaccidity and leaving families no room for sand castles or towels.

Timmy stalked the shack, looking it over like a rum soaked pirate with a vague notion that somewhere beyond the dunes he had left his treasure. He approaches with a weary trepidation that teetered on cautious excitement. There was something special about finding the patriarch of the Gods, a God that knew God when God was just a baby and knew Mamma God when she was tight and feisty instead of burnt and stretched beyond our world.

The place was packed, shorts and polo shirts keeping company with shockingly skimpy.

The men swore up and down that they were rich.

The women swore, with backward arching shoulders, to be only as easy as their wallets.

The men trumpeted their machismo, swearing theirs was the biggest.

Eyelids fluttered in response, that's what they all say, still with the right wine and fat enough wallet, I'll give you a try, though next time it will cost jewelry.

Khaki screaming, don't worry there won't be a next time.

Timmy knew nothing of the game, for him lust was just a word that rhymed with dust. But now was no time for rhymes, ahead of him, nearly within his grasp, was the ass-biting-crustacean God he'd been searching for so fervently. He could nearly taste him. He felt sure that God lobster had to be better than eggs and toast, though nowhere near as good as God eggs and God toast. The very idea of scrambled God and brown and crispy ultimate toast served with butter-slathered omnipotence made him drool. Which he was sure was some kind of blasphemy and figured Old Man God already knew what he had thought and how he had drooled.

Old Man God probably knew about Timmy's thoughts and the drool well in advance, eons ahead of his thinking, which made Timmy sad that anyone would know for eons that a young boy in a fisherman suit on a search for his lobster incarnation would someday believe that he would be more delicious as eggs and toast. That's a hell of a burden and Timmy didn't blame Old Man God one bit for crawling into a tank, surrounding himself with a shell and biting people in the ass. The main drawback of course being that God always knew he'd end up that way and that too was depressing.

But it was hard to stay depressed when he was so close. He hadn't come all that way to feel sympathy for an aging God that could do little more with existence than be a lobster. He'd come to find a patriarch, one that had some power or some knowledge that would help him save his family and probably, though not at the very top of Timmy's list, the world.

Timmy found the tank he was looking for among dozens that contained condemned prisoners from the sea. It was teeming with lobsters, the best New Jersey has to offer.

I know you're in there. He controlled the yell his hoarse voice desired. He'd yelled into lobster tanks before and no one seemed to care much for it.

And I know you knew I was coming, possibly for some kind of eternity, which I'm sorry for, but that doesn't change the situation. I am here for you and if I have to do the bit on the ass routine then I have to be bit on the ass. But I got to warn you, it isn't as large as it may seem. Though you probably know that, just like you know that if I keep talking to this tank they will throw me out. But I'll only come back looking like someone else. Unless of course someone has already or is already eating you, in which case I'll have to guard this tank with an ear on the bathroom listening for an almighty scream. Unless they take you away from here and drop you in some Manhattan toilet, in which case I'm out of luck and I gotta get back to walking. So I guess what I'm asking, just like you knew I'd be asking is…

Sir, will you be ordering or just talking to the lobsters.

Just talking today, thank you.

Then sir you really must move on. This is not a lobster social club. This is a restaurant and I will have to ask you to leave.

Just one more minute, I've almost finished.

If you're not a customer you'll have to leave now, before I call the police.

Really, I'm just about done.

I'm calling the police.

Fine, I'm a customer!

Very well sir, then please give your name to the hostess. There is a ninety minute wait for a table, but for you we'll make it a nice round two hours.

Then give me two minutes. I'll know the one I want if you just give me two minutes.

I'm calling the police.

As I was saying, Timmy turned back to the tank as two men, much larger than Timmy was pretending to be, appeared and Timmy decided his best bet was to go quietly; no ants, no beavers, no dinosaurs.

He could hear the call going to the police. I'll be right back. He whispered to the crustaceans. They ignored him and continued a never ending game of king of the mountain as Timmy allowed himself to be escorted out of the restaurant. Alone in the parking lot, he promptly disappeared.

The police showed up minutes later. They're never far from the beach. They parked right in the doorway as the self important ones like to do and out of the car rolled an overstuffed shirt, wearing dark glasses despite the fading sunlight and a pencil thin mustache only appropriate in porno or police work. He talked with an authority only known by those never questioned, only experienced by those paid to enforce the law, but this cop routinely threw in an ego driven, power hungry, dick to anyone he decides looked at him the wrong way.

He strutted, part cause he felt it and part because his thighs rubbed together unbearably when he walked normal. He spoke like every word was a national treasure. He asked for a quick description of the fisherman and demanded to see the lobsters.

I know you know it's me, Timmy said into the tank. And I know you knew I'd be back, just like you know that I'll keep coming back if necessary. Even if I'm just talking to a tank full of lobsters. So for God sake, if you're in there, please let me know. I've traveled the sand for many days hoping I'd find you. I really need your help. So if you're in there, please, please and I hate to use the cliché but please give me a sign…

To Officer Timmy's surprise, a medium sized lobster climbed to the top of the pile and waved its claw at him, giving him an improbable wink.

Timmy nearly leaped with excitement and despite himself yelled. I'm going to need assistance at the lobster tank now!

The men who kicked him out came at a run. Is there a problem officer? Did he do something to the tank?

That's hard to say. Timmy gained control of himself. But I'm going to have to take that lobster as evidence.

You need a lobster as evidence?

Are you questioning my authority here?

No sir, it's just… strange.

Not as strange as you in the county lockup! Timmy heard that on television once and always wanted to try it out.

Of course sir! I'll wrap that one up to go.

Timmy took the bag and high tailed it out of the restaurant, vanishing as soon as he was alone in the parking lot, hardly a moment before the patrol car pulled up to the front door and a fat, lazy, doughnut-filled slob-of-a-cop hobbled his way into the restaurant as uninterested as he had ever been on any call. He was completely unaware of Timmy, casually absconding with a bag full of old-time God.

Mother's Garden

Mother God, as the name would imply, was first and foremost a mother. She had been raising her son for near an eternity, a son that had grown into manhood well before conception. It was not an easy job being Mother God and if she'd had anything better to do, she would never had done it at all. Which brings us to the second of the things which Mother God was, namely bored. The third thing she was, was her son and the forth thing was a lobster, but we'll get to that later.

Mother God had been getting a bad rap since Adam and Eve. She'd often been accused of being the apple-tempting snake and sometimes the snake-tempted apple. But deep down, she was very sweet and nurturing, the only problem being that she was not that deep.

If you are going to last forever, the first thing you must get rid of is the deep, after that the sweet and then the nurturing must be thrown out the door. Depth only leads to empty ponderings and answerless questions. The best thing about ponderings and unanswerable questions is that they are usually contemplated and asked by people who have the luxury of death. Death is really the only relief for the nagging of the soul. Ideas like why am I here, who am I supposed to be and what am I meant to be doing are only answerable by death, or, for those that just can't wait till their final moments, by the next sentence. The answers are, you are not here, you will never be anything and just don't do it. These answers are approved by Mother God, who has given up all forms of contemplation and knows that the best answer is always shut up.

Her husband had once been fond of these questions. It was a weakness in his character that made him think that philosophy had meaning and wasn't just the meanderings of the insipid. It drove Mother God crazy. He'd ponder himself into comas that lasted for eons and left her alone with a boy that was both ancient and childish every second of every moment. He'd drift off into the infinite possibilities, dreaming long chains of whys and what ifs that would compound and then implode, a dreamlike look upon his face as she'd kick him and kick him, often for centuries on end to no avail.

It was toward the end of one of these long, lost, mental lapses that she decided to take decisive action. Revenge can be cathartic and if done correctly, hysterically.

She timed her revenge to coincide with Father God's reemergence from his not so deep thoughts. Awakening from near oblivion, her husband was always very hungry, so hungry and so dazed that he would have eaten a black hole had it been served with some attractive garnish.

Taking advantage of his ravenous hunger, in an attempt to teach him the difference between dreams and reality as well as to get a long deserved laugh at his expense, she turned herself into a lobster and fed herself to him.

She intended to speed through her husband and bite his ass on the way out. Only she didn't realize that her husband's intestines didn't actually lead anywhere and she spent the next two thousand years taking too many left turns and not enough rights to ever be free.

She was stuck inside. Her revenge amounting to little more than heart burn and, for her husband, an overwhelming sense of relief at having exited one dream world directly into another, as can only describe a world that exists without the naggings of a wife.

Finally admitting defeat, she turned back into herself, possessing her husband long enough to make him dance a can-can before he managed to spit her out. But not before she was able to implant in his mind the overwhelming desire to turn into a lobster, be eaten and bite people on the ass after exiting.

It was during her time away, stuck in the never-ending bowels of her husband, that her son, left alone and feeling abandoned, first started dressing like her and blaming his worst deeds on his indisposed mother.

As the years past, he grew to love wearing the wig and the dresses and would often be seen in raging arguments with his cross-dressed reflection. It was in these arguments, while abusing himself unmercifully, that the first seeds of mother resentment were sown. He said terrible things to himself. He felt tortured and abused. He called himself a dirty no account louse and a pathetic failure. So by the time his real mother returned, their relationship had long since become irreparable. He would never forgive her for the things he said to himself while in her clothing and she would never again believe he was anything other than an idiot.

God had worked hard, in her steed, destroying her reputation. She was blamed for plagues, pestilence and poison ivy, when in reality she had more in common with the simple blue-haired old lady bravely managing to live on her own, who enjoyed gardening and cooking as a way to pass the days. The only differences being that her home was Hell, she planted lost-souls into fiery holes and cooked up misfortune. But none of her evil deeds were ever done with evil in mind, she was just in continuous need of freshly fallen souls that could be planted, with love and care, in her garden, by her Lake of Fire home.

She was far from demonic per say. She was just bored and like pretty things and there is nothing prettier than the way the damned bloom in the springtime, when the weather in Hell is fair and the fire rains gently down from the deep-black sky. In the springtime, the howls of endless torture mellow into song and there are always freshly cut damned decorating her kitchen table, where she liked to drink tea and hum along.

So she wasn't really as bad as her son let on and only played with mankind to keep life interesting and to keep her son from putting on that damn dress and wig and making a mess of everything.

When her son demonized mankind in drag, he left too much unrepentant evil in his wake and Hell would flood. There was nothing Mother God liked less than monsoons in Hell. She could never properly plant all that misery and Hell would go to weed and bramble. Every time it happened, it took her nearly an eternity to cut back the demons and groom the ill fated.

Call her wicked if you must, call her foul. Think of her as an overprotective mom or a bad parent if that is your particular damage. But if you were to know her, and many of you will, you would know that the name she prefers is Grandma. And if from time to time she has been testy or demonic, it was only because that vagabond, cross-dressing son of hers won't settle down and give her the grandchildren that all old ladies need to make their lives complete.

Old Man God Comes Out of His Shell

Away from the beach, within a hollow, amongst the sheltering vale of a small stand of, well, beech trees, Timmy crouched with his prize, a crumbled brown bag folded over at the top that had been banging against his knee for a quarter mile, far enough to be away from flashing lights and the confusion of police and restaurateurs alike, as the story of the crusty old fisherman who talked to lobsters and the officer that seizes them was told.

Timmy was content knowing that no one was out looking for little boys, at least no one he was intentionally hiding from and the other kind are not to be discussed in this story. Gods, though fundamentally flawed, at least in this story, are not so flawed as to let bad things of an erogenous nature happen to little boys who are too young to know what to do with their wives.

So on to the little cove of beeches, not so far from a sheltered cove, where waves beat down upon a beach in the hopes of getting at a shack where they boil its crustaceans and cleave the heads and tails from creatures that certainly need them.

In this small oasis, Timmy squatted, rendered nearly helpless by the cool shade upon his back, a back on which he had layered sun burn after sunburn, till even his marrow had begun to blister.

He could have dropped, giving himself over to hundreds of hermit crabs that had been laying in wait for years for so large a body to scavenge, large enough that every hermit would finally be able to afford a night on the town. But Timmy was not ready to drop and the crabs were forced, with claws full of depression, back into the grottoes they carry on their backs (they were as yet unaware that a grey-haired, rolly-poly, unwanted fool calling himself Skipper (not because he was a captain but because that is what he'd like to do) was only three drinks and one annoyed bartender away from making all their dreams come true).

Each crab secretly believed that if they could only muster their numbers, they could easily take the boy. At least that is what they thought until Timmy open the bag and a light as bright as anything man, machine or God could muster exploded from its open mouth. Timmy dropped the sack and fell away, the clinging bits of sand in his hair, eyebrows and eyelashes, under his nose, coating his mouth and neck, cheeks and jowls turning instantly to glass.

A look of horror froze on Timmy's face, concealing a greater look of horror, that would, if it could have only gotten out, expressed how much it sucked to have an expression of pure pain frozen on one's face. Falling against a beech tree, Timmy nearly shattered, saved only by the strength of the glass that was killing him.

Say kid that was really great! I mean top notch! The whole tank shit and the fat cop and the ride here with a knee hitting me every other steps and Christ you should have seen your face when I did the whole divine light bit. That's the one! I see you still got it. Freakin' fantastic! I mean really kid, good show!

The lobster climbed out of the bag and onto Timmy's face. Cheer-up kid, he chuckled poking Timmy's horror with his claw. We're probably through the worst of it. Though it's hard to tell. I try to keep surprising myself by doing what I don't expect, which gets to be a real hassle if you can conceive what I mean. Most days, seems the thing I least expect is exactly what I'd expect, so I do what I'd expect just hoping I wouldn't expect it, if you follow me. Ha! He clunked Timmy's glass noggin again, enjoying the shades of purple and blue the skin underneath was turning.

The glass really makes the colors shine like a distant nebula. Old God rang a quick ditty against Timmy's chest and said. What's the matter kid? Crab got your tongue? Again he laughed, much louder and with far more cackles then you would expect from a lobster.

Of course you wouldn't get that one, not being in tune with all things and all, and having absolutely no idea how many things, at this very moment, wish to eat you. Ha! Wish they'd eat me! I damn near like being bit as much as I like biting.

Timmy turned a shade of green that displeased Old God. The light through the glass reflected something pukey and of all things in this universe, including his ex-wife and in-laws, Old God did not like things looking pukey.

Guess we're done with the pretty part of dying. So I'll tell you what… Always knew I'd do it, but I'm gonna do it anyway. And with a sharp left, Old God smashed the glass with his claw, sending tiny shards spinning through the air. Then with a wink he turned the splinters into biting flies, little can't-see-'ems with glass shard teeth that Lobster God sent to the seaside shack where his fast-friends were being baked, boiled and fried.

There's gonna be some butt biting tonight, one way or another! Lobster God yelled cowboy style, slapping four knees as Timmy gasped for enough breath to turn green to purple, purple to blue and with a few great heaving convulsions blue to red. Burned and blistered he rolled with the pain and tossed with intracellular agony. He kicked and clawed, sucking for air like a man three-days drowned.

Timmy knew how it felt when all the king's horses and all the king's men proved inept. He knew how the egg felt as it dropped into sizzling butter. He would have screamed if he could have afforded it. He kicked and moaned, clawed and bit, digging what could have been his own grave, stopped from casket depths only by beech roots, kept from burying himself alive only by assimilation, an instinct to grow, to dig down and tower up. As his breath again eased through his lungs and his blood turned back to red, Timmy towered high above, swaying gently over God, his plumage rich and his bark insect free.

God could not have been more impressed.

Boy kid that was some show! I knew I didn't let you die for a reason. I mean you can know things and then there is knowing things and kid let me tell you, sometimes it's good to know what you know if you know what I mean.

Why? Timmy creaked, far more damaged than his gentle sway made it appear.

Why what kid? If you gonna ask questions of the ultimate being you should be more precise.

You know. Timmy moaned.

Of course I know! Jesus kid, we ain't talking about what I know, we're talking about respect.

You tried to kill me.

Never say try son. I do what I do and that's how it goes.

Why?

Why is not a real question and all answers are made up. If you'd like me to make something up for you, I can, but I'll warn you, whatever the answer, it's gonna bore me and when I'm bored I do things that only I find fun.

Help me! Timmy choked through a knot. His leaves were turning brown, his limbs growing weak. He shrank from hardwood to sapling. His roots shriveled. His bark took to disease, inviting vermin and showing potential to woodpeckers of various shades of red.

Please, he withered.

Fine, fine! God snapped his claws and flipped his antennae in disgust. But understand I only do this because I always knew I would and not out of any sympathy for your wood.

Timmy's tree collapsed back into a boy; his sand was blown away; his blisters and burns smoothed. He had never felt so good. The distance his current pain was from his previous pain, when he had wished only to be split into kindling and forgotten, was near joy in itself.

Timmy was scared, deep down, beyond God scared or Mother God scared, more afraid than when he had plunged into the sun or been buried in snow. That was one mean little lobster sitting before him. But he'd come for a reason, not just himself, but family, safety and happiness. He shook and trembled but he was going to make Old God listen if it killed him.

Nearly did, you know.

Did what?

Killed you.

No you didn't.

Listen, if you want to play this whole you-already-know-crap game with me, then there ain't no sense in any of this. I'll get bored and who knows what will happen.

You.

Do you talk this way to my son?

Don't you know?

Really, honest, son, knowing ain't all it's cracked up to be. All I really got is seeing things through. The power kick wore off a long time ago. What I gots is the little moments to keep me happy, so don't go ruining that!

Sorry. I just don't get why you would do that to me. I didn't do anything to you and that was the single worst thing I've ever experienced.

You're welcome.

I wasn't thanking you.

Hell kid, don't you get it? That was awesome. Someday you'll have told this story to so many people, that the pure joy of telling the story will even everything out. That's why I bite people in the ass. To give them a good story, something to share. I gots hundreds of people walkin' round talking about the time they shit a lobster whole! They swear they know it's impossible, cross their hearts that it's not a lie and then say how they didn't even know they'd done it till the lobster reached up out of the toilet and bit them on the ass! Now that's living, that's real surprise, like that sand melting light. You never saw it coming. God you should have seen your face! You looked so alive. It's shit like that that makes you alive. It also the same shit that makes me not.

You're not alive?

Surprised ain't ya, knew I was dead the moment I was born. And that's the hardest way there is to live a life that doesn't end and never started.

And the wife and kid. It's all a game.

Without the game, what's the point? If you can't pretend…

Then you can't have choices.

And without choices…

You're not alive.

You catch on quick.

I teach college.

That's why I'm amazed you caught on so quick.

And that's why you pretend you're amazed.

It's the only thing that keeps me going.

How long can you pull that off?

Till we're all together again.

Your wife and kid?

You gotta think way bigger. There are lots of us and lots of you and eventually there will only be us.

And?

And then we won't have to care no more. Nothing will happen. There won't be anything to know. And we'll all be happy, better than happy, we'll be content.

Why are you telling me this?

It's what you wanted to know.

The meaning of life?

The meaning of your life.

The meaning of all life.

Whatever.

Content beats happy?

Happiness is just another Hell. You can never keep up with it. It takes too much effort. Content is what you can be when you stop.

What I need to talk to you about is your son and wife and how to get them to start stopping.

Kid, just because the process is all I have left, doesn't mean I want to repeat the process. As far as God Jr. and my wife go… been there, done that. And as far as you go, I'm bored. You came a long way to waste my time. Now, if you come looking for me again, before the end, I promise to leave you in splinters.

The crustacean grew to small boy height. Its legs bulging with muscles. Its tail a flexing bicep. It spread its armored tail, swooshed it up and down like a wing and Lobster God began to hover. He stared at Timmy, nose-to-nose, eyeball to beady little eye and slapped him with his antennae.

Red welts lined Timmy's face as the giant flying crustacean swooped low, pulled up hard into a barrel roll. He circled behind Timmy, thrusting a muscular claw into the seat of Timmy's pants as he swept by. He cleaved away half a buttock before speeding through the grove back toward the sea shack. Timmy was left screaming in pain as a rolly-poly, grey haired man skipped into the clearing. Skippy took one look at Timmy's bottom, smiled queerly at the way it half smiling up at him and promptly passed out. The hermit crabs were delighted.

Sledgehammer of Trash

The Trash Man could think of nothing, would think of nothing, every time he thought his mind went back to bubbling. He drooled for two days, enough to overflow the bathtub where he lay as a fragmented ball. A golden hammer was all he wore and he clung to it feverishly, as he waited for the next tray of ice to freeze. Perspiration oozed from every pore, a furnace still boiling in his core.

It was three days before the pruning reached his bones, he ceased to sizzle and allowed thought to once again wander through his mind. One thought, he allowed one thought in, not even a thought, what he allowed to enter his mind was a deadline.

One week, he had one week to turn Timmy's world to trash. How long had he been in the tub? How long had he been gone? Where the hell did he get a tub? The floodgates had opened. He remembered the trash bag he assumed would be his greatest trophy. He recalled the burning. Even the thought of it made him steam. He tried to shake it off. He tried to leave the tub. He couldn't stay there any longer. He wasn't sure when the week started, but he was sure it had. He wasn't sure where he was, but knew he had to leave. He knew that he hadn't a speck of hair left on his body and he knew, that if what he recalled of the hammer was correct, he was a God.

He stood up, heaved the sledge over his head and drove it down upon the edge of the tub. It crumbled. Dust flew like locusts. Metal returned to a primitive state. The floor gave way. The walls blew out. The ceiling carried itself and the floors above to a new zip code and the Trash Man road the crumbling heap to the ground, the hammer glittering in the sunlight.

He rode the debris like Neptune riding a tumultuous sea, rubble barking at his heels, the garbage heap applauding as it tumbled down.

His mind's eye opened upon a world full of the fire and lust that comes with the belief that one is indestructible, that one's own image of the world will be the world's image of itself. He felt sure of at least two things; first, that he was finally going to be able to put that holier than thou father of his in his place, even if he had to turn every piece of rock in the world into waste. And second, he was going to need a really bitchin' costume. No longer would he hide. He intended to shine, brighter than the world he intended to demolish and sweep into mounds. He would make the one that had betrayed him look like little more than a discarded match crushed under a wino's foot.

He could hardly wait to start destroying, but all good things must wait, at least until he was properly attired.

He heaved the hammer upon his shoulder, his slight skinny frame bulging with muscles. He adopted a strut and an evil sneer as he surveyed all and knew that he could destroy it. He swaggered, the most confident naked man in any city whose junk below doesn't hang low, but much can be made when you swing a mighty hammer above.

Junk to Junk

The Trash Man was in some sort of ghetto. He could tell by the way no one seemed to notice him, naked and bulging, stopping every other block to invoke the power of the Gods, banging his chest, hollering at the air, declaring himself the most powerful man in the world. Though, as full of himself as he was, he was careful not to bring God's mom into it, for underneath his sledgehammer bravado he was still just a boiling puddle of nothing. And the way the crowded streets continuously ignored him was doing little to restore him to a solid.

Even the pimps, whores and pushers ignored him. A man with no pockets is in no hurry to pay. All they saw, all they knew of his passing, was the giant side of bling that rested on his bare shoulders. All eyes followed the brilliance that glimmered in the sunlight, almost too gold to be gold and too large to rest on someone so invisible. Where does a man with no pockets get something so fine? It made the pimps feel plain, the hookers ordinary and the pushers turn to their own products just to alleviate the pain of not having.

Every eye danced along with the sparkling hammer. Heads swayed when it swayed. Necks bobbed with every step, the street was mesmerized from first glimmer to last glance, hypnosis reaching the brain, whispering to all who saw - You want me. You need me. You deserve me. You can't live without me. So baby, come and get me.

Those with little minds stalked closed behind. Those with enough cool chose side streets and planned to intercept, oblivious of the throng they crept among.

Thousands converged. No one was willing to let that out of the Ghetto, oblivious to the shiny white man and the masses of men and women planning the same attack. Eyes bulged toward golden. Fingers grasped. Feet stumbled wildly, near out of control from one-thought-frozen minds. Get the gold drooled from mouth corners. Thousands lost bladder control and thousands more had begun to twitch.

The Trash Man stopped within the epicenter of the storm. He had never seen so much garbage in his life. Trash littered ruined streets. Buildings were crumbling, held together only by a thin layer of graffiti. Thousands of the trashed circled him like a toilet tornado. Brown gained momentum, surrounding in an attempt to ensnare, to drag him down. While inside the cyclone of waste, the trash man saw bits of sparkle, things that glimmered and things that shown bright enough to lead wise men to a newborn bastard.

He smiles despite himself, strangely attracted to what shone among the rubble, while unexpectedly affronted by what he had always assumed he loved, the most decrepit element, the people, with their claws out, ripping at the air in an attempt to get closer to his hammer, lust seething out of every poor. These, should he call them people, the rotted, the decomposed, the smashed, the bashed, the neglected, so at home among the trash, should have looked to him like gold. If he loved garbage, if this degraded slop was his true calling, then why hadn't he come to this place first? And what made matters worse was that he didn't know what to do with a disposable storm whose sole aim was to steal the only thing that can keep a God's mom happy and prove to your father that he should have treated you better.

The quandary - How do you wreck the wrecked? What was the point and what was the meaning and how was any of it going to make things better?

Rage bubbled through his arteries as he brought the hammer down upon the street, rupturing, renting, opening up a crevasse, a gorge, a canyon.

Tens of thousands were heaved mightily skyward. Bodies propelled through the crumbling dust of buildings and possessions they had once mistook as homes. In the sand paper storm layers of skin exfoliated, hair dislodged and clothes became a fine mist that burned eyes and clogged orifices.

Miles away, in the still quiet suburbs, the skies darkened as thunder shook the old Victorian and Federalist homes, thunder that could have been confused with the screams of the masses until the clouds opened and rained miscreants down upon the finely trimmed lawns. From the sky fell the beaten, bruised and bleeding, each one more heartbroken over the loss of that mighty shiny piece of gold than broken from the hundred mile fall.

Where once had stood the seedy undercurrents of the city, now lay a hole. And on an island, in the middle of the last patch of asphalt for a mile in any direction, The Trash Man lay in a heap of his own. He was not having fun. This was not trash collecting. He would not sweep up these remnants and compare them to the ones he had collected the night before. This was rage and this was anger, years of hiding behind garbage to prove to his father that there was more to life than the stone he collected, loved, living for and treating his only son with all the warmth of.

He shook upon the mound upon his island. His hammer lay beneath him as he seethed with rage and uncontrollable laughter. This was the greatest worst thing he'd ever experienced and it made him feel so much better and much, much worse.

He rose to his feet, muscles bulging a little more than before, eyes bubbling red. He surveyed the pit that surrounded and saw how it glittered, how it shone like the moon had snuck beneath his feet and refused to stop shining. It was bright enough to make the sunniest day look like night in comparison.

In the hole, everything nice the Ghetto had accumulated, the expensive nothings that kept the ignorant poor, the prized trophies of the masses; gold, silver, platinum, diamonds and rubies, rings, bracelets, piercings, bedazzled grills, flashy belts, silk, opals, pearls, necklaces, money clips, armbands and nameplates, shone to perfection, buffed of blemishes, resounding to the point of nearly ablaze.

He had blown the garbage away and left behind the remnants of a sparkle obsessed mankind. Nearly sneering, hardly laughing, possibly crying, but no more upset than he was tyrannical and no more put out than he was enthralled, The Trash Man descended into the radiant pit of his own self loathing, content and determined to find the proper attire for a God. He required bells and whistles from head to toe. He would make the moon gasp and the tides freeze in their tracks, which was only the beginning of what he was now sure he deserved.

Timmy Roll

If it wasn't for a grey-haired, rolly-poly man passing out in what Timmy now thought of as Old God's Clearing, the hermit crabs would surely have taken him away and sold him for spare parts. The rolly-poly man's only movements were labored breaths, while Timmy maintained a constant speed, equivalent to a hermit crab's sprint, which in reality was a slow roll.

He didn't know he was travelling, but as soon as Old God had left, he'd fallen into an ever-moving heap. He was pointed toward home and just out of claw's reach, his pathway lubed by a hysterical sweat, a well-oiled fever that gave him no rest but kept him searching for a cure that rested solely in his mind.

Inside his little prepubescent mind, Timmy knew everything. He could see cause and effect. He could taste what was happening and he felt, through deep chilled shivers that pushed his body through its roll, that knowing, being controlled and allowing were all at odds. There had to be some agreement or simple destiny. It terrified him to think that everything Old God knew might be different from the everything God knew, might be different from the everything that was known by God's mother, causing a boy who spent most of his time Anthropomorphizing his imagination to ponder reality. It was enough to raise anyone's core temperature, pumping up blood pressures till veins pulsated evil genially.

His mucus flowed exponentially, leaving behind a slug's trail as he slowly somersaulted away from Old God's Clearing and into the street with the many dangers it poses to those that salt and sweat through their preponderances. To all those who aren't versed in the comic book of philosophy, this amounts to little more than a cracked egg, a humpty dumpty of cracked metaphors coming from the academically lazy and the financially over endowed. But to tiny Timmy it was all too real. He had conversed with more Gods than anyone living or dead, more Gods than the Gods had talked to in a God's age. And the Gods had only one thing in common that Timmy could see. They each brought pain that threatens him, his family, everyone else and everyone else's family. Pain was the legacy of the Gods and even Timmy's fever knew that it was unfair for a boy, already responsible for the life of a man, to be left to answer such questions and fix such problems. His body, out of sympathy, shut out the infectious influences of the outside world.

Crust formed over Timmy's eyes. His nasal passages swelled. His tongue grew to rooftop proportions. His ears built a wall, heavily fortified in case of attack. His prostate tied his small intestines into a knot and his nerve endings all took two steps back.

He rolled through the last shards of daylight, the near spotlight that for the last few minutes of day makes the world intolerably clear, illuminating Timmy sufficiently for cell phone talkers and seaside partiers alike to swerve in time, all in clear agreement that they had just saved the life of some crazy rancid badger.

As the last drops of sunlight went around the corner that leads to night, a collection of pine trees reached out and pulled Timmy from the road.

The pine trees caressed the troubled boy and offered nuts to a community of squirrels to guard him safely.

The squirrels refused the nuts but took the boy. They scurried, a hundred strong, to a family of beavers.

The beavers thought nothing of building a sleigh, knowing very well the squirrels could never fell the number trees they offered in exchange for the boys care and wouldn't hear of it anyway. They dragged the boy near a mile before they found the herd of deer they were looking for and promised them every leaf from every fallen tree.

The deer just smiled and took the boy away, dragging him through the forest like Santa had just opened for business and was still only offering local service. They pulled him to a swamp where a thousand birds and their thousand friends ate ravenous on the tall seeded grains. The deer offered nothing but a wink and a prance, which was all the birds needed.

The birds tore reeds and thistle from the waters, weaving them tightly into a nest, with a thousand latch points and a thousand more for their friends. They loaded the boy and away they flew.

Timmy rolled and eeked in the nest without enough room left in his throat for regurgitated worms and barely enough room for barely enough air to keep him barely enough alive. His pores closed their doors and black heads developed so the world couldn't get at him by following his grease upstream.

His somersaults had given way to a malcontent slither that any crab could collect. He was treading like a maimed slug when the thousands upon thousands of eager helpers saw the sun once again shine its spotlight on all that might be wrong with the coming day. Under such light, no self-respecting bird was willing to be caught netting small boys. But luck had the final word, they had arrived and it was left to a crow to ring the buzzer before flying away.

Timmy Gets an Infusion

It was daybreak when Timmy's brother brought him home. He had witnessed the scene at the lobster shack while dining after a day at the beach with his son. He enjoyed the spectacle of the captain and the police, but could see the deeply scared remnants of his brother underneath, trying desperately to keep things together. He was broken and blistered, salt-caked, cut and shell imbedded. He tried to intercede, but he had never been that quick. The captain was out on his ass too fast and the cop was gone long before he understood who he was. When he tried to follow his brother from the parking lot, Timmy proved too good at disappearing, even for his knowing eyes.

It was hours later, following reports of a road bound beaver, that he found him, in the final spotlight of day, a sandy, suffering, sweaty ball rolling along the side of the road.

Timmy was shifting shapes quickly. His brother barely managed to put the badger in his back seat and patch the bleeding. It was nearly impossible to find the wounds on a boy who appears to be a badger then a rock then a snake and the noises Timmy was making, made him fear for all three.

He knew no hospital could hold him. They wouldn't know what to do with all those trees and would never accept that many squirrels. Even if they fixed him, it was sure to be trouble. There would be official inquires, federal meandering and visits by the vet.

No options were good. So he drove as fast as he could, as fast as he dared, with beavers chewing his car into a dam and deer prancing and leaping through his dashboard. He held on tight and pointed the car towards home.

He had always heard that Timmy was the greatest, could be anything, anytime. He had joined his crusade, feeling the family had always been missing the joys of blind loyalty. But beyond that, he honestly loved being part of something, of working towards a better world, his mind was set; his heart was determined but he was not prepared for the birds. He could not, even after hearing so many Timmy stories, stories he had half-chalked up to exaggeration, handle watching his car becoming a nest that flew threw the night.

His driving slowed to a crawl. His son screamed a mile for every foot they travel. He told himself over and over that there was a road and they were on it. Telling himself and his son that the boy's life depended on him staying on that road or they'd never be able to fly the nest home.

It was his son that saw the way. Just follow the birds he told his father. And they did, arriving home with Timmy gasping for air through the throat of the sparrow.

Man Becomes a Boy

Urgent knocking was not one of Corrinna's friend. Timmy had been gone for too long. Her nerves were too shot. So after tearing the front door from its hinges, she didn't waste time being surprised by the boy she found, limp as a rag in the arms of a brother. His system had nearly shut down, his defenses had built up and no one could blame them for it, other than that the walls were killing him.

She wasn't surprised to see him and she wasn't surprised to see him so damaged. She was mortified. She was panic stricken. But she wasn't surprised. Everything in her that could pulsate with trepidation did. Her only shock was seeing how small her man had become. Not that she didn't know, over time she had found it easier to see through him, not physically, but as love can see, only together were they whole and she knew her other half. Still, when her so-called husband showed up at her door, broken and shrunken, she acted maternally, clasping him tight in her arms and pulling him to her bosom, where in her embrace, he finally stopped his travels.

She had never seen him so small. She wept. She rained down upon him. It washed away the ocean. It cleaned away the grove. It chased lustful crab eyes back into their shells. It felt like home. He curled up to his wife, his throat as wide as a robin's, his black heads beginning to pop. His gasping quieted and he looked like he might be having a happy dream.

He wasn't. Not that they were bad dreams, just a little too transcendental of his tastes. In his dream he was a wallet in a purse flying too close to the sun. He tried to control the purse, shaking his change till it turn ever so slightly, just to stay another second away from being cooked. This was not Timmy's kind of dream. He liked dogs and chalk, dogs with chalk, chalk drawn dogs and more recently girls chasing bikinis that always floated too fast.

He didn't hate flying through space in a purse. He'd already flown through the night in a nest, so who was he to say what was real, what wasn't or which was better. Fresh air was pouring down his cat-wide throat, making things tingle he hadn't felt in a while. It was nice and he was able to sleep, now that the birds had brought him home.

Timmy slept through seven doctors and twelve siblings that had been pretended to be doctors for some time. He slept through eight surgeons and one anesthesiologist (that felt left out since putting someone to sleep that won't wake up is not a good idea). Timmy circled the sun shaking his change, despite thirteen hours of surgery. He curled into a ball on his wife's lap. They were too afraid to move him. He was sure it was where he belonged.

Two days later, Timmy was taking air into his deepest parts through the throat of a young boy. His shell had gone and his breathing had returned to normal, but his ass would never be the same again.

Love Makes the Cow Girl Sing

Four in a bed is a hard way to find the peace necessary for restful sleep when there are no other beds to be had. Four to a bed when each person in it needs the others is what peace and rest is made of. It builds a warmth no chill can permeate. Timmy slept the tranquil sleep of those that have nothing to hide, in a world that's constantly searching for what you did wrong.

He thanked the birds and the deer, the beavers, squirrels and the pines, holding tight to a word he couldn't get enough of - mine. His family had come so far, trusting him, staying with him when the powers of the world wanted him destroyed, but this was the first time they'd seen him as frail and fallible, which only made them cling on tighter, forcing his walls to crumble, his nose to clear, his eyes to open and his ears to listen.

He woke up once again as the man, knowing everyone understood that every man is only as good as the child inside and as far as his family was concerned, his child had been more than approved. He was thankful and knew what he had to do.

He was revived, refreshed and packed so full of eggs and toast that his decisiveness nearly wavered. He grunted to his feet, his tongue licking fetishly at the back of his mind as sweat dripped feverishly into the pit of his stomach, fighting a desire for lobster Florentine even though he didn't know what it was, but feared a bite in the ass for merely having thought it.

He squeezed his cheeks together, declared himself well and asked for some time alone, making a point of telling them that, while they cannot always perceive him, he saw them coming however they hid.

No one followed, though he limped and his face showed cracks. It wasn't so much respect for his privacy as fear he would try to run and that that would be too much. They restricted themselves to casually walking the streets and peering from street corners.

They pretended not to keep track and Timmy pretended he wasn't being kept track of for several blocks. But, when he drew near his destination, he disappeared, playing chameleon with the street, mimicking building so well that the buildings themselves did not notice anything askew. When the searchers were not looking, he slipped into a costume shop, blending through nuns, ghosts, giant chickens, princesses, Frankensteins, slutty bunnies, buff studs and revealing witches. He reappeared, secure and alone amongst the westerns.

Timmy picked out five gallon hats, suede leather vests, a short skirt with fringe, bandannas, high stomping boots with jingling spurs, six guns with live action and gun belts already notched from killin'.

He moved through the store like a breeze, dropping money on the counter and disappearing through the door.

She was waiting and worrying. She was tired, tired of worrying, wondering how many more surprises she could stand, how much further her love could be stretched, amazed at how much she had invested in little things, her home, her security, her simple little rise and shine life that she didn't remember living, because she had never lived it. None of it mattered. She'd given up living so many years before. First for her husband and then for her sons. There was always a reason not to live. Until the boy... so clearly not the man she married that even his true form was no real surprise. He was her true love, her heart. He had brought her back to life. But she worried that life might kill her.

When he came through the door, she didn't know whether to cry from happiness or sadness. His disguises had become nothing to her. She didn't notice the man turn back into the boy. Tears were rolling and Timmy put his arms around her. They wrapped around her stomach and she didn't care. He was back. They were safe for another moment.

Timmy stepped back silently, opened a bag bigger than he was and disappeared within. He emerged, a sly smile creeping across his face. His look turned soft as he proudly held, in outstretched arms, a cowgirl suit, fringed in suede. Attached below the lapel was a silver star that read Sheriff and twinkled seductively. She reached out and took it warmly, putting on the vest then the boots. They fit just right and the hat was cute and sat preciously on her head. She had to bite her fist to keep from choking on her overwrote emotions. She had to swallow them whole when Timmy unzipped his jacket to show her his own sheriff duds. They were torn, blood stained and tattered. His skin shown through, blistered and shredded. He grew two sizes, so proudly he beamed. She spat out her knuckle and loved him all the more.

He pulled two more outfits from the bag, smaller than his wife's. They were for the boys, for their family. They would round up the wicked and bring peace to the savage land, together.

She couldn't have been happier. Then again, some people just ain't right.

God Breaks Stone

There's not a pebble within half a mile of that boy and that's hurtin' him how?

No bricks, no pavement, no sidewalks…

Do I need to repeat myself?

I guarantee you his feet are always dirty.

So?

So! So! So what? All he has is wood, plaster and plastic. Nothing is better than stone! It's solid. It makes you feel secure. His whole world is flimsy, flimsy I tell you!

I hired you to make his life hell.

Hired me! You didn't hire me. I've been pushed and I've been threatened and for your information I've already been to Hell and I'll tell you straight out, your mother is way scarier than you!

You don't want me to be scarier.

I don't want you. Why do you want me? What do you want from me? I'm a Goddamn stone klepto. It's what I do. It's all I do. What did you expect?

More!

More?

Lots more.

How do you figure?

My mother already has your son.

Has my son?

Gave him a golden sledgehammer and a week to get things done.

My son? The garbage thief?

Your son of the golden hammer.

Hammer?

Sledgehammer.

Sledgehammer?

I know, corny huh. What kind of God borrows from other Gods? And the Norse! They couldn't even conquer England! How pitiful is that?

He has a week for what?

To stop Timmy.

To stop Timmy from doing what?

Doesn't really matter.

How can it not matter!

We'll make that part up later.

How are we supposed to do the things you demand when you won't even tell us what they are... when it's all imaginary!

It's not all imaginary.

What part. So far all I've seen is imaginary and not yet determined.

The or else I assure you is real.

Or else what?

It's really not important, just so long as you know it's real.

What is she going to do to him?

Use your imagination, it's my mother.

Oh God!

No, really, use your imagination cause we have to do better than a sledgehammer.

And better than a week?

You got it. The seventh day is for resting. I invented that.

Jesus!

That's mine too. So what do you think about lightning?

That's Zeus.

Yeah, but he's a way better God than Thor. Greeks actually got shit done. They didn't just grope and pillage. They conquered shit.

The English conquer the world and their God was you.

Yet, but I've been done, floods, plagues, pestilence, kid in a whale, where's the pizzazz? We're competing with a sledgehammer here!

And what am I supposed to do with lightning?

You melt shit or burn it.

Why would I want to do that?

Okay, how about the lightning turns shit into stone.

I can get behind that. But six days?

I've done more in less.

Six days to do what?

Take down Timmy. Why don't you make him into a statue?

I'm a thief, not a killer.

I'll be the moral bench mark here, besides it's just a scare tactics. I'll turn him back later. Oh and if you can get his whole family, do it!

And if I can't get any?

I'll figure that out later. I got resources, things up my sleeve that make Hell look like Nantucket.

And if I do pull it off?

Some riches or something.

That's a little vague.

Nothing is a great reward compared to what I'll do to you if you fail.

182

What about my son?

What about him?

If I win, he loses and I gotta figure your momma's gonna get burning mad.

I'll take care of my mother.

You haven't yet.

Once I get Timmy, everything will fall into place.

And until they fall, my son burns in Hell?

You're all going there anyway, despite what my mother says. But I can always make it seem like heaven, if I choose. Remember, I invented Hell, she just summers there.

I guess it's a deal.

I wasn't negotiating.

Stone Age

After God left, at least as a physical manifestation… but again the Omni discussion gets a little tiresome; omnipresent, omnipotent, omnivore, omni-vision, omni-ferrous, omnibus, we could easily omni ourselves right out of a decent plot line, when all we really want to know is what the hell happened with Stone after God left.

Well what do you think would happen? Like a damn child just given a magic stick that turns everything it touches into toys, the dang rock loving fool went crazy with lightning. First he zapped the stove to stone, then the fridge, cabinets, tables, floor, television, sofa, air conditioner, window shades, bed, dressers, bathtub, light fixtures, a cockroach, three bananas, a shag rug, the ceiling fan and a whole bunch of shit that was already stone, though he was convinced that after the lightning they were somehow more stone then the stones they were before.

He chased a cat around his apartment, shooting wildly as the cat slipped stealthily away from each lightning strikes. Enraged, he summoned a storm, stoning end tables, magazines, curtains, the pantry, a six pack of Dr. Brunner's cream soda, little old hunchbacked Mrs. Daisy Lambert from apartment six G who stuck her head in to see if everything was all right, the front door, his freshly folded laundry, the walls, the ceiling and finally that damn slippery cat.

Choosing to over look Mrs. Lambert, who, except for how her dentures flapped when she spoke, had never bothered him one bit, he had never had such a good time.

Stone crouched close to inspect the lionized cat. He liked how its claws spread. He had caught it mid leap and the damn thing had landed on its back. He laughed joyously. He'd been trying all his life to make a cat miss its feet and had never been successful. He'd even taped their feet together and still they landed on all four, but not anymore. He was more powerful than cat balance.

The description God quickly entered his head and stuck. Clearly he was a God, his power were unique and supremely supernatural. Now, he wasn't claiming to be The God, or even God's mother. He wasn't that kind of crazy. But always with great power comes great crazy and he was crazy enough to consider himself some kind of God, enough of a God that his ego needed to grow exponentially and he decided that his life of anonymity would no longer do.

It was time the world learned of his greatness; the greatness he always knew existed but was much easier to explain to the world through lightning. He would create the rock and they would build him a temple clear to the sky and beyond if that is what he wished, so sure was he that none could resist.

But first he would need an outfit fit for a man God, yes, Man God, that was what he was. He would need the clothes of a Man God or Lightning Man or Lightning God, maybe Stone Man or Lightning Stone Man God. He shrugged. What he should be called would become clear soon after he was attired. One look in the mirror and he was sure he'd know. Well, he would have been sure, if the mirrors hadn't been lightninged into stone, like the rest of his apartment, including the walls, doors and windows, making him wonder momentarily how he was going to get out and show the world how great he had become. But that too was bound to become apparent once he had on the clothes of a God.

What outfit could possibly be better, more appropriate for the God of rock? He liked that, God of Rock. He knew the name would come if he didn't push. What could possibly be the suit or armor so to speak of the God of Rock? What could be more apropos? The definition of which he didn't know, but the answer to which was clear. Rock, he was to be gilded in rock! Indulging a fancy from his younger days, he hummed the fairy Godmother tune from Cinderella as he waved his finger about dramatically.

Salagadoola-mechicka-boola bibbidi-bobbidi-boo
Put 'em together and what have you got…

He turned his lightning upon himself, vulcanizing his boots, pants and his favorite LL Bean, button-down fleece into one hundred percent pure, made-in-the-USA, genuine rock. It looked badass, tough as the day was long. It was perfect, or would have been, had he been able to move at all.

That was when Stone first understood that not all Gods are created equal and some still need to go number two.

Alarm for a Hole

Four sheriffs sat by a fire taking turns being different. It had become the family's favorite game, except for Timmy, who didn't know it was a game. For him it was life and what he knew of it. They called his abilities a gift, but he couldn't imagine what they meant. If he'd had his way, he'd be playing with blocks, or cars, video games or puppets, anything real that he could grasp. His life was a charade and he'd never been far enough away from it to look back and see how his gifts had led him directly to the greatest parts of his life.

For Timmy, putting on an identity was like putting on shoes, but his family thought it was much, much more. They appreciated that it was a survival tool, a necessity for the life they were living. They knew there was consequences if you were not what you needed to be at the time you need to be it. But they had not spent years as a coin purse just to get milk. They could pretend, but they couldn't be, not in a way that would allow them to ant away if necessary. So Timmy drilled them relentlessly, though they thought of it only as a game.

Ono formed a dog that barked like a boy, a great dog with a terrible bark. Timmy worked him till the boy yelped and yipped well enough to get a bone from any butcher (except Asian butchers who would easily recognize the boy as being succulent). The boy never knew it was work.

Jack went inanimate becoming a dresser, but he couldn't open on cue. On his sixteenth try, he got it. Judging by the look on his face, you'd have thought he'd won the Noble Prize when Timmy gave him a high five.

It was then that Corrinna got risky; imitating Timmy and growing him from the boy he was to the man he pretended to be, so naturally that the children applauded.

A lump stuck in Timmy's throat, a feeling that his perfect world was the destruction of theirs, nearly reducing him and to a little crying boy. They'd already been through so much and because of him; they were being forced to become him. This fact alone would have led him to despair, had they not all looked so happy.

So as the applause died down for mother's grand Timmy impersonation and the turn became his, he gave them what they wanted; eggs and toast, hot and steamy. The toast tumbled like a million-flea circus into a yolk that sprayed Fourth of July high into the air, complete with pops and whistles. It was beautiful and electric, at least that is what Timmy figured the bear was thinking as it back-flipped onto the table, catching the yoke-fantastic in his mouth as it zinged through the air, landing on the plate and licking it in a dizzying long-tongued twirl that made the plate spotless. The bear looked up at the boys, smiled, winked and with a roar, ate the plate and vanished.

Ono laughed until he peed, which made Jack nearly throw up as Corrinna searched for Timmy hopelessly. She knew he was right in front of her, but that didn't matter. She rested her hand on him. She didn't know.

Fool the eyes; fool the person. Timmy smiled, appearing as the professor to take her hand softly into his. He was happy being part of a bunch of sheriff's, sitting by the fire and playing everyday Halloween, when the door exploded.

Rock God Crumbles

Stone was sure he was going to die. Which came as a mighty let down after recently concluding that he was a God. But after sitting for 24 hours in a self-made sarcophagus that filled slowly (not that slowly) with waste (he'd drank a full quart of orange juice and ate a can of Hormel chili for lunch). He had little to do but waterlog (his television had been turned to stone) and contemplate his own foolhardiness. He compared himself to King Midas whose true riches were found not in plunder but in the beautiful daughter he could never touch.

Stone turned his thoughts quickly to his great Aunt Madeline's hair lip. Thinking about daughters and touching had quickly become a bad idea. Some things were not meant to move against stone. They also weren't meant to seep in a cesspool for hours, but a second wrong never makes the first wrong any less sick.

He thought about his son and how he loved him and hated him, mostly for the same reasons. JP reminded him of his wife and worse than that, JP reminded him of himself, stubborn, obsessive, closed-minded, stunningly beautiful and neurotic. But these were not the kind of things he would ever admit, even to himself, even if the depth of his own wastewater hadn't already reached his nipples.

He had no fear of drowning and wasn't sure that was something he should be thankful for. He'd probably stop going soon and there was a slow leak in his left shoe. In the end he'd be left damp, rancid and trapped. He had no hopes of being rescued. He couldn't yell through stone and even if there had been a chance he'd be heard, his nearest neighbor was a statue in his entryway and though she was caught by surprise, he was sure he saw hate in her stone eyes.

He regretted throwing his son out, like he might save the day. But the odds were just as likely that he would have zapped his ungrateful, junk-hording son first or if stumbled upon in this state, the disrespectful kid would have laughed himself to death. He could hear PJ telling him he never looked better before playing a few games of handball against his shirt.

Stone would rather die than be found by his son. Not that he didn't love him. He just didn't like him. He didn't like anybody, which is probably why no one showed up to his parties or his rescue. He knew if he ever made friends, ever chose a companion, that the person would, at the very least, have enough dynamite to free him from his tomb. That is the kind of friend he wanted. That was the kind of son he'd hoped for.

Hours past. His muscles ached. His soggy flesh cracked. He wanted to call out to God, to damn him. But he knew from past experiences he'd only be damning himself.

Timmy Hears a Hole

A herd of brothers and a gaggle of sisters stampeded through Timmy's front door, their mouths leading the bedlam, their lips flapping in unison - Timmy! Dozens of urgent tongues bit into the air as the shrieking herd surrounded the family of sheriffs. Instinctually Ono and Jack shrunk. Timmy was proud of them even as he grew large enough to seize control of the situation. He worked at picking out the words each mouth yelled in common. He found hammer, hole, smashing, ghetto, destruction, golden and possibly but not definitely dingo, bling and Santa.

Quiet! Boomed the boy, his muscles bulging with authority as his face became bearded with wisdom. Andy, what is all this about?

The voices began again, throwing words like bedazzled, glimmering and upheaval. Timmy held a giant foam finger before a face comprised entirely of shushing lips and passed the big foam finger to Andy, a man who liked to feign Alexander the Great, but in reality stood nearer to Socrates, after the hemlock. Powerfully, he stepped forward, by making it seem as if everyone else had step back.

You must come right away, Andy urged. The Junk Man has grown. He carries a golden hammer that shines so brilliantly that one can see nothing else, until it falls and destroys all for blocks uncountable.

And what are we doing about it?

We are re-projecting the blocks nearest to the blast.

Results?

It seems to be holding him at bay. Seeing the fringes reappear time and time again is enraging him. He tries to destroy it over and over again by hammering continually downward.

And our people?

Lots of injuries, maybe worse, but we're holding up.

Is he weakening?

No, but he's digging himself a hole deeper than any I've ever seen. The further down he gets, the more city we're able to re-fabricate, the angrier he gets.

How many do we have out there?

About a thousand working on the building facades, another thousand evacuating the surrounding blocks and somewhere around twenty-five hundred on their way as of fifteen minutes ago.

Put everyone available into evacuation. I need at least a dozen getting the kids out of here. I want you to load them in a car and keep driving till you hear from me. Corrinna come with me. It's time for you to be a sheriff.

Corrinna turned red, her eyes getting large, her mouth drooping open. But, but, I can't do what you do... I mean... I'm just pretending.... I don't...

Timmy stopped, shrunk and faced her. You're already one of the best. You're smart and kind and the only one who's ever seen through me. You don't have to save the world, but we need all the help we can get... and really we don't have the time.

Let's go! She straightened her hat and her badge before taking Timmy by the hand.

Where to?

Helicopter on the roof. He's destroying the hell out of everything down there.

I'm right behind you.

They ran out; Andy first, Timmy hot on his heals, pulling Corrinna behind. Her eyes focused ahead. She began to grow. Her plastic guns turning to steel, engraved with roses, inlaid with mother of pearl. Her spurs sharpened and her hat gained 5 gallons.

Power coursed between the two, pumping them both up till they bulged and had to imagine themselves a little smaller to look like they would fit within the helicopter.

They were on their way to a crater to meet a man that, until recently, had been stealing their TV Guide's. Now, he threatened how they viewed the world in ways they had yet to imagine, at least until they saw the hole.

God Bends Stone

Never one to ease suffering, God waited a little over a day before he softened trousers, boots and flannel enough for Stone to escape.

Stone awoke, sprawled on the cold stone floor of his apartment to find himself free of his clothes but unable to move his limbs or even roll out of his own puddle.

The pain of standing in his-own filth for what might have been his entire natural life had not lessened from the time he spent upon the floor. His muscles had tightened into rocks, his tendons into sprung steel. He could barely roll his neck in agony and scream. His voice bounced off the walls of his self-made cave and blasted his ears. It was more than he could handle and he blacked out.

When he woke, pain had given way to a piercing throb, annoying, yet controllable. Slowly, tediously, feeling like a hungry alligator pinned to the swamp by a hungrier crocodile, he moved from his waste. Each movement hurt a little less and by the time he reached the backside of his puddle, he was mainly fighting stiffness. Club footed and steel fingered, he pulled himself up to have a look.

He was starving, but his food was all rock. He was filthy, but there would be no turning igneous fixtures. He was naked, but again, I think you get the picture. All that remained, the only thing he hadn't turned to stone, was a simple track light in his living room, whose glow gave him no clue as to what time of day it had become.

The windows showed no light, not a single one had been left open or been missed by his lightning bolts. He had no idea what day it was or how long he'd remained trapped. His stomach growled that they'd been there for days and his eyes swore they saw no way out.

He pushed at every door, threw his weight against every window and searched every dark corner. He combed the walls on hands and knees for so much as a mouse hole. There was nothing.

Enraged, he struck the wall with his fists - twice. Once should have been enough of a lesson, but he was near angry enough to level his skull against the front door. Nearly angry enough? Hell, he was leveling. One way or another he was getting out of this. Either he was the bull, blood on fire, ready to burst through any confinement or else he was the china shop.

His head swayed back and forth, hypnotizing the door with his crazy eyes. Hot air blew in angry bursts through his nostrils and lightning danced from his fingers as he yelled rabidly at his own echo.

What have I done? He screamed.

You acted like a damn fool. Came the answer.

The bull became distracted by the clown. It turned, eyes full of blood on the khaki wearing form sitting comfortably on the plushest recliner any bull could imagine.

I give you six days and you immediately imprison yourself. Jesus Christ! If I'd said it once, I've said it forever. You can teach a smart man to be evil, but you can't teach an evil man to be smart.

Now that just hurts. The bull shrank to a mouse without a hole.

Did it hurt more than a stone suit slowly filling with excrement?

It, it hurt different.

That's not what I asked. What I wanted to know is, did it hurt more than being entombed during what should've been your finest moment? Did it hurt more than pure power turning into the inability to stop your Rock God bladder from emptying into your Rock God armor?

It didn't hurt more.

I give you six days to please me and I have to leave you confined in your own pants for a day and a night just to try and teach you to stop being so stupid.

That was only a night and a day?

Now, if you please, imagine how long that same period would feel in Hell.

Stone whistled.

Hell will be your lightest sentence if you don't have some kind of control over Timmy in the next four and a half days. Am I making myself clear?

Crystal!

Even your jerk-off, junk-collecting son is doing better than you. He's been destroying shit all morning while you've been wallowing in it.

I get it. I fucked up. I've been through enough without you yelling.

Not even! He flared dark and cold. Now get your ass out of here and win one for God!

Yes sir. He yelled unable to stop staring at God and trembling.

Move!

Yayayayayayes sir. He stammered, staring at his feet. Ummm…
could you… umm… opened the door… umm… God, please, sir.

Timmy to the Hole

They flew above the crater. It was breathtaking, volcanic, a mile in
diameter and lipped by rubble that jutted savagely toward the sky. From
above, the edge looked sharp and reflective, like razor teeth on a redneck
shark. But the closer they flew, the more the teeth turned into an upturned
city. The sharp angles dulled into street blocks thrust high into the air or
thrown as if by a drooling child, a cliff of buildings becoming as formidable
as the Rockies.

Upon the crater's crest a strange game was playing out. The city was
being built at an incredible speed. High-rises burst from the tattered
landscape, growing like vines on steroids, twisting their way toward the sun.

But before the city towers were rebuilt, well before final floors were
finished, the earth would shake, the crater would smoke and rock would
blast into the sky, following bums, pimps and dealers toward the suburbs.
The rising city would be blown into thousands of tumbling men, women,
boys and girls on their way down the mountain. They clung to displaced
road signs and mountain slope hydrants. They grasped at doors to nowhere
while rolling over and clinging desperately to each other. Those that could,
scampered back to the crest to build once more a city made only of
themselves, while those that couldn't were carried away and replaced by
fresh recruits eager for their chance to be toppled.

My God! They'll all be killed! Timmy sat rigid, sweat cold against his
forehead, his face purple with strain.

We have to get them out of there!

They're the only things holding him at bay. If they leave, he'll
destroy the whole city. We'll never be able to evacuate in time.

I'll do it.

You can't make them all leave. We have an army that can't get them
all to leave. The news and the governor can get them all to leave.

No, I'll be the buildings.

All of them?

All of them.

But you'll die. He's near killed men ten times your size. If we lose
you it's over. We can't risk you getting that close.

I'll do it from here.

Andy and Corrinna looked at each other in sparkling amazement.

Can he do that?

She shrugged.

Can you do that? Andy turned to Timmy as the earth shook, a cloud rose, rocks migrated to the suburbs and men, women, boys and girls tumbled down, breaking crowns, releasing torn skin into the wind with confetti cloths and feathered hair.

Timmy was no longer there. He was the city on the hill standing tall. His family, the city's would-be-builders sat too astonished to move or help those too hurt to care.

Radio below. Tell everyone to get out of there, way out of there. Andy screamed to the pilot. We need shelter and lots of it. He turned to Timmy's wife, is he here or is he there?

She shrugged.

I'm here. Answered the air.

How?

Not now. Too hard.

Right! Let's get this bird down.

Junks Journey Down

He'd been so happy. Happier than he'd ever hoped. He loved blowing a hole in the earth. He loved watching trash fly. But he never realized how much he liked shiny things, or how great he looked in them. He sparkled more than the hammer and felt his God rising. He was sure that he was no longer simply a man possessed by a beautiful hammer, but a beautiful man, a beautiful God, possessing a hammer.

He was in love with the idea. He was in love with himself. He gathered a pile of silver and struck it smooth as a mirror, just to see how he sparkled. He noticed how light struck the golden bands on his bulging arms. He admired how the clef in his chin had deepened. He fell in love with the way an insanity he called God sparkled in his eyes.

He needed more. He struck smooth a pile of gold and admired his image cast in bronze. Truly he was magnificent. The world would surely love him as he smashed it smooth. When he was done, all that was lovely would surely make him their God, for when beauty believes in you, you know you have transcended the garbage heap.

He twisted silver and gold around gems and bent them into a fishnet tuxedo. He examined his gluts and his abs and admired the festival of rocks that glittered about his body. He loved what he had done with his feet; bands of platinum tapped into a sandal - God's sandal. At least they would be, if God weren't so lame and tacky. He admired his every crease and crevice. He ogled his every glint and gleam. He was finally perfect.

While Hammer noticed every single detail about himself, what he did not notice was the city that was rebuilding itself upon the highest bluffs of his greatest achievement. Looking away from his own image was painful enough, but then to see a mockery of all he had done rising toward the sky, rising right before his sacred eyes was… was… was blasphemy!

Enraged, he drew his hammer back to his heels and screamed like a Scotsman whose kilt was chafing at the exact moment he'd finished drinking all his money. He arced the hammer high over his head and slammed it down upon the fractured hole.

When the dust cleared, he enjoyed the satisfaction of well-placed rage. The buildings were gone, the hole was wider and deeper and power surged through him like meth through the gay community.

But the victory was far from total. His mirrors were sideshow warped. His body and all the perfection that adorned him were covered in dust, pockmarks and filth. He had believed that beauty was meant to be forever. But then again no one ever said being a God was going to be easy. So starting over, he carefully taped himself smooth and with glancing blows restored his mirrors, both silver and gold, to a state of bliss.

He regained his perfection. He was once again a prim and polished God. Self-satisfaction pumped through his veins, up until, he once again, looked upon the sky and saw upon his craters rim, a city on the rise.

The Hammer had always assumed that he could never hate anything more than his father. But what he felt now was like nothing he'd known when he was a lowly collector of trash. Back then, in a time that felt so long ago, he had a game. He would see how much trash he could collect in a day and then try to beat it. Then God showed up and then God's mom and Jesus Christ, for the first time in his life he had no control. Sure, he'd been angry before, mostly with his dad, but he'd never felt like destroying the city he loved with a sledgehammer just because it had the audacity to keep coming back.

The Hammer narrowed his eyes at the rising city on the rim and drew his sledge back. With a howl and a mad leap he brought it down again upon the bottom of the hole that had no idea why it was so hated.

Tons of granite flew through the clouds, some never to return, while most was destined to surprise farmers in lands far beyond falling bums.

He felt great, except for the pock marks that needed smoothing, the mirrors that needed shining and the dust that made him look damn near tarnished if not nearly like the junk he'd begun to hate even more than the civilization upon his edge.

The modern world grew and he smashed it. The modern world climbed and he blew it to smithereens. His hole became deeper as the fringe's lip bulged full of collagen.

The mountains rose and the riff plunged downward. his only satisfaction becoming the rage that determined to destroy the city before it had a chance to grow. His hammer pounded away. What had been a city on the apex was beat down to urbania.

Still he swung, digging himself further down in an endless attempt to cripple the rise. His hammer rang in ways that haven't been heard since John Henry.

Then something changed. His hammer continued to pound, but the city on the hill no longer fell, nor did it shutter. It stood firm, in silent mockery, unchanged.

Roaring, Sledge leaped into the air toward the cliff's base, a thousand feet below the city. He struck the granite upon a rift, blowing into it a ravine a quarter-mile deep. Above him still loomed the city, unshaken, as water rushed in through thousands of cracks in the bedrock.

Water fell along deep fissures. Sledge hammered at the water, blowing up geysers, but it flowed in and raining down too quickly. He had to club his way to safety. Striking a staircase into the cliff, he climbed to a ledge above the water line and watched how the water continued to rise and the city continued to stay and wouldn't you believe, after so much glory, that that was the moment his dad decided to show up.

Father Finds a Hole

PJ was made just hard enough to make it through the stone at the rate that God propelled him. He flew up and out and up some more, through the apartment building next door and up over the city.

Yesterday, when he was so sure he was rock, he would've taken it as another sign that he was indeed a God. He would have been sure of landing on his feet as the whole world applauded.

Today, entering a young woman's apartment through the front and exiting through the ceiling, his only hope was that he'd eventually stop going up and his greatest fear was that he was bound to start coming down.

He flew through a flock of sparrows that whipped and darted out of his way. He was sure that he'd heard cursing but was unsure if it was from the birds or his own scream shaped mouth, forced open by wind currents well past screech. His lips fluttered against the round of his face. His tongue flapped into his ear. He began his descent and knew he had already lost his mind, for below him, where he knew a city should be, was only a hole.

The sight of the hole eased and cajoled him. Clearly he had already landed. Certainly he had made that hole, had not survived and God being sorry was ascending him to Heaven. He smiled despite velocity, thinking of a place where the streets are paved with rock, your days are endlessly peaceful and the countertops are all Italian marble.

Descending. The word struck him like a wayward pigeon and at the exact same time, the pigeon hit hard enough to fill his gaping mouth, skirt his fluttering tongue, streamline through his stomach and intestines and emerged from his behind without missing a flap.

Father Rock gulped too late to help the bird leaving his ass. He knew how wrong he had been about ever seeing Heaven. He was accelerating so he could enter Hell the hard way, head first, reducing him to mush before becoming barely a puddle, set to boil for the rest of his days.

What burned him the most was that he wasn't going to burn for being a remorseless crook, but for being a terrible mercenary. If he had the time, he would have considered it ironic. But he had only time to scream at the way the ground approached him quicker than he felt was fair.

Rock hit face first, causing him to ingest much of what appeared to be a random assortment of city. He noticed mainly rock, which he would have usually enjoyed, had the rock not been charging past his tonsils, leaving behind him a trail that would have sickened a pigeon.

He skipped like a stone through buildings that did not break or bulge, coming to a stop in an alley at the crest of a mountain range, a range, densely built, but sparsely populated.

The city was built around what might have been a volcanic ring or maybe a meteor crater from a space rock large enough to bring back the dinosaurs. But he wasn't thinking of that now. The only thing going through his head was asphalt and teeth.

Apparently, he had been made just hard enough to hit a mountain at sonic speeds, while remaining just soft enough to pass a ton of gravel without internal bleeding, at least he hoped there was no internal bleeding. When everything hurts, it's hard to differentiate traumas. He'd been made hard enough to crash but soft enough to feel the smallest pebble. He was Hercules the Precious Flower, laying amongst rubble that he knew a bit too intimately. He was buried under buildings both broken and sublime, his head making it clear through the destruction where it dangled over an abyss that dropped straight down, a thousand feet above a lake.

He struggled to work himself free, as the mountain shook with rage, boulders rising up from dust-sheltered depths, pummeling his unprotected face. He imagined himself being born, as first one arm than the other wiggled free. He wormed his torso through the rubble as the contractions came more rapidly.

Stunned by a cracking boom that burst his ears and blew his hair away in the wind that followed, he watched the far side of the precipice move skyward as the rock hurdling past him became a wash with ice-cold water. Dirt turned to mud and he was able to slither his extremities free. He came out of captivity both burnt and frozen, conditions that were uniquely and individually painful, each seeming a pleasure when compared to the other.

Free and peering into the precipice, he wondering why God would send him here, why he sent him so painfully and why a God, so obsessed by pants, had sent him naked. The rumbling, the booming from below now sent only water that cleaned as it froze and then stopped all together.

The dust cleared under a dwindling rain from settling spray and a bright noonday sun shone down into the massive hole. It was then that he saw, sprawled upon a tiny ledge, above a rising lake; pocked, pimpled, dented and clenching a beautiful golden hammer between his bejeweled thighs, his son. The sight appeared to his eyes stranger than his emotions remembered his son to be estranged. It had been a long time since he felt anything but rage towards the boy. But his rage had flipped and he remembered clearly the love they shared before great loss drove them apart.

This Hole's Not Big Enough

I see you've given up trash for giant holes. Father Rock yelled into the abyss, no longer remembering the words that caring brings.

And I see you have given up rock for droopy, old-man balls.

Children who hang from cliffs should talk nicer to the only droopy old balls left in this city.

I don't need you.

I've been hearing that since you were seven.

When I was seven I said it because you were no longer there. Now I am a God and Gods need no one.

I thought the same thing yesterday… And I know I'm no good at this… These are the kinds of things I always depended on your mother for.

Leave mother out of this.

Christ son, there's some bad shit going on here, more than I think either one of us is prepared for.

You haven't seen what I can do with his hammer.

I think I have. I think I'm looking at it.

This is my trash collection all over again.

Kid, I know I ain't done so good, but I've learned a bit in the last couple of days.

So have I! The Hammer yelled. Pushing away from the cliff, he raised the golden hammer and struck. The hammer, glistening, rang its way through the cliff wall, crumbling the earth below his father's feet. Together they fell, father and son riding an avalanche down. It was the most they'd done together since mother left so many years before.

Hammer swung and swung, turning boulders about his head and feet to pebbles and then to dust as his father bounced from rock to rock, his body molding around each new boulder as he was pounded by the splintering stone from his son's constantly swinging hammer.

The son swung and the father molded till the son has nothing left to hit and the father had nothing left worth a collision. Together they fell and fell. The bottom seemed a lifetime away, far enough that they had enough time to get to know each other all over again, had that been on their minds. But all their minds understood was that a son had tried to kill a father and a father had never tried to love a son. Unreciprocated love and patricide combined with accelerating rock to become a hatred as red hot as any love. They had finally become one and the same, father becoming son becoming father. The only difference left between them was that one was trying to beat his way into becoming a God and the other had already had the God beaten from him.

The water rose toward them at a dizzying speed and for a moment they forgot to love hate and thought only of terminal velocity belly flops. Father Rock grabbed his junk, twisted feet side down and prepared for pain. Peaking through fear clenched eyes he saw his son, falling only a few feet below, surrounded by sand and weighed down by a ton of preciousness. His heart softened once more at the sight of his only child about to meet a watery grave. He used the only thing that God had given him, the only thing he had left.

Lightning struck, shooting from fatherly fingers into the awaiting pool. The waiting waters turned to stone just in time to not make much of a splash.

They say at terminal velocity water is as hard as cement, well, at that speed, cement is as hard as water that is as hard as cement. And while you may not be sure what that meant, I guarantee you that father and son could each sing a few verses of that song as their splash hardened around them and their pancake bodies were rolled upon by rocks still tumbling.

They lay devastated, within feet of each other, as close as they'd been outside of freefall in years, having more in common than they'd shared for more than two decades. Together they hurt, beyond yells, beyond anguish. They felt that every break in every bone was broken in two more places but neither God nor mother had given permission for them to shatter. They only authorized the pain, abundant pain, a bumper crop. They would have curled into balls and crawled back to mamma had any mother been available. Unfortunately there were none and all they had that functioned, in bodies dredging through pain, was a tiny part of their minds.

The father was firm in his belief that he had saved the boy who tried to kill him from an underwater grave and that surely made up for at least part of a terrible childhood. Not that he allowed himself to believe it had been terrible. In fact, the more he thought about it, their troubles had always come from an ungrateful son and he was, in reality, the bigger man for not letting the boy drown.

He vaguely looked forward to a thank you. It would take the edge off. Off the hurt and off the gift of power that brought him only pain, encapsulating him and sending him into a hole. Why would God give him the gift of rock and send him to a hole? Sure, at the time, it seemed like the greatest gift any man could have, till he's launched naked into a land of rock where his only son, who clearly hated him, had a sledgehammer.

Such are the thoughts of an old man, rambling and disoriented at best, while his son, young and crisp, kept his mind on course. At worst, he thought poignantly, the droopy-balled bastard had tried to kill him. He chose to ignore completely how he had tried to kill his father first so as to keep his mind uncluttered. His young blood boiled and he longed for the moment when his arms would once again function and he could teach the old man the folly of playing with the Gods.

A Family Hole

The hole lay quiet. Brothers and sisters, girls and boys emerged from tattered city crevices where they'd pretended to be mice, but could not resist the lure of peace on the mount.

198

Timmy let the city fall away, reappearing next to his wife.

What's going on up there?

I don't know.

You couldn't see?

I wasn't there. I was just pretending.

I never thought of that.

You're not supposed to. No one is. It's my main advantage.

She took Timmy by the hand as the copter put down. Shall we have a look?

With understanding comes doom.

You're awful smart for a kid.

I'm just pretending.

I never thought of that.

You weren't supposed to.

Timmy rebuilt the city. He wasn't convinced by the calm, neither was he convinced that the city on the hill wasn't what was causing the momentary peace. Regretfully he let go of Corrinna's hand. He had far to go and felt it best if she not see what he must find.

There was standing room only in the coliseum. Every seat was filled. People stood in the aisles, desperate for a glimpse, eager to see the match of the century. A father with the power of lightning and a sullen bitterness that comes from the loss of God stature, verses the incumbent, a boy, who despite the pain, despite the damage, still insisted that he was a God.

Thousands of eyes stared down wondering if curiosity would in fact kill the cat. Each fearing they might be that cat, but despite fear they were unwilling to gaze away. The wise stood behind brothers, the cowardly behind sisters, each on tiptoes, peering into a pit too wide and too deep for any show to be clearly seen by crowds so crescent perched. Still they stared and swore to one and all that they could see movement deep down in the hole.

Having God as a father, (God venomously denies this, claiming their father was a drunken sailor and all he contributed was the fertility) made his children want to root for the son, if he hadn't killed their siblings and attacked the city they called home. Most wished they could kill him themselves. Thousands inconspicuously played footsy with boulders, 'cause if dad doesn't get him an act of God might.

Smoky on the Mountain

It was not quite the same as trying to see out of a cloud. It was more like a cloud, stuck within itself, trying to see through the sea. That was how the world looked to a little boy trying to be a city on a hill. He felt stretched to say the least, like a rubber band on Prozac, ready to snap with or without medication. It is far easier being very small than it is to be as large as Timmy had ever been. He could no longer feel. He was as everywhere as he could muster. He was the least shakable thing ever seen on the edge of a pulsating precipice.

His mind strayed as the helicopter landed. If this was what it felt to be stretched thin, if this was all it took for numbness to sink in, he could nearly understand how God and his mother so easily missed the plight of man. He could feel how they could allow and even insist upon pain and humiliation, torture and degradation as being a part of everyday human existence.

At least he could imagine he could understand, could feel through not feeling what it might be like to feel even less, to find oneself not only empty but somewhere profoundly below. He could nearly grasp the cruelty that would result, until he stepped from the copter into the cruelty it hath wrought.

His family, brothers, sisters, nieces and nephews lay strewn about his feet in tatters, burned by steam, flattened by rocks, limbs missing and faces deranged. Timmy's feet stuck to the ground they so freely bled upon. Dozens of hundreds of siblings worked desperately to stop the flow as hundreds more abandoned the mount, steaming down the rubble, supporting, carrying and dragging those that made a city of themselves.

Timmy was glad he was so scattered, built high and strong far away from himself. But looking upon the faces of the family he had begun to call friends, as well as those he'd only known from a distance, seen maybe once raising their glasses at an egg and toast recruitment, seeing the pain and death in these faces made even his city begin to shake.

He shadowed through the twisted wreckage of many blocks and even more livelihoods, against the tide of siblings, against the flow of red, taken in by that which lay natural amongst so much gore. Peacefully sitting on the twisted remains of a bed lay the odd teddy bear. A door to nowhere stands perpendicular. Little square windows remained intact despite the destruction of house and home. Dresses lay gently upon uprooted signs waiting for a night on the town. A set of teeth still soaked in an epervescent glass. A wino, missed by the savage cleaning and the unforgiving collapse, snored.

Timmy climbed, claiming ignorance when confronted by bits of family flesh. He could no longer look at anything but the summit. He refused to see, whether it was a tea pot still intact and steaming, ready for grandma, or a brother, no longer intact and losing warmth.

Timmy sent the crowds away. He wasn't ready to lose anymore, but despite the risk, he had to know what Hell looked like. He braved a look over the edge and down into the hole. He expected little less than demons, hating and smashing, but found only an overstuffed boy with a hammer and a too hard, too old man. For the first time Timmy wished he was a destroyer. Then he would have brought his city down, making a tomb of a hole.

Life on the Bottom

Timmy watched the hammer strike, saw the two men fall in an avalanche smashed to dust and strike a lagoon that in a flash became a parking lot. He watched the rubble fill the hole, saw the boulders hit hard enough to crack, witnessed his dream of destruction coming to fruition. He felt less than glee, not so much as retribution and had no sense that they had somehow gotten what they deserved after inflicting so much pain upon those he nearly knew and those he had begun to love.

Watching the dust settle on the rock strewn bottom, Timmy wanted far worse for those that had been responsible, even though he knew that the two men buried along the bottom were not to blame. They would never have acted such upon their own volition. They had been held down and pumped full of callous.

Even the one man Timmy had encountered with enough vicious self-absorption to hate and destroy based solely upon his whims, did not do so indiscriminately. Even Gargantuan stuck to his target. Only God and his mother felt no need to justify means or be concerned with ends. With immortals there are no ends, only infractions. The harder they pushed, the more they felt they were right. And while he did not have room within his grief to feel pity or compassion for the men in the pit, he allowed his city to blow away, slowly in the gentle wind of a tattered day.

His head dropped to his knees. Hot tears streamed into the void. This would never stop. It was only going to escalate. And why? Because he was the greatest hider? A boy wishing anonymity forced to create, forced to grow, to become a leader of a new direction that had no chance of success as long as he remained.

He considered hurling himself into the void. He braced himself along the line of here and now and shall never return, teetering. There were no good decisions. Alive or dead he was in the hands of the Gods. If they wanted more from him, all they need do was wish it, command it, or think it, casually, in passing. They loved the game and that's all it was, a game. They played to see how little they could do to get as much from you as possible. They were the deep pockets manipulating the market, making living or dying neither here nor there.

Timmy teetered, but knew it would do no good. While below, rocks were subtly shifting, fingers were breaking through and torsos scraped upwards. The dead were restless, too infused with callous to stay below where they belonged.

Part of Timmy wished to leap upon the heads of the destroyers, smashing them, doing what so many boulders had failed to do. The rest of him wished to leap to the sky, to bring war to the theoretical home of the Gods. In reality, he could do neither. He felt helpless, hopelessly rooting for the water that streamed from every seam to hurry up and engulf them while they still seemed helpless.

Timmy stepped back from the edge and began to pace. He watched the son collapse after freeing his hammer, his eyes always on the old man whose leg was twisted and wedged between two great stones. The old man tugged. The bejeweled boy clamored to his knees and collapsed. Timmy paced. The old man freed his leg with a yell that trumpeted from the hole. The boy pulled himself back to his knees and collapsed once more. Timmy paced, helpless, unless…

In his most honest projection, Timmy appeared upon a boulder between the faltering men as himself, all four-foot two-inches and sixty-five pounds of him.

You have killed so many of us.

Better talk to the boy. I was just thrown here.

I was made, raged the boy, gasping for breath, for a reason. I was chosen for my gifts.

We all have gifts and look where they have gotten us.

I am a God!

You're not that bad.

Always exaggerating, that's what he is.

You never saw what they see.

Anyone can smash things.

Can you?

You're missing the point. Timmy tries to gain control.

He's missed it his whole life.

Oh and you haven't? What have you done since mom died? You haven't even talked to anything that wasn't made of rock?

You leave your mother out of this.

You're missing the point! Both of you!

You're the point. If it wasn't for you he'd still be collecting trash.

And you'd still be a dick!

It wasn't me. Timmy pleaded. It isn't me! It's them! They did this to you. They're using you.

Better to be used than to be nothing.

They've made you a killer, a destroyer, a ruiner of lives!

And a real asshole!

You're not helping.

You're not helping. Before you we just didn't get along. Now it's all swinging hammers and rocks that rise and meet you while you fall.

I told you it's not about me. They set us all up!

Actually, they set you up. If you stick around I'm dead.

Me to.

A common ground, The Hammer smirked.

The hammer crashed as lightning sparked and then thundered. The dust glowed red, melting in the air and dripping in hot sparks of lava. Burning light sizzled through the clouds. Deafening booms bounced between the cliff walls.

When the hammer finally stopped and the lightning resided, the old man and the boy stood upon a fractured lake of glass and before them floated Timmy. His rock was smashed yet he remained, causing the boy and man to shake uncontrollably.

Are you him? Or maybe her?

Are you them?

They said he was a tricky son of a bitch.

Maybe that was the trick.

If I was them, I'd have destroyed you by now.

That's what they would say.

No they wouldn't.

He's right.

Whose side are you on?

You don't want me pickin' sides old man.

I'm here to try and save you.

What's that supposed to mean?

Mean's I've been wanting to put a sledge aside your head since I was nine!

Listen to me!

Just try it little boy!

There goes common ground.

Gone like the wind.

The More the Holier

Sledge griped his hammer.

Stone's fingers glowed red hot.

A specter rose from the lake of glass as a God rained down from the sky.

Hot and cold, burning and all wet, divided the two men.

Stone raised his lightning palms above his head and sunk to his knees.

Sledge wet himself, shaking uncontrollably and dropped his hammer on his foot.

Oh God!

Oh Mother!

Children! The Gods of above and below mime together. This does not make us happy. This is not what we had in mind. We sent you to find the boy and bring him over to our side and this is what happens? You destroy our creations? You waste your time in holes? You attack each other? And when you finally believe yourselves close enough to your objective, you stumble over each other trying to destroy him? Hasn't either of you enough sense to realize that a child can't get to the bottom of a hole? A hole whose depth is only surpassed by your combined incompetence.

I'm sorry! The father cried. I thought...

Please don't make me bubble.

When you threw me at this hole.

This hammer...

I tried to keep on track.

I thought you wanted destruction.

And my bastard son...

Why would you give me a hammer?

He tried to kill me.

He tried to kill me first.

He needed discipline.

I don't even need him.

It's probably too late for discipline.

We don't need him.

Should've been firmer with him when he was young.

I can do this by myself.

Can't blame myself really.

Get rid of him and let me have the time you promised me.

Was his mother's fault really.

You leave mother out of this! Sledge's eyes flared bright, the red and puffy tears giving way to flame. In one fluid motion, he scooped up the hammer and hurled it at his father's head. It sheared off his left ear before spinning head over shaft into the cliff wall. The wall exploded, burying father and son neck deep in rubble.

The old man smiled wryly, flashed his palms to his son and winked.

Throwing away you weapon huh, didn't learn that from me.

You always were a bastard.

A bastard that's still armed. Stone waved his hands and grinned wider. Guess who's going to be stone.

Like father like son.

At least we'll finally have something in common.

Hello! Gods' here! We have ways of garnering your attention. And if you kill each other, it just means you get us fulltime. The Gods seethed, smoke billowing from their nostrils, volcanoes erupting from every pore, blowing puss, ash and black smoke. Their veins throbbed, threatening the world's smallest holocaust, the extermination of all men buried to their chins in a pit too deep to be reached by the noonday sun.

Wound tight egos gave way to free-flowing bladders. It was easy to imagine molten being what death had waiting for them and each man secretly hoped that molten was the worst they had in store. They'd heard about the angry Gods, severe punishments being handed out for light infractions. Moses struck a rock and lost the holy land. Jonas got the belly of a whale for not wanting to bother people in distant lands. Sal's wife became a pillar of salt for not wanting to miss the best show in town. Sodom was destroyed for playing a rusty trombone. Lot went through hell just for being too close to a Devil and a God when they had a gambler's itch. There are no stories that tell what happens when two men pissed God and his Mother off till they're ready to explode. It may be, that though it's happened before, there was no one left afterwards to tell the story of how the Gods wrath burned, blasted then salted the land so nothing could ever again grow. It could in fact explain Utah.

Regardless, the father and son groveled and wept, apologizing relentlessly. They pleading, working themselves free from the rocks stone by stone, desperate to prostrate themselves before the demonic mother/son tantrum of fire. They swore they would do anything, eat rock, fill the pit by hand, mend their ways and never, ever screw up again. Never had they been so sorry. Never had their bladders been so empty nor their faces pressed so hard into gravel.

Placated, the throbbing Gods cooled. Volcanoes became dormant. Dark clouds escaped their eyes. Together they eased into a Zen, a melancholy. They perched golden above the sprawling men, calm as two fifty-foot Buddhas.

Rise only enough for your ears to clear the rock and listen well. They echoed, two sides of the same mirror. You have done tremendous damage. We speak to you, the son, so overwrought with power, you sought to destroy everything in your path, killing countless innocents.

That was very wrong son.

Silence! He never would have done it if you had been a father. All of this could have been avoided had you only unlocked the love you squirreled away. Instead you demonized your existence and gave yourself to the worst that grief can conjure.

We are very sorry Gods. We are ignorant and ask you to help us understand.

That is why we are here, to help you upon a better path.

That is very generous, though, I hope you don't mind me saying, very strange. Especially after all we know of you.

We are Gods of war and Gods of peace, as fickle as the wind.

But why are you both here? And why do you talk together?

We are as the same as we are different, as together as we are apart.

That's not what you said this morning.

Dad's right, that ain't what you told me.

What is time to us and what is time to you will never be the same.

What always stays the same are the signs of a dysfunctional family and I don't care what time it is. A rift is a rift and even if a day is an eternity, that rift ain't filled since morning.

And why you always talking the same?

You cannot separate immortality.

You could this morning.

You telling me that ain't God.

That ain't even his mother.

You don't want us to prove ourselves again! The Gods fill the hole, maliciousness dripping from quaking mouths.

Talk separately.

Yeah, one of you drink water and one if you sing Oh Susana or something.

Are you making us into a sideshow act? Gods howled and trembled with furry.

I'm callin' you a figment and bettin' my life you can't prove me wrong.

Timmy Out of Bounds

Timmy would have liked to prove them wrong. But the hole was too deep for individual banter. It was easier to be a city on a hill than two Gods in a hole. He had never projected into such overwhelming darkness.

Depth and darkness were the one thing Timmy had going for him. Since he had little idea what the bottom looked like, he figured they weren't that sure themselves. As long as they were yelling, they were still alive, but for how long? And if he couldn't calm them down, there was no telling what they would do. At least while arguing they were preoccupied with their own grudges and not destroying aimlessly. But then again for how long? One was bad enough. What if they were able to focus their rage beyond themselves? Hate is only backwards love after all. With family, things can change in a heartbeat. Then he'd have two to deal with. It could amount to more than twice the trouble.

Timmy had to think. The boy was dumb and easy to trick, but the old man had many years on him and while they may not amount to wisdom, they could at least add up to less dumb or at least not irrational enough to waste his time pounding a hole to the center of the earth.

There didn't seem to be any way out. There was little he and his family could do to stop such powerful creatures. That was what brought him to the edge of the hole and convinced him to project himself to those he hated. He had to persuade himself that it wasn't their fault so he could try and talk some sense into them, instead of raging abuse at them, using the cruel and nasty words he'd learned in the faculty lounge.

It was the first time he'd let his own form stray so far away and he was amazed at how vivid everything was. He could hear. He could see. He could plead. But he could not convince.

The God thing was just a stall, to give him time to think. But he didn't even have the chance to consider. The projection was too complicated and he couldn't take his mind away for even a minute. It was almost funny that as a boy in a pit he could finally see but as two Gods in a hole, he couldn't make out anything at all. In that there was something ironic, but he did have time for irony and didn't know what it meant anyway.

He'd liked to pat himself on the back, congratulate himself for how clever he'd been despite his lack of years. But childish cleverness wasn't going to cut it. Blindly impersonating Gods, even in a sunless pit, could only last so long and then what?

He had nothing. When he saw the lightning flash and recognized the gleam from the falling hammer, he knew the con job was over. His apparitions had been vanquished and the family squabble was back on. Timmy did the only other thing he could think of - sure he had let the family down and the world just behind them.

Tussle in Great Depths

Stone was shocked to realize what life had brought him to. It had happened so fast and gone so wrong. He suddenly understood that the Gods were going to keep changing the rules. Everything he was ever going to do was wrong. If everything he did was wrong than Hell was where he was going no matter whose team he was on, no matter which way was right and which way was wrong. He knew, from somewhere outside himself, that this is how he had raised his son. He had left him damned. He also understood that this did not change how he felt about the boy. The flip side of love is hate and hate was all he had left.

Stone shook off thought. It was too late to try anything new. He had left only one burning question. What were these creatures before him? He had his doubts about the Gods in the hole, the synchronized speaking, the mixed messages and now they seemed to not know what to do or say next. It all added up to them being impostors.

He believed they were fake, but after the rock suit incident, he'd really begun to second-guess himself. Then one last thought entered his dull little brain. What's a few extra days tacked onto an eternity in Hell. He was ready to take eternal damnation into his own hands.

The lightning flashed and passed straight through the Gods without them so much as s complaint. Stone rose from prostration and hurled strike after strike, an angry smile taking over his face as he threw bolt after bolt into nothing. The knowledge brought him no satisfaction, it was akin to beating the marshmallow that burned you.

Consumed, he hadn't noticed his son's dash to recover his miss-thrown hammer. He continued to throw bolt after bolt until the hammer rang and the lake at his feet opened and he splashed downward into a rock tumbling crevice.

A hundred feet down his fingers scratched deep enough into the stone that his body came to a halt and his feet found a jagged out crop.

I give you credit father. You sure got some balls. Fake or not I wasn't going to test them.

You always did have your mother's balls.

Men clinging to cliffs should watch what they say.

Boys with no balls should watch who they pick fights with.

I would have taken those Gods out myself and sooner, had I my hammer.

Your aim is as accurate as your recollection.

Your head was nearly mine.

Shame you missed. You could use a good head.

And you could use a boulder. Sledge brought down his hammer and the cliff splintered, filling the precipice with coarse rock and his own tangled body.

Made hard by the Gods, encouraged by rage, the two men defied the jagged falling fill. Unearthing themselves as quickly as they were buried, they glared at each other through rock caked eyes and yelled brutalities through rubble munching mouths, demanding each other's blood.

From cat strike stances, eager for first blood, they found that they had beaten themselves there. They found, crowding the hole, hundreds of fathers, hands arcing lightning and hundreds of sons, hammers bent to their heels.

The hole was filled with fathers and sons, back-to-back and shoulder-to-shoulder. Rage turned to confusion and back to rage and back to confusion, back and forth on face after face after face.

It was Timmy's last trick and it stopped the men in their tracks, leaving them echoing the perplexed looks on their cloned faces. They turn from face to face to face to face to face to face, desperate to find something real, something to strike.

Hammers fell and lightning flashed. One by one the hundreds made moves that brought no doom. The rocks did not fly. Nothing and no one was turned to stone. Father and son darted and dodged among hundreds of dodgers and darters. Imaginary men ran from imaginary trouble, while being watched out of the corner of every real and imaginary eye. Father and son, their heads ducked, their feet flying, hide even from themselves.

Mayhem ran rampant. Stone passed lightning through all the wrong sons. Hammer swung through dozens of heads that were not attached to his father. Tired and overwhelmed, they crouched amongst a few dozen squatters, watching the best pretend war they had ever seen, searching the crowds, trying to find one real threat, eyes keyed for something different.

It was hard in the crowd to find differences, but they began to notice similarities. The runners looked like runners, whether it was father or son. Their faces were fixed the same way and their paths become predictable. The crouchers shared a wariness. The sons swung from their heels and the fathers threw from behind the ear. The two men weeded through the sea of similarities, knowing now, at least, what they weren't looking for.

The father saw it first. The son, tired of looking, brought his hammer down, showering the imaginary with rock and knocking a hole into the rubble. It gave the old man some direction and he began to throw, striking every clone around the hole with ragged edge fire. His shots passed through son after son, unable to find what was real before the son redirected his hammer to open the land at his father's feet. Once again Stone found himself clinging to the sheer of his son's cliff.

Funny how we keep meeting like this. Sledge flared from above as the fakes disappeared.

Of all the yous I've seen tonight, you have got to be my least favorite.

You ain't seen nothing yet old man. I almost wish there were hundreds of you just so I could smash them all.

You with your mother's balls ain't got what it takes to smash a potato.

I said don't talk about my mother! Sledge leaped into the air howling, his hammer glowing red above his head as Stone pushed away from the cliff. Freefalling, the son closed the gap, teeth bared, eyes wide and veins pulsating across his forehead.

The Hammer descended as the lightning flared.

The hammer shattered the father. The boy turned to stone. He cracked and crumbled as bits of fast moving father eroded his statue. On the ravine's bottom, son mixed with father in a dusty pile, deep beneath the city's newest tourist destination, the soon to be Lake Hammer-Stone.

Father and son gathered sediments, destined to share an unfortunate, though eternal embrace. It was as close as they'd been since the loss of a wife and a mother had left their hearts too empty and their emotions at a constant tilt toward rage.

Timmy Leaves Half Whole

Timmy saw the end as a blinding flash. Stunned, he almost felt ashamed that he never foresaw such an obvious end. He couldn't have been more relieved or more miserable. He felt exhausted with glee and energized by a nagging depression.

He didn't like death, even when it involved people he wished would die. He secretly wished but hadn't hoped for such an end and only wished for it at all because of the bloody terror that lay about him. His eyes were blinded by the light of destruction. His mind went black to shield him from how the city of his sibling had been ripped asunder again and again by freaks fronting for Gods.

The worst part was that things could hardly have gone any better. In the worst of circumstances, he felt lucky they all hadn't died. But lucky was a terrible thing to call what had been done.

Timmy sat and closed his eyes. It was too much for child. Ability was just ability and was never meant to mean he could take all the pain. He was too small to contain it. He froze, near comatose, ready to choose never knowing again over any more feeling.

What he needed was a soft shoulder and a lot of tears. Fortunately for him, it wasn't long before the softest shoulder crested the mountain, held him tight and cooed to his cries. He collapsed in her arms, trying desperately not to become smaller than his tears.

Airborne Gargantuan

Gargantuan could not believe a mere two cranes could lift him. He had held off attaching the third, hopeful but not convinced. He thought hope was all it was, but he hadn't been so light, so free, in over a decade, since before he had been enclosed in the shrine that he believed would one day be his tomb. He never believed he would again see the outside world with his own eyes. He had amassed the world's greatest riches, but it never occurred to him that he might get to see them.

He rose through the domed roof and his face met the forgotten breeze. His eyes looked down with a tear upon the mausoleum, the Taj

Mahal, the last great building he owned, the one that had been his prison. Looking up, his eyes witnessed the vast and barren landscape where all the world's treasures once stood. It was so beautiful; he couldn't help but quake with rage. He had never been happier and he couldn't stand the lost. His anger grew larger than he had once been, sending his heart into a frenzy that threatened stroke and melted fat. The cranes engines eased as the fat dripped away, filling the pools and fountains of his once luxurious incarceration.

One man had taken his treasures and chased away the gluttony he had for so long called home. One boy, enemy of enemies had sent him skyward for one purpose and one purpose only. No longer was he contends to rule as a bystander, coercing power through palatable fear, a well-deserved reputation for destroying all that crossed him unmercifully and a lust for punishing with thoughtful cruelty those who failed him.

He was determined to oversee his own revenge, to inspect each and every implement of destruction he had amassed in exchange for the world's possessions. He would give the orders and inspect the results. His army would be his. He would know every officer and pilots, every commander and bombardier. He would hand pick the best from the bottom, carefully watching them rise, trusting no one, leaving nothing to chance. He'd been fooled once, only once and he wasn't going to let it happen again.

Oh he'd been lied to before and he'd remove those tongues before the lie was finished. He'd been stolen from before and had a pile of hands to prove its futility. But he'd never been tricked, infiltrated and destroyed. He had never underestimated his prey.

It brought back a ferocity he hadn't known since the tender age of three, when the other preschoolers had tried to play with the toys his teacher had clearly laid out for him. There wasn't a child in that class, a teacher in that school, or a family member of an affronting child that would ever forget his name, so deeply had he branded it into their backside and so they would never forget what they did, the word 'mine' was dug deep into their chests. He still had their fingers tucked lovingly in the fold of fat nearest to his heart.

Since then no one had challenged him. Over the years there'd been plenty of thieves and grifters, but they were always easy to spot, being either too stupid to know better or too headstrong to give into the fear that should come with reason. In the end there was no difference between the two. Both types were, in effect, too stupid to live and were never missed by anyone. But to be straight out fooled and betrayed from within his innermost circle. It had never happened before.

Mammoth really began to enjoy his newfound rage. It felt so much like being alive for the first time. He breathed in the fire and enjoyed the swelling of hatred in his throat when he saw his near empty compound. All that remained with the George Jefferson Memorial, the Great Wall of Japan, the Leaning Tower of Puerto Rico and the world's largest omelet, all of which had been deemed worthless by the world.

The rest of what he had once owned, the world ached for. The Russians bought most of America's prize possession. The United States purchased most of China's artifacts. North Korea owned South Korea and vice versa. Everyone wanted a piece of England; each country swearing the purchase was to be used as a public urinal.

The world's treasures sold readily to the world's enemies and made Gargantuan rich enough to buy much of the world's destructive capacity. Navies, air forces and armies, he bought direct. Equipment and manpower he traded for or stole. He bought a Malaysian battalion and an Italian brigade. He traded much of the Ming Dynasty for an American Air Force carrier. He stole Soviet subs, Afghan rebels and ten thousand Somalian's with spears in their left hand and machine guns in their right.

His army was second in size only to China's. It had cost him near everything, but for the first time in his life he was saying money be damned, stuff means nothing, reputation is everything. He was no longer a collector, but a hunter. His quarry, one elusive little boy and he felt deep in his enlarged, fat-clogged and blackened heart, that he had more than enough dogs to sniff out this particular pest.

Break the Eggs, Pop the Yokes

They buried their brothers and sisters and cried. The city sobbed. The state wept. The country mourned openly. The world heaved heavy. It took a cemetery to bury the dead. It took a city to house and feed the mourners. Tens of thousands came to pay their respect carrying enough flowers to bury the cemetery six feet deep.

Such was the impact of the family on the communities of the world. They were chasing out the evil spoilers, imprisoning the rapers, thieves and pointless abusers. They'd cleared streets and liberated towns, block by block, and when necessary, crack house by gang lair.

Tens of thousands had at least a taste of what it was to be free. Doom was down, friendliness up. Most were simply amazed that they could leave their homes without running. Block parties broke out and neighbors met and shook hands, coming together after living so far apart.

The debt they felt at the family's time of morning nearly buried them in cards, wreaths, condolences and tears. The outcry was so great that doves released in tribute had to dodge bullets shot in reverence.

It made Timmy's hearts swell as it collapsed, fluttering along the ground on tattered wings. The confusion in his head was deep, dark and muddled. Little voices came from everywhere, haunting him, twisting his features, aging him, wrinkling his mind till all he could imagine being, looked like it was dying.

His family wouldn't leave his side. Someone was always close enough to him that they could have shared his pants. His children became his voice. He made only little noise and all of them were pain.

His woman, his compassion, his heart, shared embraces, wiped tears, helped in the healing of everyone in her path except Timmy. Little Timmy, so lost in blackness, he could only see what he was unable to prevent. Tormented, broken, surrounded by love he couldn't embrace, he kept a wall of emotion bottled up behind a locked mouse-hole door. Many felt worse for him than those they came to mourn. At least the dead's cliché pronounces them to be resting in peace, while Timmy's cliché had left him in pieces.

It took everything Timmy had left to call together the family council for an egg and toast meeting, the topic he would only say comprised the yoke.

Chicken Beats Egg,
Egg Beats Yoke
Yoke Beats Chicken

Brothers and sisters, I thank you from the bottom of my heart. You have given me things I never thought I would be able to call my own. I had assumed as a toddler that our great numbers were our greatest liability, when in reality it was to become our greatest strength. Once such burdens as egg and toast were resolved. Once we understood how much we could do for each other. The good that can be accomplished when family becomes more than just enormity and can grow to include our neighbors and then beyond that, to any stranger that needs someone in their corner. That need for someone to care, being the one thing I believe we can all understand. I thank my wife and my children for sharing this truth with me. Before I was lucky enough to fake my way into their life, I really hadn't seen past my own daily needs.

Things have darkened. My family has been targeted, all of you are now targets and too many of us have paid the ultimate price. And for what? Because of me and my obstinace? Because I have refused to be a willing pawn in a game that the Gods have invented for me? Because of that we're missing sisters and brothers.

I don't confess to understanding the game, but I do admit to knowing that it was being played and I swear, if I had known it would go like this, I would have given myself to them immediately.

What every you say God! We'll do it your way or your mother's just leave my fucking family alone!

And that is exactly what I'm going to tell them. I'll be whatever you want, just let my family be. And I can do that knowing full well that leaders like my wife and Andy and Sarah will lead the way, so that our work can continue unhindered by the wanton destruction my resistance to God has brought upon us all.

Forgive me. I love you all.

For the first time since the mountaintop, the mouse hole exploded and shattered the wall. It blew with all the makings of a tsunami. It threatened to flood the meeting hall. Inches of sorrow covered the floor as Timmy broke for the door.

One hundred eyes echoed the wave, adding a foot then more upon the floor, spawning fish, as birds swooped, cawing hungrily. The ocean in all its fury flowed heavily about Timmy as he hit the door, his back to his family so he wouldn't have to see them any more. They deserved at least that much for being the best damn family any child ever had.

Carried along by a surging tide of sorrow he reached the door and nearly drowned in bewilderment upon finding it locked. Surprise turned to shock as the current ripping him back toward the open embrace of his family.

It was only then that he noticed, his boys had never let go of his legs, nor his wife his neck. Such had it been since he'd come down from the mountain that he'd forgotten that they were not him.

His family swept in, replacing some of his tears of sorrow with a pathetic, wrenched happiness, love rising to the surface through a swamp of pain. The salty burning nearly pleasant as it coated the bite of loss.

Arms desperately searched, crushing, pulling, tearing, beautiful and healthy. Monkey in the middle, pig in a pile, the weight crushed breath, but the little breeze that squeaked through brought light to the darkness that had overwhelmed Timmy. The voices inside, the ones that cursed beyond his years, the ones that blamed beyond his tears, began to be replaced with the whispering of a hard-clinging family.

215

This is all because of you.
You brought us together.
You made a family of strangers.
You made us better than we were.
We love you.
We will never let you go.

They decided before the pain of loving so strongly could break them, that they would find another way. That if they kept their minds and themselves together, they could survive and prosper no matter what the Gods had in store.

Timmy protested. He cried and he pleaded till the resistance in him died. He wasn't willing to believe that he had made things better than he was making them worse. But he understood that the love around him would never let go without an unforgivable betrayal on his part. A betrayal that could echo through the kindness they had started, bringing it to the ground.

He swore he would stay. The egg had been cracked. All that was left was the yoke.

The Yoke

The family sat down, having, as we already said, cracked the shell and Timmy told them in detail everything he knew. He told them how he had first met God in a closet and how a fire and God's mother soon followed. He told them about a ridiculous war by God on pants and how he learned that pants didn't matter. Then he told them what he thought of Gods and what he believed Gods thought.

He thought Gods were too large to care and despite the magnitude of their power and comprehension, they were the most piteous creatures in a universe they claimed to have created. He felt bad for them. Even after all they had put them through. He could still say he felt pity. The pain they had created, in and about his family's lives, was far greater and strangely better than anything they would ever be able to experience. They felt no love, no hate, only an endless longing to fill the great eternal void, their only respite coming though a continuous and pointless competition.

It was like they had their own religion. They adhered to a set of rules that have nothing to do with and are in fact dismally opposed to what they understand and can accomplish. They wish only to make their lives less empty, to which end they continually fail. Theirs is a joyless existence and

216

the real kicker is that for us they care nothing, to the extent that Timmy would wager, that they, mother and son, are more interested in being the first to make him cry uncle than in humanity as a whole.

And there lies the yoke of the problem. How do you convince all-powerful beings that care nothing for you, to leave you alone?

The answer was clear enough. They needed to find God and his mother something better, something that made the void appear shallower than it did when filled by Timmy.

This much was settled on immediately - if it meant making other people's lives worse, then the family would just have to bear the brunt of God's boredom. Timmy felt that he should bear the brunt since he was somehow responsible, but the family was adamant that none of it had anything to do with him, that the real problem was the constant need for distraction and without Timmy, the Gods would quickly find other ways of torturing humanity. It could even be much worse, since most communities aren't capable of weathering hardship without choosing an ancestral enemy to focus their frustrations upon.

It was a fine conclusion that left them all feeling momentarily good about themselves. But brought them right back to the yoke. How do you distract God? You cannot trick God. You can only make him do what he wants to do and then only as long as he was already going to do it.

Out of Corrinna's mouth it sounded like this:

Since the Gods already know what they've chosen and what they've rejected, it may simply be our role to submit something, so that their game may continue along their rules. The result is predestined, hinging not on what we may decide but the fact that we decide something.

While everyone agreed that this was the case, they also agreed that they should bring to that hinge something they believed the Gods might want.

After such theological nonsense was agreed upon, brainstorming came as a welcome relief. They started a list:

Things God Might Like To Do

Nascar – The Gods could compete within the confines of Nascar's rules and regulations.

Smash up derbies - Two Gods go head to head in a redneck arena, forever.

Poker - If they can obey their own rules, what about the rules of chance?

Which led to carnival games, two-hand touch, hacky sack, marlin fishing, largest pumpkin, skeet shooting, trick shooting, most eggs eaten in an eternity, longest fingernails, a chili cook off, largest pancake, most new life forms, most planets farted on, most stars farted into, battleship, jumping contest, best collard greens, best NY times editorial, who could be quiet the longest, spam carving, sand castle building, pigeon licking, cake decorating, best animal rock band, billiards, largest cannonball, smallest insect, best in show, biggest bubble, worst smell…

…And on and on and on, reject after reject, nothing stood up to the lure of Timmy's God-given, unsullied, self-determination. Nothing even came close, nothing animal, vegetable, or mineral could compare. Neither could paper, rock or scissors.

It looked hopeless, when Timmy's wife was able to look past concept to reality, concentrating on why the Gods did what they did. She figured that while God may seem interested in Timmy, he's really only interested in his mom. The same with the mom, she only cares about the son. Who's missing in this formula for perfect family dysfunction? Given the whole - as earth as it is in heaven shit, what's missing was the deadbeat dad, and if there is one thing a mother and child can come together on, it's uniting against the deadbeat dad.

Timmy hugged his wife and whispered in her ear. That son of a bitch almost killed me. Now I know why. I'm the hinge that lets his family back in. Personally, I would have killed me too. He tried to kiss her, but fatigue overcame him so quickly that he could only deliver it in his dreams.

Ollie! Ollie!

Believing it symbolic and even healing, Timmy climbed the mountain that led to a lake that filled a hole that was once a city to call the Gods to convince them that mankind was a hole and the Gods were mountains. At least that is what he was thinking as he climbed the hill that had risen too fast and too jagged for too many of his brothers and sisters.

Ollie, Ollie Oxen Free! Was all he could think to yell.

Answers came from both Heaven and Hell, their voices coming in unison.

Little boy! Little boy, where have you hid? God descended like a lead butterfly as Mother ascended like a rabid naked-mole-rat.

I thought you hated each other. Timmy tried to hide the pain that their simulcast rekindled.

With all you've come to understand, you still believe that. I suppose next you'll think this is all about pants.

So it's only boredom.

You're learning tires us.

You sure are playful for being so hopeless.

We aren't hopeless, just over informed. We hope someday to know a little slower.

You know enough to know you're doomed.

As do you. Yet you're here with a near impossible idea.

It's not my idea. It's just the one I'm supposed to present.

See how smart you're getting. God broke the unison.

It doesn't make you any more interesting. Mother God glared.

I can never be more interesting than how you made me.

Don't blame your flaws on me.

It's like you're begging for an ugly oblivion.

Some things are better than what you got.

God we fucked you up.

Children should be talking about lollipops.

Don't tell me I'm surprising you.

Just following the dialogue.

I suppose that's all I'm doing.

But you're having more fun.

Sorry to hear that.

If it was worth our time, I do believe we'd hate you.

I didn't make me like this.

Imagine how we feel.

We gave you more than we have.

You didn't mean to.

We didn't know.

Ignorance is bliss.

What you don't know often turns into the cruelest truth.

So you feel sorry for yourself but not us?

Didn't someone yell Ollie, Ollie, Oxen Free. Now forgive me if I'm wrong, but in little kid lingo that means essentially that we've been set free.

So?

So you're deliberately being a pain. We have your word. Slack must be given.

You're not giving me any slack.

We didn't call Ollie, Ollie, Oxen Free, we only responded to it. Our mere arrival comes with a don't waste our fucking time clause.

Missed that clause.

Ah Jesus Christ! You know we only put up with your shit this long cause we have so little else to do.

Now we're as bored by this as by anything else.

Next thing that bores me makes you a rock.

Then let's get back to business.

Boring, but I'll withhold the rock for now.

Out with it.

It's a change in the game I think you'll enjoy.

But we're enjoying this game very much.

At least as much as possible.

The new games better.

I think you're selling yourself short.

I think you're selling me long.

I don't know what that means. Do you mother?

I don't. Do you Timmy?

Not really, but it is the first agreement we've ever had and that's got to be a good sign.

We're all about signs.

Good, then hear me out.

Just because we agreed once, doesn't mean you can get bossy. Does it son?

No Ma, it don't. Besides, these days the signs I'm into are more ominous and less the every thing will be okay sort.

I can work with ominous if you would just please let me explain.

He did say please.

I suppose we might as well listen then.

As I was saying, I'm just a child really, should be talking about lollipops and all that.

You're pretty bad-ass for a child.

I'd call him an old soul wouldn't you?

Old soul for sure.

But there are much older.

You don't mean?

Surely you're not talking about…

He wouldn't!

He shouldn't!

He oughtn't!

I think he's going to.

Old God, father God, husband God, whatever you want to call him.

I call him Hank.

Bad daddy works for me.

I like that. I'm changing my answer to Dick Head.

Then I'm taking Omni-Ass.

That's good!

You like it?

I do.

I'm blushing.

You're always that color.

No, you're always that color.

I got it from being in Hell.

Hell got it from being near you.

It was quite nice before I got there.

Damn near paradise.

Ah, now paradise would have to be my new garden.

Burning corpses do not a garden make.

I planted them.

Point taken.

I don't even understand why you two are pretending to be at war anyway.

From time to time forever feels like an eternity.

That's so damn corny.

He asked.

So it sucks to always exist. Wouldn't eternity be better if you were pleasant to each other?

Can't imagine anything more boring.

Have you ever tried to be pleasant long term?

I'm pleasant most of the time.

Try it for a millennium than talk to me, right son.

Boring, boring, boring, boring, boring… I'd rather spend the next thousand years saying boring over and over than be bored by pleasantries at all.

It's just like not being alive.

Alive! Is that what you are?

Are you?

If you say I am, I suppose I am.

Ditto.

What if I say you're not?

Then you die.

Because you'll no longer exist?

Oh hell no.

We just think it would be funny.

You keep getting me off track.

We got time.

Might as well.

That's my point exactly. We need to fill your time with something better.

Ah, but Timmy you're the best.

Aces in my book.

What you need is something more challenging.

You can't give up yet.

You've lasted longer than anyone, ever.

You're not making this easy.

We got time.

Might as well.

Your dad has never given up either.

He's a lobster.

What do you call that?

I don't know. But listen, who do you hate the most?

Alyssa Milano!

Scrappy Doo!

I change my answer to Scrappy Doo.

I change my answer to Alyssa Milano.

Who's committed the greatest evils against you throughout eternity?

Clint Eastwood!

Mother Teresa!

She really did railroad you.

She's the Clint Eastwood of the nunnery.

Clint Eastwood is the Mother Teresa of Hollywood.

Now that's just mean.

Glad you liked it.

Wish it weren't true.

You two are driving me crazy.

It's a bit of a hobby.

I'd call it a specialty.

Who is currently living as a lobster?

Harry!

Bad daddy!

Dick Head!

Omni-Ass!

Let's call him Hairy Ass for now.

Agreed!

Agreed!

Twice in one night! What do you say we go for three? Who strips bikini tops?

Harry Ass!

Who bites your ass on the way out?

Harry Ass!

Who's living comfortably on the Jersey Shore, while you two fight over Heaven and Hell?

Harry Ass!

Who's a big dick that needs to be put in his place?

Paul McCartney!

Socrates!

He's dead.

Still needs a good place putting.

He's in my garden.

Extra fertilizer?

The shittiest.

Then I change my answer to Hairy Ass.

I'm keeping Paul McCartney.

You already broke up the Beatles and gave him a one-legged woman who likes dancing, what more can you do?

I change my answer to Hairy Ass.

Then I say he's the one you should torment and play with. He'd be a challenge and better than that, he has it coming, so there's a chance you may even enjoy it.

It has been thousands of years.

And we may actually enjoy it.

You always knew you were gonna do this.

Since before we were born.

Don't ruin the moment.

Remember how high and mighty he used to act. Blah, blah I know everything. Blah, blah do what I tell you.

Now he's a lobster.

And a pervert.

Hangin' in Jersey.

Remember when he knocked you up with me.

I'll never forgive him for that.

Me either.

Hated him even before we were married.

I'm going to eat him first.

He'll just bite your ass on the way out.

I'll make my ass a mouth and chew him on the way out!

That's gross.

You got a better plan?

I'm gonna hot glue every bikini directly to the skin and sandstorm the barbecues.

Won't matter if I eat him first, then my ass eats him, then I eat him again.

Then it's a race.

In your face.

The God's disappeared.

Years of pain and frustration melt from Timmy's face. So great were his turmoil, worries and tribulations that by the time he's fully relaxed, even his face has washed away. He's shrunken, his years shedding off till he's an early embryo, enjoying the formation of his thumbs and mouth and how the two like to meet for a good suck.

He hadn't felt so good since he first put toast to yoke. Or maybe it was back when he was just a little purse in his mother's satchel, a short commute from milky nipple.

He melted into a deep glob of goo. He could have stretched a towel down by the Lake of Fire and enjoyed it. Such was the purity of his relief. His family was safe. They no longer had to hide and could concentrate on helping those that needed it most.

His ooze soiled and sprouted as a glow emanated from deep within his wellbeing, a light that grew and grew into green foliage and clear blue streams, ripe fruit and abundant wildlife. His heart opened. He experienced the birth of a new world, the promised sprouting, the gift from God. The one that was meant to save the world was saving him. Within his new, found peace, he felt the life and beauty of a new Garden of Eden coming to life. He felt utopia. Unrealized potential blossomed before him and he knew that his family and all those they touched were destined to become life's rich fertilizer, which only sounds shitting if you've never helped something grow.

Timmy absorbed the garden back inside, carefully of the leaves and the toads, securing it softly so it could continue to grow. The feeling of freedom and infinite potential overwhelmed him. He felt he might burst. The only thing that could make him feel better would be the right pair of arms.

Hello Goodbye

A light rain cooled Timmy's brow. Water from the garden he thought, lifting his face to embrace the cleansing liquid, his smile grew too large for his face. If the last few years had been different, this would be one of those moments when he'd offer thanks to God. His life being what it had become, Timmy decided to leave God out of it, even if he was as close to a father as he would ever know. He'd also, of late, seen where the father-son relationship could lead when mishandled, so instead he spread his arms wide, palms to the sky and thanks it.

The sky answered immediately with an arm that pendulumed downward, a hand of rock that laid into the side of Timmy's face as if swung from the moon. The left side of Timmy's face impacted the right as he moved through the air, pin-wheeling head over legs over the canyon lake, twisting around, his smashed form an apparent boomerang that carried him over the great lake and skirted him along the far rim where his little body impacted the rubble with such ferocity, that the crumbled bits of humanity never stood a chance.

He cleared a runway, long and wide enough to remove his broken body by 747, assuming there were any bits left. There were, but they were scattered, his pieces still breathing and bleeding, but purely out of habit.

The cooling rain became a downpour, washing pieces and fluids away.

The day turned dark. Timmy's eyes rolled downhill, missing neither rock nor drop. They settle against a bolder in time to see the hand reach its pinnacle, turn palm side down and descend like a freight train fired from a cannon, traveling with such vicious intent that lightning moved fearfully from its path. It descends in haste upon the mound, grazing the runway in a torrent of sparks, melting rock and metal, paving the airstrip as it sent Timmy's bits hurling into the far wall of the canyon with enough force for reconstruction.

He was encrusted with rock and metal, but in one piece, breathing air that fed blood that ran through intact veins, into present limbs, leaving Timmy sure of one thing. It hurts far more to be put back together than it does being ripped apart.

He peeled from the cliff wall, wishing he were numb enough to feel surprise when he didn't fall but hovered. But the pain was too great for him to hold any other feelings. He knew exactly how many cells he contained, as each one cried with a pain large enough to fill an entire man.

Agony was all about him as he floated to the highest point on the crest. Lightning struck in circles about his feet, the thunder bringing blood to his ears. But it was too late for him to be effected by the sideshow. He was the lion in the cage, thunder, lightning, dark menacings, blinding lights, these things he was beyond.

The light flashed in rapid succession and the thunder crashed mercilessly, telling him what he already knew. Inside the lightning raged the face of Old God, within the thunder bellowed his voice.

You should have learned from our time at the beach. If there is a Devil among the Gods, it is I. If I take a boy moments from death once and he comes back to bite me in the ass, then shame on him, but if I take him to the brink of death twice… well… might as well leave him there. That is the most generous of my positions. I mean Jesus Christ boy! What the hell were you thinking? Even my child and my wife didn't treat you as callously as I and still you send them to me. Did you really think you'd live happily ever after at my expense? The lightning glared and sizzled.

Shit kid! I know you're young, but every schoolboy knows to stay away from the bully. Don't you know what happens to tattle tales? Tattle tales that tell on the bully! I'll tell you. It's this. It's pain. I can hear your cells screaming from here. So you go ahead and tell them they haven't seen anything yet. This ain't over and it don't matter which side of life you're on. I'm gonna make it painful.

The lightning burned from heaven to earth, moving in on the encrusted Timmy, melting the rock and scraps of metal imbedded in his flesh into a bronze and glass mosaic of Timmy, frozen in horror.

Timmy clung to life through a crack in his lips where he could still pull a faint wisp of air. He was burned from head to toe. A thin layer of sweat and puss lubricated him, slowly collapsing his frame within the metal and glass sarcophagus. His failed strength and slipping form stifled further the strand of air he was still able to suck from the crack. The only thing keeping him alive was an overwhelming sense of hatred for a certain side of his family that had never shown him any love.

Father and Son Reunion

Few men could have prepared Timmy for how quickly fluids fill a tomb of your own dimensions. When the rain stopped and God appeared, the fluids, a yellowing brown, had already filled to his knees. His body slunk downward till the metal and glass about his crotch had crept as close to his spleen as his taint would allow without splitting. He wasn't against splitting and being done with it, but his nipples were smelted in place, his nose still held out and his hairs still had a great number that hadn't yet torn from his flesh. His lifeline contained a slight lip crack, one taint, two nipples, many hairs and a half-God nose.

The world outside his shell look to Timmy as a mixture of dark shadows and ashen blurs, but Timmy could tell God was smiling as he wrapped on his cage.

I know. I know. God said. I should have told you about daddy. He'd been banished to the Jersey Shore for a reason. I know. I know. I never mentioned banished before, but to be honest, you never asked. Really, you've always expected me to be interested in your life, death and destruction and all that shit, but when did you ever express any interest in mine? It was always you, you, you and still you played along perfectly.

I know. I know. I've known what your thinking since before, so if it makes you feel better, we can do this as a monologue.

You'll say something like, you knew this would happen all along didn't you?

And I'd say, yeah well...

Then you'd be outraged with all this how can you do this too me shit.

And I'll go back to the old what else do I have to do routine.

Then you'd try and be cleaver or witty or mean or something and I say what happens, happens and that is why this happened. And even though you're a child, we've been doing this long enough that you should know better. Don't ever, never, no way, no how, at no time, mess with a God, even to get rid of two. We were just playing with you, but dad's pissed.

I'm sure now you'd get all intellectual and say he always knew he was going to get pissed, but I'm here to let you know that doesn't matter. We don't even know the future, we just register what is happening so much faster than you, that it seems like we know, so I'll repeat, for the thousandth time the only truth there is, if that's what it takes to make you happy. We are only looking to have some fun and our very being is set up to make that near impossible.

Which brings me to why I'm here. I have come to thank you. Believe it or not, for the first time in a long time we almost had fun. And I'm not just talking about your present situation, though this is kinda fun too, but still not the point I'm trying to make. What I'm saying is that you were what was fun. Christ you should have seen some of the looks on your face. Beats the hell out of Abraham and the whole kill your son routine or the Noah why don't you build a massive boat in the dessert stick. You were classic, like when I was playing the pants thing and kept showing up in your closet, then mom came and burned it up. I almost pissed my robe. Maybe I do see something of myself in you kid. Maybe that's why you're so God-damn funny to me.

But seriously kid, you've been a lot of fun.

I know. I know. You'd say some shit about how I'm the only one, but blah, blah, blah, if you suffer for a lifetime it's nothing compared to never ending boredom.

But I'm not here to be nasty. I came with a gift. Because you've been a good time, like it or not. I know. I know. Just try and shut up for a minute. Give me a chance and listen. Really listen cause you'll like this. Given that you survive daddy, what I'm gonna do for you is reverse age your wife, so that every year you get older, she will get a year younger, till you meet in the middle, then you'll be free to grow old together. Again, assuming you survive. Which bring me to the catch. If at any time you perish, like say any time now, before the two of you reach the middle, your wife will continue to grow younger till she becomes an egg. And I know how you love eggs.

Leaves a lot up to you don't you think? I know. I know. But that is the game. The reward for amusing me is in part, that if you stop, your world will suffer. I learned that from my dad and now I'm passing it on to you.

My best advice, suck as much through that hole as you can and try not to bleed. You're already flooded passed your knees and your family is just reaching the mountain now.

Anyway, I see you're dying, so I'll let you be. But understand, just like daddy said, in the here or in the after, we will meet again, cause that's were the fun's at and having a little fun is as close to not living forever as I'll ever get. So until then I'll leave you with a little ditty.

A gentle lullaby entered Timmy's head, warm and soothing, and despite his pain and fragmentation Timmy had to fight off sleep by leaning hard against his smelted nipples.

We'll meet again
Don't know where
Don't know when
But I know we'll meet again some sunny day
Keep smiling through
Just like you always do
Till the blue skies drive the dark clouds far away

God's voice faded, leaving only pain as the fluids rose over Timmy's pants, past his navel and then crested a tiny surf upon his nipples before moving towards his chin. Timmy gritted his teeth and concentrated on hatred. This was no time to die. He could hear the voices rising from below. His family was nearing and all he knew was he was too much fun for the Gods to let die and his wife was too wonderful a woman to be turned into an egg.

228

His anger was all that kept him alive. His pain had become greater than his fear of fire, greater than the dread that filled him when he pictured burning eternally with devils prodding his ashen bones. He sucked at the hole and tightened his taint, hoping that help would arrive in time.

www.ingramcontent.com/pod-product-compliance
Lightning Source LLC
Chambersburg PA
CBHW060916180626
46817CB00004B/1284